"I'm going to find what makes me happy, Sam. And then I'm going to do it." Avery tipped her chin up and met his stare. "Dare me."

She might as well have been seventeen again, but the feelings he had were so different. Instead of wanting to beat her in whatever race they cooked up, he wanted to help her, to encourage her. A breeze sent one curl over her forehead to land across her eyes. Before she could brush it away, he smoothed it aside, happy to see the spark of determination in her gaze. "Do it, AA. You're the only one who can."

Sam knew there was never going to be another moment to try it—the kiss that could settle everything. The woods were quiet. The water was turning golden with the sunrise. The two of them belonged in that spot at that time.

So he slowly pressed his mouth against hers, the sweet taste of her lips completing the most perfect moment...ever.

Dear Reader,

Sometimes the only way to move forward is to go back.

In *Smoky Mountain Sweethearts*, the first book of my new miniseries, I have a smart, formerly fearless heroine who desperately needs something to shake her up, and a hero who has never failed to push her higher.

After experiencing a tragic, heartbreaking loss, Avery Montague returns home to her small town, searching for what (or whom) it will take for her to become herself again. Meanwhile, childhood friend Sam Blackburn's certain a new firefighting job is the challenge he's been looking for—until he rediscovers Avery. Add in family, friends and the hiking that they love, and special things start happening for Avery and Sam. I hope you enjoy spending time racing up the trails of east Tennessee with them!

To find out more about my books and what's coming next in the Otter Lake Ranger Station miniseries, visit me at cherylharperbooks.com and find me on Twitter, @cherylharperbks.

Happy reading!

Cheryl

HEARTWARMING

Smoky Mountain Sweethearts

———

USA TODAY Bestselling Author

Cheryl Harper

HARLEQUIN® HEARTWARMING™

Recycling programs
for this product may
not exist in your area.

ISBN-13: 978-0-373-36857-0

Smoky Mountain Sweethearts

Copyright © 2017 by Cheryl Harper

Printed in U.S.A.

Cheryl Harper discovered her love for books and words as a little girl, thanks to a mother who made countless library trips and an introduction to Laura Ingalls Wilder's Little House stories. Whether stories are set in the prairie, the American West, Regency England or Earth a hundred years in the future, Cheryl enjoys strong characters who make her laugh. Now Cheryl spends her days searching for the right words while she stares out the window and her dog, Jack, snoozes beside her. And she considers herself very lucky to do so.

For more information about Cheryl's books, visit her online at cherylharperbooks.com or follow her on Twitter, @cherylharperbks.

Books by Cheryl Harper

Harlequin Heartwarming

A Home Come True
Keeping Cole's Promise
Heart's Refuge
Winner Takes All
The Bluebird Bet
A Minute on the Lips

Visit the Author Profile page at Harlequin.com for more titles.

To the men and women who protect and preserve America's wild places, open spaces, and the plants and animals that call them home, thank you.

CHAPTER ONE

BEING ROUSTED OUT of bed like she was thirteen again wasn't how Avery Montague thought she'd start the last Friday before her thirty-fifth birthday, but her mother had never let little things like closed doors stand in her way.

If she'd wanted to sleep in, Avery never should have gotten hotel rooms with connecting doors.

"Get up. We can't miss that flight." The long *a* in "can't" sounded so much like home that Avery had to wait for a second to let the wash of homesickness fade. Every one of her mother's *cain't*s used to drive her crazy. On the few occasions she'd managed to talk her husband, Robert, into a visit at the holidays, they'd locked eyes to communicate silently whenever her mother said it. He'd been amused at Avery's pet peeve.

Homesickness was chased away with the

dueling realizations that he was still gone and she was free to do whatever she wanted again. That freedom wasn't a gift most days.

After almost ten years of marriage, including three years of being his nurse, she'd spent the last two years adjusting to the realization that she could step out the door without fearing that life would never be the same when she came back home.

No matter what she did from this point, her life would never be the same. The dream of building a family with the man who'd derailed the plans she'd made at eighteen was over.

But her life? It kept on going, one hour dragging into the next. Some days she had to brush away the thought of how much simpler it would be to just…stop.

"We won't miss the flight, Mama. I'm packed. Let me put on some clothes and run a brush through my hair and I'm ready." Avery slipped out of the adequate sheets the airport hotel preferred and ignored her mother's gasp as she padded barefoot across the floor.

"Gonna bring back a toe rot or something, girl, if you don't put your shoes on."

Her mother was fussing with the large bag of cosmetics she almost never let out of her sight.

The laugh that bubbled out surprised Avery. Trust her mother to say something to make it easier to go on. "Toe rot? That's what you're worried about?" Avery studied the carpet from the bathroom and realized her mother might have a good point. The suspicious stains had clearly been cleaned more than once, but who knew how long it took for toe rot to disappear?

Her mother was wagging a perfectly French-manicured finger at her when Avery wrapped an arm around her shoulders. "You don't watch enough news programs, Avery Anne Abernathy. I am telling you, there is funk in that carpet."

Whatever funk she got from walking un-protected across hotel carpet might be worth it for the way her mouth held a smile as she headed back into the bedroom. For so long, she'd had nothing to smile about, but now she was going home.

One quick glance in the mirror was all it took to know she was leaving in the nick of time. The dark circles under her eyes were familiar. So was the gray in her short hair. Only the small curve of her lips, which surprised and pleased her, seemed out of place.

If she didn't hurry, her mother would barge back in with a can of hair spray in one hand and her leftover cheesecake in the other. She'd be forced to eat while her mother teased and sprayed. Then they would definitely miss their flight into Knoxville, and Avery wasn't sure how well she'd weather a setback like that.

She quickly slipped on the jeans that were so loose they were uncomfortable and yanked on a sweater. For years, through Robert's treatments and hospital stays, Avery had learned never to leave home without layers. It might be October, but the cold had become a permanent part of her life.

Her mother was still fussing when Avery stepped out of the bathroom. Her view from her room into the connecting room showed a whirlwind of destruction. "Mama, you only slept in that bed for one night. What in the world were you doing?" The sheets were tumbled into a ball while all the pillows save one were stacked against the headboard in a teetering tower. Avery was worn out just studying the mess.

"Hunting for the bedbugs." Janet Abernathy rolled her eyes. "Hotels are famous for bedbugs."

Avery almost argued with her. If hotels were famous for bedbugs, no one would stay in them, ever. And this airport business-class hotel might not be big on amenities or renovation, but it was clean enough. Arguing wouldn't change her mother's mind, though. Janet Abernathy never missed a news program. Because of that, she knew the world outside of Sweetwater, Tennessee, was filled with dangers. Only constant vigilance would do.

Avery's suitcase was still on the side of the bed where she'd left it. If her mother's room was an after shot of a crime-scene investigation, hers was barely disturbed. At least she'd slept through the night. She was beginning to depend on that.

With a shove of her hairbrush and the clothes she'd slept in into her bag, Avery was packed. She quickly zipped up the suitcase and slipped on her flats while she smiled again at her mother's relieved sigh.

"Do we need to call a cab?" her mother asked as she looked one last time in the mirror over the desk.

"No, they'll get us one downstairs," Avery said as she moved to stand next to the door.

"I can wait if you'd like to put on lipstick," her mother said with an encouraging nod. "I have choices."

"And I still don't care to see them," Avery answered as she pulled open the door. "We better hurry." They were still two hours before boarding, but it was important to both of them that they get home soon. And coffee was the only thing that would make this day bearable.

Avery handled the checkout while her mother fiddled nervously with her bags, her hair and her rings, both eyes locked to the muted cable news channel running in the hotel lobby. "It's okay, Mama. We'll be home soon."

Instead of fussing back, her mother reached over and squeezed Avery's hand. "And I'll be glad to know you're safe, my girl."

The tears that sprang to Avery's eyes were disappointing. For months, she had been fighting these stupid emotions that blindsided her when she was least expecting them. She'd gone to therapy and used antidepressants and self-help books. Still, the tears were there, under the surface. This wasn't like her at all.

If she was going home and planning on leaving the house at some point, she had to get that control back. The day she'd been packing and opened the front door of the house to find her mother standing on the step, she'd buckled so badly under the weight of the tears that she was certain her mother would never look at her the same.

Avery Abernathy had only cried when she was mad or when her father died.

Avery Montague cried at the drop of a hat.

Herding her mother through Chicago's O'Hare International Airport was the perfect distraction from any worries she might have. It was a bit like keeping up with a teenager who had a credit card with no limit. When they finally sat down at the gate, Avery was on her second cup of coffee and her mother had a load of shopping bags.

"Watch my seat. I have to go to the ladies'."

Probably to put on more lipstick.

Avery wrestled the lid off her cup and

blew to cool down the coffee she desperately needed.

At least she'd done the hard part. The bags were checked, except for her mother's airport must-haves. When they landed in Knoxville, Avery would do her best to hustle her mother right to baggage claim and on out into the parking lot.

The businessman seated opposite her pointed at all the bags stacked in the chair. "Forget a few things?" His charming smile was easy to answer.

"I think it was more about killing time." Avery sipped her coffee and watched her mother meander around the newsstand across the way. She had two magazines in one hand already.

"Is Knoxville home?" the guy asked as he set his computer aside.

"No, over an hour away." Her home had been in Chicago for almost ten years, but it was easy enough to understand his question. And Sweetwater was where she was headed to stay.

"I'm based out of Knoxville." He reached for his wallet to pull out a card and hand it to her. "I'm Chuck. Nice to meet you."

Chuck Armstrong was a liquor distributor, apparently. Why would she need his card?

"Nice to meet you, too," Avery said and laid the card carefully next to her on the seat. She'd drop it in the trash somewhere to avoid hurting his feelings. Maybe he thought she had a restaurant or something.

"Lookee what I found," her mother crowed as she plopped down next to Avery. "Cute actors. Cute singers. Cute designers. And cute dogs. If you can't find something to read in this stack, you ain't even trying." She dropped the magazines in Avery's lap and pulled off the one on top. "This one's mine."

"Cute couches. That's what you're going with?" Her mother devoured decorating shows, books and magazines, and occasionally decided to revamp the house Avery had grown up in. "What color is the living room now, Mama?"

Her mother sighed. "You don't remember how many paint chips I tested?" Their conversations for a while had been all about her mother's projects, mainly because Avery had stared at hospital walls and nothing else for days straight. "Colonial gray. That's what I've got right now." She tapped the white sofa with splashes of bright red flowers. "This would be darling."

It would. Years of study meant Janet Abernathy had a good eye. "Have you ever thought about opening up an interior-design business?"

Her mother straightened in her seat and shot her a surprised glance. Then she laughed as if Avery had said the most amusing thing she'd heard in a while. "It's a hobby. I don't have any training. And who in Sweetwater's going to be hiring an interior designer? No, ma'am. Right now, my focus is on you. Once you're home, everything will be okay." She turned the page slowly and then folded the corner down so she'd remember to come back to it. If she'd been in a better frame of mind, stronger, Avery would have insisted they talk about this. Her mother needed more in her life.

At this point, Avery was not in a position to argue, but having her mother's attention focused solely on her? This could be a problem.

"I like working at the school part-time, here and there as needed. It's never dull," her mother said with a careless shrug. Since her eyes never met Avery's, it was hard to decide if she meant what she was saying. "Are you thinking of opening up a…something? Going into business for yourself? It ain't easy. I mean, I don't know why you can't go back to school, but…"

This was her mother's subtle way of asking what Avery was going to do with the rest of her life. Since she'd been mainly focused on tying up all the loose ends left by Robert's death, closing up and selling their two-story house, and sleeping sixteen hours a day, Avery hadn't had much time for career planning. The first several times her mother had asked, Avery had shut her down. Sharply.

Going back to law school? All she could imagine was the stress and terrible grief from the memories it would no doubt provoke.

That was where she'd met Robert.

She couldn't go back.

Her mother would continue to ask what Avery planned to be when she grew up. She needed a better answer.

And after almost two years, she should have one.

"Maybe. I don't know yet." As long as she was happy living with her mother, Avery could float for a long time without any income at all.

Her mother wouldn't be satisfied to leave her alone for more than a week.

"Girl who put herself through college..."
But never graduated law school.

Her mother's mutters trailed off, but it was easy to see that she disapproved of Avery's lack of focus. At least she'd learned a bit of control.

As the gate crew called the first group to board, Avery slipped the magazines in her tote and the business card fluttered to the ground. Her mother picked it up to hand it to her. "Leftover from some other trip?"

Avery shook her head and pointed with her chin at Chuck, who was waiting in the line with the priority passengers. He was scrolling through something on his phone. "No, that guy introduced himself and gave it to me. I didn't want to give it back or..." Avery blinked. She still wasn't sure what had happened in that weird conversation.

When the next boarding group was announced, Avery stood and grabbed her mother's shopping bags. Her mother was shaking her head sadly. "What?"

"He was hitting on you. That was an invitation to call him when you're in town or something." Her mother dropped her purse on one shoulder and took her armful of bags from Avery.

The wave of people heading for the line flowed around Avery while she processed what her mother had said. "Hitting on me? No way." She wasn't dead but she might be half a step away. It had been months since she'd applied mascara. "What man in his right mind would be hitting on me?"

Once upon a time, that had been a common occurrence. She never would have missed Chuck's interest at twenty. Then she'd fallen in love, gotten married, and that all stopped.

She was technically single again, but how could the world tell?

After she'd lost so much weight that her wedding rings had slipped on her fingers, Avery had taken them off and put them safely away. Did she need to find them again?

"Any man who likes smart women would be hitting on you, sweet girl. That hasn't changed." Her mother wrapped a hand around her arm to urge her into the boarding line. "And that won't be the last time, either."

"I'll get my rings resized, put them back on. That'll help." It hadn't stopped every flirt through the years, but she'd lost the knack of understanding a man was flirting and the ability to answer properly. Chuck had deserved a better conversation than the one he'd gotten. She still wouldn't be calling him for a date, but she could have given him his card back without a trace of guilt.

She wasn't in the market for Chuck or any other man.

"Not to come back to life, it won't," her mother snapped before graciously handing a member of the gate crew her boarding pass.

Avery did her best to respond to the attendant's pleasant greeting and then nodded in a friendly manner at Chuck as she passed. He tapped his phone in a nonverbal signal that she should call him. Once all the bags were stuffed overhead and her mother had settled with her neck pillow, her blanket and her magazine, Avery tipped her head to say, "I'm perfectly fine without a man in my life for now."

"Thing is, you better not lose something

that will make you happy because you got your head buried under a pillow." Her mother pursed her lips. "Grieving is important and only you know how to do it for you. It's been two years, and I love you too much to let you grieve yourself right on into the grave."

Avery closed her eyes and inhaled slowly. "This isn't grieving. This is…"

"…being confused." Her mother turned to catch Avery's stare. "I get it. I've been there. Let me tell you something. The more time you lose figuring out what you want, the harder it is to go for it. Once you stop, it's hard to get started again."

"I'm not confused. I'm sad, Mama. Heart-broken. I can't even believe this conversation." Avery yanked open the magazine she'd picked up off the stack, the cute-dogs one, and flipped it open to study the table of contents, a weak sizzle of anger fizzling quickly.

Her mother cared even if she didn't understand.

The short flight to Knoxville was so easy that Avery had to sit back and think how long it had been since she'd flown. At least seven years. Maybe her first step should be a real trip, one without her mother. She did not want a weeklong lecture about the dangers of *foreign* toe rot.

The Knoxville airport was easy to navigate, but Avery was breathing hard and feeling the strain all through her body by the time she and her mother made it through baggage claim and to her mother's small SUV. With the last push of her strength, Avery loaded the bags and staggered around to the passenger side to flop down in the seat.

Her mother, instead of showing signs of fatigue, was perking up. "Want to eat before we head home?"

"No." Avery covered her forehead with one hand. "Let's pick something up, if you want."

If she had to get out of the car anywhere other than her mother's driveway, she'd stumble. Her mother didn't need to deal with that scare right now.

As they left the city behind and the road wound through the rolling hills toward the Great Smoky Mountains in the distance, Avery breathed deeply and memorized the dense forests, the running streams and the way the mountains rose behind Sweetwater all over again. If there was any place in the world that would feed her the energy that had been slowly drained over years of distance and struggle, it was this one.

"Need some rain. Fall color's off, all the dry, dead leaves," her mother said, "but it's still the prettiest place on the planet." Avery had loved so much of Chicago, but it was impossible to argue with her mother.

Avery turned on the radio and the country music that flowed out of the speakers made it easy to relax through the curves that her mom handled like a race-car driver. Whatever came next, this was the right decision.

"Thanks for coming to get me, Mama," Avery said softly. She might have stayed in that house until they'd kicked her out and in Chicago until she faded away. Already Avery could feel the color in this world.

"I should have come sooner." Her mother's lips trembled and she flapped her hand in front of her face like she'd done anytime tears threatened for as long as Avery could remember. "And I want everything for you, Avery, all you ever wanted."

"I was fine. I'm *fine*." Avery had assured her mother she was coping with every phone call.

Her mother's snort was easy to understand. "You're not fine, honey. But that's okay. You will be." The grim set of her lips was worrying, but Avery didn't have the right words to convince her otherwise.

And the way she felt, she needed to conserve her energy. They passed the tourist draw of Gatlinburg and wound north before turning off to stop outside Sweetwater. As her mother drove down the lane to her farmhouse, Avery was relieved that almost everything outside was the same. "What happened to the oak?" It had once been home to a rope swing and the beginnings of a tree house that her father had started but never finished.

"Storm came through. I told you that." Her mother waved a hand as she slid out of the SUV. "Maybe not. I thought it might depress you."

And we both know I don't need to be any more depressed.

"Had to call in a tree service. Sammy was too concerned about how close it was to the house to try to take care of it himself." Her mother yanked open the back of the SUV and started unloading the bags. "Plus, it was in the park's busy season. Kid works as many hours as he can."

Kid? Samuel Blackburn was exactly Avery's age, definitely old enough to have outlived "kid." He'd been the thorn in her side growing up, but his mother was still Janet Abernathy's best friend.

"After we get you settled, I'll run over and let Regina know I'm home. She's been watching the place for me." Her mother hustled up the four steps to the wide front porch and unlocked the front door. "Need to get you a new key made. Had the locks replaced after I had the renovations done." She paused in front of the grand entryway and said, "The new foyer."

"It's lovely." The old wallpaper was gone. Gleaming hardwoods were stained dark, and the front room was done up in grays and blues. "I could spend all day in here with a book."

Her mother pointed up the stairs. "Your room is ready. You go take a nap. You look tired. I'll see about dinner and let Regina know we made it in."

Before she could disappear, Avery wrapped her arms around her mother's shoulders and squeezed. "Thank you for letting me come home."

Her mother sniffed. "Girl, if you make my mascara run, we will both be sorry."

Avery squeezed her again and then let go. "Now, do I need to be worried about toe rot in my room?"

"Only if you brought it in," her mother said as she narrowed her eyes. "You bring any rot at all into my place and we will have words." She waved and then stepped back out on the porch.

Avery was still smiling when she opened the door to her old room. The linens and paint were different. All her awards had been boxed up, but the afternoon light through the window that warmed her favorite spot in the world, the window seat that used to overlook the old oak, was exactly the same.

Her phone rang and she didn't even pull it out of her purse. She knew who was calling, the only one of her friends who still made the effort. Maria Benton had been one of the lawyers fighting for people who needed them most in Chicago's Legal Aid. She'd spent the time Avery had volunteered there test-ing her and encouraging her, and when Robert had been diagnosed, she'd been Avery's most loyal friend.

And for two years, she'd called and left messages and never once accepted Avery's excuses for why her return calls were so very few. It hurt to talk to Maria. It hurt to remember that old life.

Today, Avery was going to put off until the day after tomorrow what she couldn't face today. She was home now. She'd have more energy any day now. That was the day to call Maria. Until then, there was voice mail.

Avery dumped her bags on the floor and sprawled sideways on the queen-size bed. A nap. Then she'd get started on figuring out the rest of her life.

CHAPTER TWO

SAM BLACKBURN HAD climbed The Eagle Nest so many times in his life that it had lost some of the thrill. Doing it in the fine mist that Sunday afternoon certainly added a degree of difficulty. Still not enough to satisfy the restless urge that had been plaguing him ever since he'd read about the opening for a spot on the Highland firefighting crew out of Colorado. They tackled the most dangerous wildfires out West.

That was the kind of challenge he needed.

Sam dropped down to sit next to Ash Kingfisher. They'd worked together for years and known each other longer than that. If he tried to start a meaningful conversation with Ash at this point, the man in charge of the Otter Lake Ranger Station might give him a hard push right over the edge.

Ash was a good leader but a terrible conversationalist.

The best thing about the rain was that it meant this trail, one of the most popular hikes in the reserve, was deserted. It wouldn't do much to alleviate the drought that had started in the spring and lasted all summer, but it was nice to remember that rain was still a possibility.

Sam clenched his hands together to keep from twiddling his thumbs and stared out over the trees. Might as well be at the top of the world on a day like today.

"Out with it." Ash inhaled deeply, his face completely expressionless.

"I'm going to apply for the wildland fire-fighting crew opening," Sam blurted as he stared hard in the opposite direction. If Ash sneered, he'd know the guy had even less faith in his chances than Sam did.

"Might as well." Ash rolled his shoulders and wiped a drop of rain off his forehead.

Then he stretched out the leg that some-times gave him trouble and moved his foot from side to side. The climb up the rocky top of the mountain was a challenge for most people. Sam spent more time going up and down trails than he did on flat land, but Ash was in the office now.

"Don't even think it," Ash muttered.

"What?" Sam asked. He knew there was no way the guy could read his mind, but Ash missed nothing.

"I'm not slowing down a bit." Ash turned his head slowly to give him a narrow stare.

"Fine." Sam nervously chewed on his thumbnail and then yanked his hand away. He wasn't a kid anymore. When he was growing up, Avery Abernathy would have snorted in disgust and pointed at him like he was a baby if she'd caught him chewing his fingernail. "Bad habit. Nerves. Knew a girl once who did the same thing but would deny it until the end of time." Nervous babbling. No good. Sam clamped his hands together. "How good are my chances?"

Ash sighed. "Gonna be competitive."

"All the good jobs are. I had to volunteer here for two years before I even got an interview," Sam said. "That your only concern?"

Ash squeezed his eyes shut. "Are we about to have a moment?"

Sam huffed out a laugh and called Ash the worst combination of curse words he knew.

"Well, I'd say you've got a real problem with authority," Ash drawled, "but no one is going to deny you've got experience, conditioning and training. If it was New Mexico, I'd be worried. You'd get sand in your shorts and run crying to mama, but the mountains will be enough like home."

"A problem with authority," Sam said. "That must be why I hang out with you."

Ash's slow blink was his only acknowledgment that Sam might have a point.

"If it comes to it, I will make sure my high opinion of you and your dedication to the job are well known," Ash said as he stood slowly. The rocks were wet but still solid. "That what you brought me all the way up here for?"

He'd thought Ash needed to get out of his cabin. Brooding didn't even begin to cover what the guy could do with free time, but there was only so much a guy could do. "Yep. That's it. I wanted to make sure I have your endorsement."

"What do I know about firefighters? I manage calm, stable reserve rangers. Those guys, the ones who parachute in to put out these fires, they're crazy." Ash shook his head. "You should fit right in."

"They're the best of the best, taking on

the worst wildfires, the ones that can destroy whole forests, not to mention everything else in their path." Sam turned to start the slow descent down the rock face. "Here, we babysit controlled burns and put out lightning strikes."

"And save lives and conserve native flora and fauna and history and put your lives on the line by standing too close to the flames when it counts." Ash grunted. "That ought to be enough danger for any one person for a lifetime. Those fires or these, those forests or these, your job is important," he said before he drawled, "sweetheart." His sarcasm had saved them both from one of those touchy-feely moments.

Sam concentrated on making it down to the trail. If he stumbled and fell, he'd never hear the end of it. Well, if he fell over the edge, he'd never hear the *beginning* of the trash talk, but his funeral would be embarrassing.

"You told your mother yet?" Ash asked as he stepped down next to Sam. They still had the hike back to the trailhead, but it would be a piece of cake, even for Ash.

"Not yet." That was the part he dreaded.

"Think I'll wait to see if I even rate an interview. You know how it goes. Postings usually come up in January, so it may take forever, but this drought…" Sam shrugged. "It's worse out West. I figure they're in a hurry to get the crews fully staffed."

Ash grunted. "Probably can't leave a vacancy for long. Too dangerous."

Spring and summer would be the busy seasons. They were here in the Smokies as well, but search and rescue got more interesting in the winter. He'd plan to spend plenty of time volunteering here at home. That would scratch the itch.

"Gonna be a job up soon in search and rescue, incident commander." Ash turned to stare over his shoulder as he headed down the trail. "Think you might be interested in that?"

Sam had the volunteer hours. There'd be hours and hours and hours of training and the competition for jobs here wasn't much less intense than it was for the few slots that opened in the regional firefighting teams.

He could consider it as a backup plan.

But he loved fighting fire.

Sam shook his head. "No, I know what

I want." He wanted a new challenge. He needed it.

Ash didn't answer as they made it back to the trailhead. Sam had no idea if getting Ash out of his cabin had made a lick of difference, but he wasn't ready to go home.

"I was thinking of heading over to Obed to do some climbing. Want to go on your next day off?" Sam asked as they made it back to the parking area.

"Nope. I like my feet on the ground." Ash didn't hesitate as he slid into the reserve's SUV. He raised two fingers in his version of a wave, backed out of the parking spot and headed for his cave.

Leaving Sam with nothing to do and energy to burn.

He turned to look back up the trail and took off running. Maybe he could beat his best time. If he did it in the rain, that would be something to brag about.

Not that he'd have any proof, but four more miles in the rain should be enough for one day. Sam hit the trail hard, clearing the first switchback easily, and ran until his heart pounded and he had to concentrate on breathing. The view was forgotten as he focused on each step of the rocky path up and then back down the mountain.

Pleasantly tired and overall satisfied with tying his best time, Sam slid into the truck and started it up. Not much for a firefighter to do on a misty day like this one. There was no lightning to keep things interesting. It was a bad idea to whine about things being too quiet. Mother Nature had a way of kicking up a fuss, but his trip back to Sweetwater was easy enough. When he parked in front of the housing for Otter Lake rangers, he could see his mother's Cadillac.

Apparently, he'd missed everything but the goodbye, though, because Regina Blackburn was trotting down the covered steps that led to the second-floor apartments. "There you are. Soaking wet."

She smoothed her sleek bob behind one ear and plucked at his gray T-shirt. "I brought over some groceries and the leftover roast beef you forgot to take with you last night. It's in the fridge."

"Thanks, Mom," Sam said as he pretended he was about to give her a bear hug. She shook one hot-pink fingernail in his face.

"Don't you do it. I've got cards with the

girls and no time for a change." She gave each cheek an air-kiss. "Now, I'd ask you what you were doing, but it was something foolish that will make an old woman have palpitations if she discovers her favorite son participating, am I right?"

Sam mimed zipping his lips and tossing the key. The Eagle Nest was safer now after the trail renovation than it had been in decades, but she'd never agree.

She raised one eyebrow at him. "How you can risk that pretty face is beyond me. You better keep it safe." She tapped his cheek.

"Yes, Mother." He ducked his head and wondered when she'd notice all the mud on his legs. He should point it out to hear her fuss.

"I should run," she said and pouted. "Wish you'd been here sooner. We could have warmed up the leftovers."

The thing about loving his mother was that he was skating dangerously close to becoming one of those guys, the mama's boys. But she was amazing.

Since she'd retired, she'd taken keeping him well fed seriously.

"I needed to get Ash's opinion on something." Sam stared up at the tall pines lining the parking lot and decided to rip off the bandage. "A job opportunity. In Colorado."

She paused midstep and slowly turned. "Ash's opinion. On a job that might as well be on the other side of the world." That was pretty much how he'd expected this conversation to go.

"Yeah, for the Highland team that's based at Copper Mountain." Sam braced his hands on his hips, prepared for the worst.

"The crew that fights out-of-control blazes," she said slowly. "That *dies* fighting those fires."

Much like the improved hike to The Eagle Nest, he could tell his mother that they were trained for those conditions and had countless successes for each accident the crew suffered, but she'd never accept that as a logical reason not to worry.

"I won't get an interview, Mom," Sam said as he ran a hand through his damp hair. "I bet there are a hundred better-qualified applicants for this one opening. I thought you'd want to know."

"Well," she said as she smiled brightly, "you know I believe you can do anything you want to do, so…" Then she marched to her Cadillac and slid in. She gave him her normal jaunty wave on the way out of the parking lot, but he had the feeling she'd be losing sleep until he got his form rejection email.

That would make two of them.

He shouldn't have told her. That had been his original plan. He always got into trouble when he did too much thinking. Sam trotted up the steps two at a time and resolved to send in his application and then eat every single bit of roast beef in his refrigerator before calling his mother to ask if she had any more.

If she was upset over his news, some of her mood would be restored by his love of her cooking. Regina Blackburn could be talked out of a funk by one needy phone call from her son.

CHAPTER THREE

THE THING ABOUT epiphanies was that they never came when Avery wanted them to. After nearly a solid week of living under her mother's extremely watchful eye, it had become clear they both needed a break from all their new togetherness.

Borrowing the car had been her first step to freedom. When her mother asked for a destination, only one place came to mind. It had been ten years since she'd made the easy hike up to Yanu Falls inside the reserve, but she would never forget the exhilaration of standing on the cliff overlooking the falls that led to a cove of Otter Lake.

Since her mother was hovering again, Avery had grabbed a water bottle, waved her cell phone and said she'd be back that afternoon. After so many years of living in the city, even driving the wide-open road winding up to the

Otter Lake trailhead seemed to roll off the weight of years.

The first inkling that not everything would go according to her plan was when she'd collapsed, panting, on the first bench along the trail, the one she and her friends had always called "Better Off Dead."

Because anyone who had to stop there to rest already had one foot in the grave.

She and her friends had been punks, obviously.

The hike that had taken her half an hour at seventeen took four times that long now, and she'd made unscheduled stops at every bench and flat rock she could find along the way.

None of that mattered once Avery reached the clearing, because she'd managed it. All by herself. Even two weeks ago, walking into the grocery store had been too much of a physical challenge.

"But either all that gasping for air has killed brain cells or the realization of what I'm supposed to do with the rest of my life isn't coming today," Avery muttered and pulled her phone out to check the time. She'd sat there, legs folded under her, for so long that they might have frozen into position.

She hadn't seen a bear or an otter, the two main draws, other than the panoramic view of old, dense woods, a wispy waterfall and the sparkling waters of Otter Lake in the distance.

Avery inhaled slowly and forced herself to stand. At least it was easier to breathe here. The cool, dry air flowed in and out, something that she'd learned to never take for granted again after too long inhaling canned hospital air and feeling the crushing panic that came from watching someone she loved dying.

"Forget the revelation. You have another problem." Avery raised her cell phone higher, hoping to find a signal, without any luck. The sun was dropping quickly, and the climb down, while it would go faster, wasn't going to be as quick as she'd expected, either.

Her mother would be worried.

In an effort to hurry, Avery stretched her legs, grabbed her long-empty water bottle and started back up the first small rise that led back down to the trailhead parking lot. The unseasonably warm breeze had been perfect while the sun was up. Now a jacket would be nice.

Thanks to the shadows of the setting sun, it was harder to see all the rocks and tree roots that bumped across the trail, so halfway down the second long rise, Avery stubbed her toe, stumbled and landed on one knee with an ugly curse.

The urge to sit down and sob over the injustices of life welled up almost as quickly as she realized she wasn't hurt, but banged up. The fact that her emotions ran away with her before she even knew where she was heading was twice as irritating as a scraped knee.

"You can't sit in the dirt and cry like a baby, Avery. People will be searching for you." The last thing on this earth that she wanted was to be the subject of a manhunt, and if she didn't get to the bottom and her mother's car and cell phone service soon, she'd have to move, leave the country and change her name.

She'd brushed off her jeans and tightened her shoestrings in the effort to convince her feet to get with the program when she heard someone yelling. Whoever he was was still a distance away and she couldn't make out what he was saying, but there was no denying that her search party was already on the hunt.

Annoyed at herself and at her mother, Avery cupped her hands around her mouth and yelled, "Here. I'm here." Then she pulled her cell phone out and checked again. Still no signal.

Determined to save the poor guy headed her way as many steps as she could, Avery marched up the next rise and had to catch herself on a fallen tree when she tried jogging over rough rocks.

"Avery." This time she could make out the word clearly.

"Here. I'm here." Her voice was breathier than it should be, thanks to the pang in her side that made it easier to stay hunched over for a second.

Then her rescuer appeared over the rise and trotted down to meet her.

"Sam Blackburn. It's been a long time," Avery said with a lame attempt to convince him she was perfectly fine and had everything under control. They might not have seen each other except for brief flashes whenever she'd made it home for Christmas, but she'd pick him out of a sea of faces. They'd once moved in the same crowd, the previously mentioned punks. She and Sam had either been friends or vicious competitors growing up, but his grandfather was the first one to bring her here to see the falls. Sam and his mother had lived with Gee next door to Avery's family forever. After Avery's father's death, he'd showed her and Sam all the trails she'd ever explored in the Smoky Valley Nature Reserve, as a way to save Janet Abernathy's sanity. When the weekend rolled around, she and Sam were dogging Gee's steps. And Sam had been the cause or the witness of most of her teenage stunts until she'd graduated from high school and moved to Knoxville to go to college.

While Avery was one more hike up to the cliff away from death, Sam was as strong as he'd been at seventeen. She was also in need of a rescue while he was barely breathing fast. Life was unfair.

"Have a seat." He wrapped his fingers around her wrist to test her pulse and handed her the flashlight. "Hold this for me."

Avery eased down to the rocky path and turned on the light as Sam pulled a handheld radio off his utility belt.

"Blackburn to base." Sam handed her a canteen. "Drink."

Avery wanted to argue but he wasn't ready for that yet.

Whatever he made out through the static prompted the answer: "I found her, headed back down to the Yanu trailhead. Good condition. Pulse is fast but steady. Hold the second group. We'll walk out."

When he turned back, Avery tipped up the canteen, took three good swallows, wiped her mouth and offered it to him. "Are you the Otter Lake ranger station's arm of a county-wide manhunt?"

Sam eased down beside her and ran a thumb over the tear in her jeans. "I'm it. Your mother called me instead of 911. Once she told me you were headed to the park, I had a feeling I knew where to find you. The fact that she couldn't reach you on your cell phone was another good clue. Worst cell reception in the area here." He waved the canteen. "Drink."

Avery snatched it back. "You know, it was a couple of hours on a beautiful fall day, not the desert at high noon." She took three more swallows to make him happy and then capped the canteen and slung it over her shoulder. "I'll hold on to this in case I need it, okay?"

"Good idea. It doesn't take long to get dehydrated, especially as dry as we've been lately." Sam checked her pulse again. His warm fingers reminded her how much she wished she'd brought a jacket. The shiver that shook her shoulders was impossible to ignore.

"Sorry," he mumbled as he grabbed the backpack he'd dumped on the trail. When he pulled out a balled-up windbreaker with a flourish, it was easy to remember every sword fight they'd ever had across her front yard. "Slip this on, and we'll get moving."

She was taking a mental walk down memory lane; he was planning his rescue. Did he remember any of those times? They hadn't been the best of friends, but they'd been more than acquaintances.

Ignoring the spear of disappointment at something else she'd lost before she even realized it was gone, Avery slowly stood and did her best to swallow the groan that bubbled in her throat. Sitting was murder. If she didn't stay in motion, her muscles would leave her here to die.

Before she'd made it all the way to the top, that would have seemed appropriate, sitting beside the trail to let whatever was coming wash over her.

Now she knew she could make it if she kept going. The only option was to fight her way back down to the trailhead.

Oh, man. Was *that* the epiphany?

"I'll follow your lead," she said as she offered Sam the flashlight. She hoped he could see nothing more than grim determination on her face. If he were a stranger, that was all she'd give him.

THE SPLASH OF light across Avery's face was a reminder of how fatigued she was. When Sam had first seen her on the trail, his immediate concerns were dehydration and shock. She was pale, the finest lines around her eyes and mouth tight with pain or something.

But when she'd opened her mouth, she might as well have been the wild girl he'd explored these trails with as a boy.

"I'd rather you set the pace," he said. "Take the flashlight. Make sure to aim it far enough out that you don't obliterate your night vision completely because you'll need to watch the edge of the trail." Falling would be devastating right now. The foliage was so thick that finding her would be next to impossible until the sun rose. Even then, the old growth along the trail could be impenetrable. "When you get tired, stop."

"Aye, Captain," she drawled, and it was enough to draw a smile to his face. She'd never once wanted to be first mate. Avery Abernathy was going to be the king, the captain, the criminal mastermind and the first to charge the enemy.

Their pace was slow and steady. The flicker of the flashlight warned him she was tiring, but she kept going. He could hear her labored breathing but it was a reassuring sound as night settled around them.

The phone call from her mother had scared him.

He'd been preparing to take a final drive through the trailhead campgrounds when his mother called. As soon as she had handed the phone over to Janet Abernathy, he'd tried to reassure her. He could remember Avery's favorite spot. It would be easy enough to check. There was no need to worry.

"She hasn't been herself lately." Janet's voice was tight and Sam knew she was trying to explain something to him without saying it. "I…I don't know, Sam."

On his way up the trail, he'd run through all the scenarios, but there weren't many that fit. She was too weak to make it back down.

Or she'd gone up with no plans of following the trail back down at all.

Suicide wasn't something any reserve ranger wanted to encounter, but they'd all experienced the fear last year when a kid, a sixteen-year-old high school sophomore, had driven all the way from his home in Samson City to jump from an overlook along the Hickory Branch motor trail. His attempt had failed, but Sam could still remember the faces of the guys who'd brought him up.

Nobody would be the same after that.

Finding Avery fighting to get back down was such a relief he'd had a hard time getting words strung together.

She tripped and would have fallen again, but Sam caught her arm in time to ease her to the ground. "Rest. We're close now."

"How can you tell?" she asked as she brushed her hands over her cheeks. He couldn't tell if she was crying, but now she had dark mud smudges on both cheeks. He reached into his pack and pulled out wipes.

"Years of experience on this trail," Sam explained as he wiped the dirt away and tapped the canteen still hanging from her shoulder. "Drink."

Her beleaguered sigh was enough like the old Avery that it was easy to laugh. "When I have to stop to use the nearest ladies' room, it will be all your fault."

"I'll take the blame." Sam took the canteen when she thrust it back at him.

"This was not how this day was supposed to go," she said quietly.

"No?" He knew she was tired. Her words were slurring, and every time she shifted, a faint frown flitted across her face.

"No. I was going to go up confused and come back down enlightened." She rested her head on her folded arms. "And you were nowhere in the picture."

"Enlightened about what?" Sam asked as he reached under her to scoop her off the ground. As expected, she squawked and tried to struggle out of his arms. At seventeen, she'd been strong enough to set him down hard on the ground. Picking her up now was like collecting a fallen branch, lightweight and brittle enough to break. As thin as Avery was, she still knew where to hit. One smack on the arm made him snap, "Settle down or I'll drop you."

"On my head?" she asked. In the dim light, he could see her lips twitching. He'd threatened that a thousand different times when they were kids.

"If I think it will help, yes." Sam grunted as she sighed heavily and dropped her head on his shoulder. "Ten minutes. You only have to suffer through this for ten minutes."

He thought she was resolved to stew in silence. She'd taught him a good lesson about women at an early age. When they got quiet, it was time to worry.

"Thank you for coming for me." She said it so quietly he had to dip his head to get the end of the sentence. "I don't know what's wrong with me anymore."

"Nothing conditioning won't solve, AA." Sam squeezed her tight and made it up over the last hard climb. "That's all."

This time, her sniff had to be tears.

"Aim the flashlight down, farther out." Sam had so many questions, but the ground team was waiting, and he wasn't sure he was ready for all the answers.

"AA. Nobody's called me that in a long time." She sniffed again. "Probably because I haven't seen you in a long time. I can't believe I missed it."

He could see the lights of the rescue vehicles as he rounded the last curve in the path. "When we get to the bottom, I'll hand you off to the medic. She's going to recommend you go to the hospital for a checkup."

Her immediate gasp made him add, "But I'll call my mother. She can bring Janet up to get you. That's what you'd prefer, right?" He almost offered to drive her home, but the report wouldn't write itself.

Besides, he needed time to reconcile himself to the fact that Avery Abernathy had come back, but she was so different from the girl he remembered, she might as well be gone.

She used to be fire; this woman was fog or mist, something too delicate to last for long.

"Yes. Thank you." She squeezed his shoulders and added, "Always the hero."

When the medic met him at the edge of the trail, Sam handed her over and waved his cell. "A hero? You said it. I'm going to hold that over your head, AA."

Her smile was shaky but she gave it her best shot. Here in the lights, it was easier to see how thin she was and the dark circles of fatigue on her face. Whatever she'd been through, she was lucky to have come out on the other side.

He wouldn't sleep tonight because he'd be filling in those blanks in his mind.

"And happy birthday." Her mouth dropped open in shock. He'd surprised himself. Remembering that today was her birthday suggested she was more on his mind than even he knew.

As he turned his back on the group and called his mother, Sam stared up at the pieces of night sky he could make out through the trees. Whatever he'd expected this shift to hold, carrying Avery Abernathy in his arms had never figured into his plans.

CHAPTER FOUR

IF SHE'D KNOWN how much trouble searching for this particular epiphany would cause, Avery would have stayed in her room and taken a nap.

But naps had gotten her nowhere.

Telling her story to the law-enforcement ranger staring down at her was also getting her nowhere.

"Honestly, Officer Hendrix," Avery said as she exhaled loudly, "I'm not sure what part of 'I waited too late to start my descent and got caught in the dark' is so difficult to understand." As Sam tipped his head to the side, Avery realized her tone might not have been as conciliatory as it should have been. "Sir."

"Actually, it's 'Ranger,' although I am a law-enforcement officer here at the reserve." He rested one hand on the gun holstered on his belt. "Your story matches Sam's, so I'll take you at your word."

Before she could argue that taking her at her word had nothing to do with anything Sam might have to say, Sam waved his cell. "They're already on the way. No one answers, so Mom's—"

The loud rattle of a large Cadillac cut him off as Sam and all the other reserve staff on hand turned to watch a yellow Cadillac lurch to a stop in the parking lot.

"Yeah, I figured it wouldn't be too long." Sam sighed and offered his hand to Avery. "If you've got everything you need in the incident report, I'll help Avery to the car."

Avery waved off his help. "I can walk. It's an easy walk. Even I can manage that."

Sam nodded as if he'd expected her to say exactly that.

Ranger Hendrix raised both eyebrows. "I hope you'll come back and take the climb when you're…better." He tapped his pen against his notebook. "Climb like this, it's good for mental health."

She wanted to demand to know what the pause was about, but she wasn't going to do it here with this crowd watching her.

Eleanor Rivera, the medic who'd checked her blood pressure and temperature, said, "I still think an ER visit might be a good plan." She pointed down at the rip in Avery's jeans. "You did take a fall up there."

Rolling her eyes would get her nowhere, so Avery gritted her teeth and muttered, "I have had worse scrapes in my own front yard."

"She has." Sam raised his hand as if he'd testify. "Uglier bruises, too." Then he shrugged. "Doesn't mean having a doctor examine you would be a waste. You aren't as young as you used to be."

For a split second, Avery had to replay his words in her head. "As young as I used to be?"

"It's her birthday," Sam said as he turned in a slow circle to address the crew assembled there. "It wouldn't be polite to tell you how many candles AA has on her birthday cake, but…"

The return of the Sam Blackburn who'd used the same tactic to force her to take dares she knew better than to attempt helped Avery settle in.

"And if I ever hear you insinuate another

woman is old," his mother said from behind his shoulder, "I will give you the birthday spankings I still owe you, young man."

Regina Blackburn had the kind of good looks that made her ageless. She could still be watching their race to the top of the old oak next door as she stood there with both hands propped on her hips. "I'd force him to apologize, but…"

"We'd both know he wouldn't mean it." Avery finished the phrase Regina had said often enough when they were kids that it brought on another flash of homesickness.

"I suspect he was trying to infuse steel in her backbone," Avery's mother said as she tightened the belt on her robe. "Dragging an older woman out into the night because you needed a walk in the woods, Avery Anne Abernathy? I do not know what's gotten into you."

Sam's mother tried to calm Janet Abernathy with an arm around her shoulders, but Avery's mother brushed it off. "And poor Regina here, she insisted on driving because I was too *upset*." The shrill last word echoed in the small parking lot.

It was funny to watch the search-and-rescue crew take a unanimous step back. Annoyed mothers brought out the same response the world over.

"Let's get out of here," Sam said as he wrapped a hand around Avery's elbow. "She's not going to the hospital."

"You going to take these ladies back down the mountain?" Hendrix asked in his official lawman's voice. "Because we are dangerously close to closing time. I'll complete the incident report and leave it in the commander's office for your review." He tipped his head to Avery, who stood next to her mother. "I hope we'll have a chance to meet each other at a more social spot." When he smiled, his whole face lit up. Dour, official Officer Hendrix made her want to stutter and promise to never speed or jaywalk again, in a national park or anywhere. Smiling Officer Hendrix sent a small flutter of the old familiar feeling through Avery, the one that said a man found her attractive and in a totally nice way. It had been so long since it happened, she wasn't sure what to do with the flutter, but if Officer Hendrix had given her a business card with his phone number, she would have taken it gladly and held on to it until she made up her mind.

"Thanks, Hendrix," Sam said as he put his hands on Avery's shoulders and turned her toward the cars. "I'll make sure they get home." His mother jingled his keys and Sam nodded.

When Avery's mother realized she'd raced to the rescue in a house robe and bunny slippers, she was going to be even angrier.

Avery turned at Sam's urging but looked over her shoulder at *Ranger* Hendrix. He was helping to pack up the gear the medic had scattered on the tailgate of one of the service trucks. It was hard to imagine what dinner with such a strong, healthy guy might be like. It had been years since she'd tried to carry on a conversation anywhere other than seated next to a hospital bed.

"Half a second ago he was ready to toss you into the reserve's jail for wasting resources," Sam muttered as he urged her toward the car, his arm wrapped securely around her hips. "Now's not the time for making heart eyes anyway."

"Reserve jail. Is that a real thing?" Avery tried to put on the brakes, pushing hard against his urging with her feet, but he was too strong. Gentle, but insistent and strong. "And heart eyes. What does that even mean?"

Sam rolled his eyes. "You know what I mean. The emoji." He fluttered his eyelashes in a ridiculous way. "Flirty, love, heart eyes." He reached around her to open the door to his mother's car so that Avery could slide easily into the back seat. Avery studied Regina Blackburn's oblivious face and then her mother's interested expression. Neither was good at pretending they weren't watching this conversation with way too much investment.

"Flirty love eyes," Avery said slowly. "I don't remember how to do that, Sam. Come on. He's a nice guy doing his best to encourage me to return to the trail."

The muscle in Sam's jaw twitched but he straightened his shoulders. "Sure. Nice guy. His wife left town with another guy. That's the kind of nice he is."

"Samuel Blackburn, you don't blame the man for his wife's terrible decisions," Regina said with a scandalized yank of her cardigan. "You know better than that."

Sam bit his lip. "Right. I'm saying he still has a *wife*."

"You were warning me away from a guy, doing a service as…what? An old friend? Nemesis? Frenemy? What were we?" Avery slid deeper into the soft leather seat and sighed with relief as her tired muscles melted into puddles. "Doesn't matter. I don't need a man and I certainly don't need a bossy one, Sam."

"Unless you're stuck on the side of a mountain?" Sam asked slowly.

Good point. Not that she'd let him know that. "I would have gotten myself down. If you'll remember, I was always able to rescue myself. No need for the knight to come racing in." Avery ignored the sore ache of her knee, determined to make sure that Sam Blackburn, his mother and hers listened. If she'd gone up searching for a revelation, it had taken getting stranded to understand it. "I've been through harder things, Sam. Tonight all I had to do was keep putting one foot in front of the other. I can do that."

He rolled his eyes. "Yeah. Duh. AA, nobody doubts that." He shut the door firmly and walked off, both hands braced on his hips. From this vantage point, it was nearly impossible to miss that Sam Blackburn had grown into the kind of man that drew women like bees to the sweetest flower. He was tall, with broad shoulders. Here in the light, she could see the sprinkling of gray at his temples, the only sign that he'd celebrated birthdays of his own. Handsome and strong, the qualities every woman stranded on the side of a mountain hoped for in her rescuer. It was too bad his personality was stuck in high school.

His tough talk had been all that had kept her from falling apart more than once that evening. He goaded her into saying and doing things she wasn't sure she could.

By acting like a jerk.

There were times when they were kids that he was no longer acting, but tonight, it was impossible to ignore the fact that he'd given her enough indignation to power through.

Neither Regina nor her mother said anything as they pulled away from the trailhead parking lot and out onto the dark two-lane road headed back to town.

And the silence was starting to get to her.

"I'm sorry I didn't start down sooner,"

Avery mumbled. When she was younger, hitting her mother with the apology before she could dig deep into her aggravation had been a good strategy. That, coupled with Janet's worry over Avery's health, might be enough to postpone the lecture until morning. "I could have driven your car home, Mama."

The tense silence that followed her statement was enough to convince Avery that nothing was going to postpone the lecture boiling inside her tiny mother.

"We will talk about this when we get home, Avery," her mother said succinctly. She didn't turn around in the seat, but Regina glanced back in the rearview mirror, confirming for Avery that her mother was in a high state of mad at that point. Only good manners and being in the presence of company were saving her from a thorough speaking-to.

Resigned to accepting her fate, Avery rested her head against the cushion and closed her eyes. They were close to the rolling hills of Sweetwater when Regina said softly, "You know, Sam's single."

Avery slowly opened her eyes in time to watch her mother thump her head against the headrest.

"I'm saying, if he'd find a nice girl here in town, the need to run off to bigger and better fires might disappear." Regina waved her hand. "In smoke."

"Good one, Ms. B. Smoke. Because he's a firefighter." Avery covered her wide yawn with one hand. "What I don't get is how that fits into this conversation."

"I think he was jealous." Regina turned down the narrow street that led to their houses. "Of poor Brett Hendrix, who is a good man. He's got kids and that woman did run off and leave him with zero help." She *tsk*ed as she shook her head. "He needs a good woman."

"But not me." Avery slowly opened the car door after Regina put the car in Park in her driveway. "Good to know."

"I'm saying," Regina said as she shut her own door, "that if Sam is warning you away, maybe he's got some interest."

Avery skidded to a stop and braced her hand against the low fence that marked the boundary between the two lots. "In me. Interest in *me*."

Regina shrugged.

"They nearly put each other in the hospital at least three separate times, Reggie," her mother said drily. "I'm not sure we want to put them back together, especially in close quarters."

The rest of their conversation was lost as Avery forced one foot in front of the other, climbing the porch steps carefully to keep as much weight off her aching knee as possible.

She'd better find a painkiller before she passed out for the night because it would be hard to sleep. The front doorknob turned easily. Avery refused to consider how often her mother left the doors unlocked.

Avery stared up at the flight of stairs that would lead to both the bathroom, home of all medicines in her mother's house, and her comfy bed. The overwhelming fatigue convinced her to make a quick stop in the living room. She'd eased down and smacked a pillow into the proper shape when her mother stepped inside.

Knowing her efforts were doomed, Avery nevertheless attempted a diversion. "You don't care if I sleep on the couch tonight, do you, Mama? My knee's making its opinion of the stairs clear." She made sure to wince theatrically when her mother paused in the doorway, her hands braced on her hips, terry robe gaping over a hot-pink sweatshirt. "If you're wearing sweats, what's with the robe?" Normally, the woman who wouldn't step foot outside the front door without lipstick would not be caught outside her home in anything less than easy Saturday chic.

"Sleep on the couch. That's fine." Her mother closed her eyes and Avery waited until the tense silence became too much to bear.

"And what is with Regina? There's no way Sam is interested in me." Avery shoved another pillow under her knee and stretched out on the cushions. "He's the one who dared me into swimming across Otter Lake in November." It wasn't impossible. She'd proved that. But it wasn't smart. A quick trip to the emergency room for a light touch of hypothermia was a significant reminder. "He'd be more likely to plot my downfall."

Her mother nodded once and then she held up a hand. "Avery, you need to get something straight."

The emotion shaking her mother's voice snapped Avery to attention. If she'd been trying to avoid an angry lecture by playing ignorant, the game had changed. Her mother wasn't playing any games.

"What is it, Mama?" Avery asked, her choked voice betraying the nerves that had rattled to life with her mother's grim expression.

"I wasn't sure you were coming home." Her mother's voice broke and she had gripped both arms tightly, fingernails digging into the terry cloth.

Confused, Avery eased up. "Tonight? Of course I was." Where else would she go? She'd been driving her mother's car.

Which was still parked at the trailhead.

"Tonight. From Chicago. Ever." Her mother took a step forward. "I've been worried sick about you, and all I get are nothing updates."

"But I'm here now. I'll get better." Avery shook her head. "I'll do better. You can see me doing whatever it is you've been dying to know but have missed out on." Lately, that meant catching up on a lot of sleep. What were they talking about?

"Avery," her mother said as she stepped up next to the couch, "do you want to get better? You don't go out, you don't eat, you haven't talked to your old friends or… All you do is sleep. Do you want to get better?" She eased down on the cushion next to Avery's ripped jeans. "Honestly."

"Of course," Avery said without hesitation. What was the other choice?

Her mother nodded. "It's that…" She unwound one arm and pinched her nose, the old trick they both used to dry up tears. "I was afraid you meant to…stop. To stop everything there in your favorite place in the world. To give up."

Avery could not figure out what they were talking about. "How would I have gotten home? You mean, sit there and…" Avery studied her mother's grim face and the tears that were making a lie of the old trick. "…die?" Nausea rolled through Avery.

"I tried to prepare Sam for the fact that might be the plan." Her mother wrapped her hands in her robe. "They handle things they shouldn't have to."

Avery straightened with a snap. "You told Sam you were afraid I was going to…" Avery paused to try one more time to figure out any legitimate reason this conversation would be going the way it was. "You told him I was going to kill myself at the Falls?" The hard burst of pain behind her collarbone shocked a gasp out of Avery. She'd been through enough pain that it was easy to live with now. She'd become a master at the slow grind of devastating grief, but this sharp jab of disappointment or embarrassment or shame or some confused combination of all three made it hard to breathe.

Aware of the ragged gasps coming from her mouth, Avery covered her lips with one hand and wiped away a tear with the other. "What?"

"I never would have believed it possible, but I was afraid I was about to lose you."

Her mom wilted in front of her.

"Growing up, you and Sam both, I worried you might kill yourselves in some kind of stunt, trying to outdo each other racing up the mountain or even climbing that oak tree." Her mother sighed. "And that would have been terrible, but losing you because you couldn't go on living… I'm not sure how I'd survive."

Since her mother had always had enough energy and firm enough opinions to fill two petite women, Avery understood immediately how afraid she'd been. She would feel the same way if she found out her mother had lost as much weight as she had.

Add to that the inability to fill her days with anything other than sleeping or staring out the window, and Avery would have checked her mother in somewhere, worried to death about the changes to her personality.

"Why didn't you talk to me, Mama?" Avery asked.

"What would you have said? You were always doing fine. I was silly to worry so much. I needed to find something else to do with my time." Her mother stood to pace. "And some of that's even true, but now, tonight, you and I are about to make a change. You cain't go on like this, Avery Anne." The pleading in her mother's eyes didn't quite match her firm tone, but Avery could tell this was important. She couldn't brush it off.

"Fine. We'll make a change." Avery ran a hand through her messy hair. "I went up that mountain hoping to find some direction, the answer to your favorite question. I don't know what I want to do with the rest of my life. I hoped for some revelation. Instead, I got a rescue."

Her mother snorted. "Think answers land with lightning bolts, do you? What did you figure out?"

"When I was seventeen, I won a race to the top of the falls." Avery ran a hand through her curls. "I cheated. I had to cheat to beat Sam by that point. He had a foot in height and I don't know how much in muscle on me, so I tricked him into heading back to the parking area for something and I started climbing. When he made it to the top, I was stretched out on the flat rock there, grinning like a mule with a mouth full of briars."

Her mother rolled her eyes. "I don't doubt it. You have always loved to win."

"That's what Sam said." Avery laughed. "As if he's ever been any better." She eased back against the pillows. "We argued over the 'rules' of the race. Since we neither one of us ever worried much about losing, they were hazy as usual, and I wiggled my way out of every one of his objections." Her smile faded. "He told me then a shark like me ought to make a killing as a lawyer."

Her mother nodded but she didn't add any of the usual comments about how she couldn't accept a girl who'd worked her way through college and law school had given up before graduation to follow a man. Really, Avery had heard it so often she should be inured to it by now.

But at this point in her life, when nothing had worked out like she wanted, it was hard to imagine how she could have let herself get sidetracked from her own plans.

"That's the first thing you do, go back to school and get that law degree," her mother said as she fussed over the rip in Avery's jeans. "You and Sam have slowed down on the dumb dares, but I was pretty sure one or the other of you would *need* a good lawyer someday." She wiggled her eyebrows.

Avery tried to imagine what it would be like to go back to school at this point. Where would she even start? She'd gotten home, her plan to never leave again. To finish her law degree, that plan would go out the window.

"I don't know, Mama. I need to do more thinking on it." It would be easy to fall back to her original plan. Her mother would stop worrying so much. She had the money to finish up the degree. But nothing about the suggestion filled her with any spark, not like the first time she'd grabbed ahold of it.

Her mother stood. "That's all well and good, girl, because I'm not ready for you to leave again, not yet. We'll get there, but not yet." Her mother studied her closely. "I'll go get you some ibuprofen and water. You need to be drinking some water. Dehydration is no joke."

"Wait." Before she could turn away, Avery grabbed her mother's hand. They hadn't resolved her worry, not really. Avery wasn't certain she had the right words, but she had to try. "You were worried I was ready to give up, and I was sitting on the fence." Avery licked her dry lips and wished for some of the water everyone was pushing on her. "But I did get a revelation, Mama. After Sam showed up, I was mad as a worn-out rag could be, but I knew in my head I could get myself down from the mountain. I didn't need him carrying me."

Her mother raised a skeptical eyebrow but didn't argue.

"I would have done it." Avery firmed her lips and raised her chin. "I could have done it because I'd already made it through the hard part. To get back to level ground and the real world, all I had to do was keep putting one foot in front of the other. Climbing to the top? That was the hardest part, and it was so challenging I'm ashamed of myself for how weak I've let myself become. But getting down? That's nothing. All I have to do is keep putting one foot in front of the other because I've already made it through the hardest part. You get it?"

Her mother tilted her head to the side. "We ain't talking about mountain climbing anymore, are we?"

"No, ma'am." Avery squeezed her mother's hand. "I nursed the man I loved. I watched him die." Her voice cracked but she straightened her shoulders. "I untangled all the strings of a life together and now… I gotta find my way back. I've already done the hard part."

Her mother bent to stare into Avery's eyes as she brushed her hair behind one ear. "That's one powerful revelation, young lady." She sniffed. "But don't you forget you ain't got to do all that by yourself. Sometimes you do need a rescue. Let the people who love you do some stepping now and then, okay?"

Before either one of them let the tears that would embarrass them fall, her mother spun on her heel. "Ibuprofen and sleep. Tomorrow you're getting out of this house or else."

CHAPTER FIVE

OVER THE YEARS, Sam had learned to get out of the way when his mother was scheming. When he saw her on the front porch the next day, conferring seriously with Janet Abernathy as he parked behind her car, he was sure he was the subject of the conversation.

The way they both jumped guiltily as he slammed the door confirmed his suspicion and increased the certainty that he had no desire to know what they were plotting.

"Afternoon, ladies," he said as he waved the empty containers that had once held the tastiest roast beef his mother had ever made. Since she was a cook from way back, that was saying something. He had his fingers crossed there might be more in the refrigerator. He'd skipped lunch on the off chance that he might get lucky on this visit. "What shenanigans are you up to on this lovely afternoon?"

Avery's mom cleared her throat. "Well…" She trailed off and shot a "you tell him" look at Sam's mother.

"Well," Sam said as he put the empty containers on the porch railing. "Someone hit me."

"No shenanigans, Sam. We were trying to decide how to retrieve Janet's car from the Otter Lake trailhead." His mother's innocent expression was enough warning that the other shoe would be a doozy. "We hadn't quite come to a decision, so your arrival is like a wonderful sign, son." She blinked wide eyes at him, her face the picture of naive motherly love.

And scheming.

"Uh-huh," Sam muttered as he shoved his hands in his pockets and stared up at the second-story window where he could make out Avery's shadow. "I'm listening."

Janet followed his stare and then heaved a sigh of relief. "Such a smart boy, Sam. You were always such an intelligent kid. You've always understood how to talk to Avery."

So we're going with flattery.

Sam propped one foot on the last step. "I believe you shouted at me more than once that I was going to get her killed." And he might have. He'd been more bravery than smarts growing up. He hoped he was getting a handle on that, but on days like this one, perfectly beautiful, sunny days, when he had nothing better to do than stare into space and wish for something, anything, to happen, he wondered. Ever since he'd sent in his application for the hotshots, he'd done nothing but refresh his email and wish for a distraction.

He glanced up at Avery's window again. Her shadow was gone.

"Tell me your plan," he said slowly. "Wait. Let me tell you mine first. You both ride up in Mom's car, and then Janet drives her own car back. Simple enough." He didn't know why he wasted his breath. If they were going with the logical plan, they'd already be on the road.

"Or..." His mother scooted forward in her chair, her expression conspiratorial, as if he was being let in on a big secret. She'd used that on him successfully before, so it was easy enough to avoid her trap.

If he *wanted* to avoid her trap.

"Or you could take Avery up, get her out

of the house, drive through town and hit some old familiar spots," her mother said as she traced an imaginary route with her finger, "and end up at the trailhead."

Sam crossed his arms over his chest. "Or you could do that." He pointed at the Cadillac. "In your car. Get lunch on the way up?"

It seemed like a good suggestion. His mother might be the best cook he knew, but she never turned down a reason to eat food someone else cooked.

Avery's mother reached forward to press her hand to his forearm. "Sammy," she said, in the same tone she'd used to ask for every favor since he was old enough to haul garbage cans or mow the grass, "she has to get out of that house. I told her that last night. I mean, I made it a threat. Still no change today. She needs time with old friends and people who aren't old enough to be her mother." Janet snorted. "And yes, that includes her *mother*."

They both watched him closely.

They might be right. If she got out of the house, some of the old Avery color might come back.

That didn't mean she wanted him to be her chauffeur.

"This is because of the remarks I made about Hendrix last night, isn't it?" Sam said as he pushed away from the porch, annoyed at himself all over again. He'd known it was an error, but he'd hoped they'd let it slide in the tense aftermath of Avery's rescue. "You're matchmaking. You think she won't see through that?" Since he still hadn't decided how he felt about the way she'd looked at Brett Hendrix, he wasn't sure if their plan was bad enough to be safe or bizarre enough to work, so the best option at this point was to destroy it with logic. "She's a widow. She needs time to figure everything out, and I am going to be leaving Sweetwater soon. I hope."

Watching his mother's joy at her scheme fade was painful, but he had to be firm about following his own plans. If not, this restlessness would drive him insane.

"And how many times do I have to say that I don't need or want a man in my life before you believe me?" Avery said from her spot near the fence separating their houses.

Her mother turned. "I don't know what either one of you are talking about. I thought someone else might have more luck lighting a fire under you." Sam had had less opportunity to judge Janet Abernathy's acting skills, but he almost bought it. "I only want to get my car back."

Avery shook a key ring in the air, the jingle of keys loud in the peaceful afternoon. "Yeah, me, too. That's why I came out. Miss Regina, can Mama and I borrow your car or will you give me a ride back to Otter Lake?" Avery smiled. "Then I'll be happy to treat you both to dinner while Sam goes to do…whatever he's going to do."

Sam frowned at her dismissive tone, uncertain how he became the bad guy when all he'd done was return empty dishes in the hope of leaving with full ones. "You afraid to spend time with me, AA? You are falling for me." He held up both hands. "I get it. I do. But believe me when I say, when I move to Colorado, I can't be bringing you along. Single guys supposedly have an advantage and I am happy for every advantage."

The tense silence that followed his dumb words, only meant to tweak Avery's attitude, was a clue that he'd miscalculated. If he wanted his mother to get with the program and root for him to get this job, mentioning anything that would further delay her plans for his settling down and giving her the grandchild she'd been going on about since before he'd figured out how to talk to a girl without punching her in the arm...that was a mistake.

Did he want her to focus on Avery? He wanted that even less than Avery did.

"What sort of ridiculous policy is that, I'd like to know?" his mother snapped. "That's discrimination. That's what that is."

Sam met Avery's stare, happy to see the wicked glint in her eyes. She knew his distraction had taken a turn he hadn't expected.

"I want to speak to your boss about that." Regina yanked her jacket down. "After you get the job, of course."

His mother never once doubted his ability to do anything he wanted to do or be anything he wanted to be. Casting doubt on his suitability, even if he had made up most of that, was one way to turn her from worried opponent to supportive ally.

"It's not a written policy, Mom," Sam said. It would be illegal even if it was never written. "It's better, makes the work easier, if the strings are limited."

Her disgusted huff was loud and clear in the sunny front yard.

"You know, Avery is *almost* a lawyer," Janet said slowly. "Didn't you take a bunch of courses in employment laws or something?"

This time, Sam knew his own eyes held a wicked glint. He'd never planned on dragging her further into the mess, but it was nice to watch her squirm.

"Labor laws, and yes, but I was concentrating on contracts," Avery said as she limped through the gate in the fence line. "And as you repeatedly remind me, I never finished that degree. Besides that, there's no way that is a policy, written or unwritten." She crossed her arms over her chest, feisty in the bright sunshine because she knew his game and was determined to play to win. "He's reaching for an excuse, Ms. B. If he finds the right girl, he'll change his tune."

Sam ran a hand down his nape, off balance and uncertain which argument to make. Avery would shut it down, whatever tack he chose. "Doesn't change the fact that Avery is about as low on the list of possible suspects as could be. My match? She'll beat me to the top of Yanu Falls." He crossed his arms over his chest, a perfect mirror of her annoyed pose. "Fair and square."

Her face had more color after a full night of rest, but she needed a push. He could push.

The atmosphere of a rousing cat-and-mouse game evaporated as Avery stomped closer to his reserve truck. "Let's go get the car. Straight there. Straight back. We don't negotiate with terrorists or matchmakers."

Before Sam had a chance to agree or disagree, Avery yanked the door open and slid inside.

He propped his hands on his hips and tried to decide how he'd lost control of the conversation and whether or not he was going to take her interference in stride. Normally, his mother was the only managing woman in his life and he loved her enough to go along with it. Every now and then, Janet Abernathy took a step forward and did string-pulling, and he could accept that good-naturedly because she was his mother's best friend and she loved him almost as much as his mother did.

The last thing he'd want, though, was to sign up for a third bossy female. Avery was glaring at him through the windshield and made a "hurry up" motion with her hand.

"You know, it would tick her off if you go for a drive through town. It's your day off. Live a little." His mother picked up the empty containers he'd left on the porch railing. "If your trip takes long enough, I'll have dinner ready and we can refill these before you go home."

"Take her by the pie place," Avery's mother said. "Girl needs to eat and you remember how she loved it." The pie place stood across the main street from Sweetwater's library. Avery had loved both.

"You two are determined one of us is going to end up in the hospital, aren't you?" Sam smiled and stepped away.

Slowly he strolled back through the grass and approached his truck. He bent his head through the driver's-side window and said, "You could ask nicely, you know. A girl who wants a favor ought to try that first."

"Okay, but a woman who knows how to make you sorry is sitting in this seat," Avery said sweetly. "Don't make me go crying to your mother."

The old, familiar threat had lost little of its

power, but Sam was happier, more relaxed than he had been in days as he slid behind the wheel. He'd almost forgotten the fact that he was waiting for an email. He was still stuck right where he was, but he could put off checking his email for an hour or two. Avery was here to distract him. "Fine, but we have to make a stop first."

If rolling eyes could have a sound, hers would. She'd always been so dramatic. That was what made it fun to pester her until she reacted. "Okay, but if there's not a fried pie in my future, your afternoon is going to take a terrible downhill turn."

Sam was grinning as he backed down the lane. Until he remembered their audience and cursed under his breath.

"What?" Avery said as she checked over her shoulder for traffic on their dead-end gravel road.

"I was acting like I was enjoying myself. We don't want to encourage them." Sam immediately assumed a scowl. Let them think whatever Avery said had wiped away his good mood. He wasn't sure why it hadn't, but he glanced over at her. "If they gang up on us, can we prevail?"

Avery blinked slowly at him. "Prevail?" She whistled. "I like it. A battle of good versus evil, all over our dating lives." She rolled down the window and stuck her head out, the breeze ruffling short gold curls instead of the long, messy ponytail she'd had at seventeen.

It took him a minute to drag his eyes back to the road. The mix of old Avery, the wild girl who'd leaned half her body out of the car to catch the breeze, and the new Avery, a woman with closely cropped hair with a touch of silver here and there, confused him. He could see the girl, even though he would say he wouldn't have recognized the woman without a clue when he'd found her on the mountain trail.

Time in Sweetwater was bringing her back to life.

She'd caught him watching her.

"What? A beautiful fall day is perfect for the windblown hairstyle. Soon we'll have cold and rain. Might as well enjoy it to the fullest." Avery ran a hand through her hair. "I haven't done that in so long. It feels good, wind blowing through my hair."

Sam nodded. "Sure. There's a lot less of it to mess up now, too. And if we don't get some rain soon, this whole place will be a dust pile. Driest summer and early fall we've had in a decade."

Sam wasn't watching but he heard what he thought might be the snap of her teeth. Was she grinding them together? "What did I say?"

"As if you don't know." Avery pulled up one leg and braced it on the dashboard like old times. "I can't tell if you really don't like my hair or you're poking again, trying to get a rise."

Sam tightened his hand on the steering wheel. It was a bit of both, if he was being honest.

Still, he wasn't a fool. Commenting on a woman's hair was a minefield of wrong decisions.

"It was simpler, less fuss. Straightening it every day was such a hassle and I had more important things to worry about." She played with the hair at her temples. "Robert didn't like it, either, but it had to be done. Believe me, deciding to cut my hair wasn't the hardest thing I did, but it sure wasn't easy. Losing that ponytail was like…"

Sam waited for her to finish the sentence

but she shook her head. Even if he'd managed to punch through the sadness that made her seem so fragile when he'd met her on the trail, some of it hovered around her now. He wanted to chase it away again, but not by his usual means.

He studied her out of the corner of his eye. She seemed so vulnerable, but every conversation was revealing enough of her grit to reassure him AA was still in there.

"It was like saying goodbye to myself, the person I knew I was," Avery said softly.

If he reached over to give her an encouraging hug, she'd make him regret it.

The urge to do it anyway was something he had to get under control.

"If we're going to the library and the pie shop, you're going to have to drive faster. The library closes at five." Avery tapped the digital display on the dashboard. "And since I'm out of the house like a perfectly normal human being who has no worrying grief or latent suicidal tendencies, I want my prizes."

That was what he wanted to talk to her about, whatever it was that had her mother so worried, but she met his stare. "I'm fine, Sam. My mother will make sure of it."

Here, in the sunshiny afternoon, it was easy to agree. Sam grunted. "Someday, I'm going to spend time analyzing how my stop for more leftovers took such a wrong turn."

"When you head to this new job," Avery said with a wave of her hand, "you'll have time and distance. That makes it so much easier to see through my mother's expert finagling."

Sam shot her a quick look and then hung an arm out the window. "Yeah, and what brings you home, then? Time and distance sound good to me."

"Sometimes you miss that finagling," Avery said as she fussed with those wind-blown curls. "Sometimes you need it, Sam."

The quick trip through Sweetwater was silent as he thought about her words. As he parked in a spot in the center of town, perfectly situated for both the library and the pie shop, Sam wondered if she was warning him. He'd never been away from home. What if he was as restless and dissatisfied in Colorado as he was here? There weren't any bigger mountains for him to climb.

Avery opened the door and then paused. "I don't know what my mother told you…

about last night, but I wasn't even thinking of how I might possibly someday want to kill myself." Her cheeks were pink as she met his stare. "You know me, Sam. That's not me."

She wanted him to agree, so he did. "Of course it's not you. That was part of the finagling, I bet, a way to get me to leave my nice, cushy vehicle and head out onto the dark, cold trail." He stretched in the seat. "They were already matchmaking. No way did I ever believe it, AA."

Her eyes narrowed as she studied his face, like she wanted to trust him but wasn't sure she could. Then she tipped her chin up. "You coming in?"

"To the library?" Sam asked in his best "you've got to be joking" voice. "I'm headed for pie and right now."

She shut the door. "Meet you there in five." Then she was trotting slowly across the small lawn in front of the library. In the old days, she might have thrown a cartwheel in for punctuation. As it was, he was glad she made it to the door without stopping. In the light of day, he could see the same fatigue in her face, but something had changed in her eyes.

And that was the thinking of a man who

was spending too much time considering a woman who would never be his type. Ever. They made better competitors than friends, but he was glad she'd pushed him as hard as she had. Right now, she needed some pushing. He could do that.

First, he was going to get two fried pies, and if she took longer than fifteen minutes, he was going to eat them both.

CHAPTER SIX

WALKING BACK INTO the library where she'd
spent so many happy afternoons after school
was like taking a deep breath above the surface after touching the bottom of the pool.
Everything was familiar and yet new. Even
the librarian had changed.

"I'd like to apply for a library card," Avery
said as she turned in a slow circle, taking in
the new paint color, the new carpet and the
same familiar smell of old books.

"Sure thing, hon," said a perky twenty-
something who hadn't existed or not by
much the last time Avery had returned her
books to this polished oak desk. "Fill in your
address."

Avery quickly jotted down all the details,
her mother's address as familiar to her as her
own face. The librarian squinted as she studied Avery's handwriting. "Oh, you must be
Miss Janet's daughter. She talks about you

all the time. When she was helping with the library's makeover, I heard all about you and your law school. I sure am sorry about your husband, but I am happy to have the chance to get to know you better."

"Uh, thank you." Avery immediately had so many questions. Her mother had helped with the library's makeover? Avery studied the walls and contemporary art. Did she mean painting the walls? Her mother loved paint.

And did everyone in Sweetwater know about her tragedy? Had her mother spread the news of Robert's death through town? Why? Who would remember her well enough to care?

The perky blonde patted Avery's hand before she placed a plastic card on the desk with a flourish. "You put your ol' John Hancock down here and you will be the proud owner of a new library card. Though I expect it cain't compare to the libraries in Chicago." The familiar sound of her mother's *cain't* was less bothersome when it rolled off this girl's tongue. That sound made it clear she was a local through and through.

"In some ways, but you don't ever forget

your first library." Avery slid the permanent marker back across the desk.

"Well, now, I guess that's the truth right there." When she smiled, a dimple actually flashed in her cheek and Avery felt like she'd immediately aged ten years. "You are welcome to pick up some books today if you like, but limit them to two. Then, after you return those, you can stack up those books to your heart's content."

Proud of herself, the blonde crossed both arms over her chest. The slight rush of air ruffled the edges of a yellow sheet of paper that floated to the floor. As Avery read the ad for a part-time children's librarian assistant, she felt the whisper of something across her neck, the stirring of something. Anxious to wave off the feeling, she turned to see Sam standing in the window, a white paper bag clutched in each hand.

"Well, now, if I had a man like that waving one of Miss Rachel's fried pies," the librarian drawled, "I might decide to come back for my books later. And I love a good book." She fluttered her eyelashes. "You and Sam…" She didn't complete the question, just raised both eyebrows.

Avery frowned as she turned back to the librarian. She dropped the piece of paper back on the spotless desk and read the previously hidden nameplate. "Astrid. That's not a name you hear too much in east Tennessee. It's nice to meet you."

Astrid shrugged a shoulder. "A little old-fashioned name, I guess. I'm a book nerd from way back, runs in the blood. My mama always wanted to name me after her favorite character in a book." She rolled her eyes like it was ridiculous while Avery tried to remember a famous literary Astrid. The librarian must have been used to that. "Pippi Longstocking. Thank the man in the moon my mama went for the author's name instead of the character. Can you imagine being named Pippi?"

Avery didn't find herself speechless often, but she couldn't come up with a thing to say to that. As she opened her mouth to say goodbye, a fat orange cat jumped up on the desk and brushed against Astrid. "A library cat? That's awesome."

"You gotta know how to frame your argument. Spot a few dozen studies showing how caring for animals, reading to animals, increases a child's confidence and sense of well-being and voilà…you get yourself a library cat." Astrid bent closer to whisper conspiratorially. "I'm gonna get me a dog next. You wait and see."

Charmed by Astrid's open personality and attitude, Avery offered her a hand to shake. "I'd like to help you with that, Astrid. Could I put in an application for this part-time position?"

Astrid frowned. "It's not many hours and those hours don't pay much." She pursed her lips. "Aren't you a big-city lawyer? I recall Miss Janet telling me that. Of course, the paint fumes might have been clouding my brain at that point."

"I never finished, but I have a degree in English," Avery said and wished she had more to recommend herself. And that was just plain dumb. She could tell stories to kids. An English major should be uniquely qualified to do so.

Astrid rocked back on her heels as she studied Avery. "Good enough for me. It's pretty much a temporary spot, so if it doesn't work out, no harm. I know your mama, so I have a good handle on your character.

And Sam? I trust your taste in men." Astrid ripped up the paper. "Can you start Monday, about two? Once school lets out, it's all hands on deck around here. We close at five, so…" Astrid seemed to be trying to apologize for the short hours, but it was the perfect start. Avery wasn't sure her stamina was up to a full Saturday of energetic kids, not yet.

But she would be up to the challenge again. With every step she took, the next step got easier. The revelation she'd been waiting for at the top of the falls was coming to her in bits and pieces, but Avery was glad to be getting it. She had a job. That would make the big step of figuring out what to do with her life simpler. Each step would get easier because she'd already done the hardest part.

They shook hands again, but before Avery left, she had to ask the question. "Sam and I are old friends. How do you know him?"

That didn't sound like a jealous girlfriend kind of question, did it? Avery smiled in her best friendly manner.

Astrid pursed her lips. "Well, he is quite a catch here in Sweetwater, but I know him best from career-day story times. We do those once a month or so. He likes to come by in his gear and talk to the kids about working for the reserve or fighting fires. You haven't seen what 'hanging on his every word' looks like until you've seen a five-year-old boy on Sam's lap touch his fire helmet. It's crazy adorable. I guess you'll find out, because he's scheduled to come in next week." Astrid pointed behind Avery at the window. "If you don't hurry, he's going to eat your pie."

"See you Monday, Astrid," Avery said before she headed for the door. "Oh, wait—I don't know the cat's name." It seemed important to know her coworkers.

"Guess," Astrid said, her lips twitching.

"Well, Pippi had a monkey... What was that monkey's name?" Avery studied the orange cat, which had wrapped both paws around Astrid's arm and tugged it down, forcibly demanding a pat. "Orange cat."

"Insanely strong for a tubby ball of fluff," Astrid said as she ran her hand down the cat's back.

"You're Astrid, so the cat's... Pippi." Avery laughed as Astrid gave her a thumbs-up with her free hand.

"I knew you were a smart one. This is going to work out fine." Astrid picked up the cat. "When I get the dog, I'm going to branch out. I was thinking Lucy Maud Montgomery. You figure Carrots works for a dog?" Astrid frowned, the question obviously important in her mind. "I already have an orange cat. Do I need an orange dog?"

Avery loved how Astrid thought and mulled over the characters of *Anne of Green Gables*.

"Marilla would make an awesome library dog name," Avery said as she pushed open the door, "or Jem for a boy."

"Jem, like Anne and Gilbert's son. That's a *Green Gables* deep cut." Astrid jumped up and down, her hands clutched in front of her. "I love it. Does the phrase 'bosom friends' concern you? Because if it does, I'll wait to use it."

Avery was still chuckling when she stopped in front of the library. Sam was completely missing, so she wandered over to the bench under the large shade tree.

Where he was eating her pie, if she was not mistaken.

Half a second before she got mad, he pulled a third white bag out from behind his back and tossed it to her. "Backup pie. I'm not an idiot."

"How did you know I'd come looking for you here?" Avery asked as she slipped down on the bench beside him, the shade cool but not uncomfortable this early in the fall.

"Here we have a seat and some privacy to wallow in our dessert. Any smart person would claim this bench." Sam crumpled up his empty bag. "You and I are nothing if not smart."

Avery thought about that as she ate her pie. "Peach. My favorite. Did you get lucky or did you remember?"

Sam draped one arm over the back of the bench, warming her shoulders where they touched. "A little of both. Again, smart people choose peach."

It was tempting to laugh at his smug expression, but she was too busy devouring the luscious goodness of Miss Rachel's fried peach pie. When she finished, she sighed, long and loud. "I've missed those."

"Yeah, you would have. I remember you out here every day after school." Sam leaned forward to study her, and Avery immediately brushed off her jacket, her face, her pants, certain she'd left a trail of evidence. "Where are your books?"

"Since I never saw you step foot inside the library, I'm surprised you know what is kept inside, but the books will be coming." Avery stretched both arms above her head, so comfortable in the late-afternoon shade with fresh sugar and fried dough percolating through her veins. "I might have figured out something to do with the rest of my life." Rest of her life? Not. "Or at least for a bit, to get me out of the house. I'm going to work at the library."

Sam studied her face. "It fits. You and Astrid will definitely be up to hijinks, but I think you might have found the next step."

How easily Astrid's name rolled off his lips. Was there something between them or not?

Why would it matter to her?

Avery took an easy breath for the first time in so long that she might as well be beginning at the beginning, learning to breathe sweet, easy air. For so long, every breath had to be measured and quiet and focused to keep the sobs from escaping that she'd forgotten what it was to be free. "Hijinks. I'm going to be involved in hijinks. I like the sound of that." She tapped his boot with her foot and decided to go for it. "Astrid seems to like you. You guys have a thing?"

One corner of Sam's mouth curled. "You jealous?"

"That's *you*, if I recall correctly," Avery said sweetly.

"I wasn't jealous. I was watching out for you." Sam shook his finger at her. "Been a long time since you had someone to look out for you? Well, get used to it. That's what happens in Sweetwater. It's a real neighborly place."

Avery dipped her chin and did her best to convince him she wasn't paying one single penny for the story he was selling.

"Do you want your mother and mine to keep pushing us together? Accuse me of being jealous of another man when they're around and you won't be able to brush me off. I'll be like a burr in your blanket." Sam crossed his arms over his chest.

"Until you leave." Avery stared over her shoulder. "What time does the pie shop close? Think I have time for another?"

"Yeah, you've got time. And you need

it." His smile faded. "When I saw you last night, I was scared. Your face, it was so pale. Today, though, you seem more like Avery Abernathy, neighborhood scourge." He wrapped one hand over her shoulder and squeezed. "It looks good on you."

Avery relaxed even further into the ease of the bench and Sam's company, his hand a solid brace holding her attention and reminding her of what it was like to be young and strong and the competitor of this focused, powerful guy.

"It feels good, too." Avery poked his leg. "I'm going to miss you when you go. When are you leaving?"

Sam's face contorted into a wrinkled frown. "Man, I'd almost succeeded in forgetting that, and here you are, bringing it up." He turned to stare at the pie place. "Better run and get your dessert."

Determined to find out more, Avery shook her head. "Spill it. I want details, and if I have to get them from my mother, those two will be sending out wedding invites before we know it." Avery was surprised at how easy it was to joke over such a thing. She didn't know if she'd ever date again, much less get married, and at this point, she didn't want to stare at the question for too long. But this was Sam. They'd known each other forever. If there was one man in the world she was safe enough to joke around with about marriage, it was him.

Sam scrubbed his hands over his face. "I sent in the application. Don't know when they'll start scheduling interviews. Until I get my rejection, I'll be all nerves and I hate it. Today, all I wanted was leftovers. Then my plan was to find some flat cliff and climb straight up so that I could sleep tonight." He squeezed her shoulder again. "Instead, I'm spending it with you, which is a lot like climbing tall mountains without a harness."

Avery laughed. "Well, I can't climb with you, not yet, but anytime you need a distraction, you come get me and we'll eat three pies apiece. Then, when both of us are awake when we don't want to be, we can blame it on the need to throw up."

Sam didn't laugh, but the crinkles at the corners of his dark eyes suggested he was amused and even happy to have her back.

"I've missed you and I didn't even know it, AA."

She knew exactly what he meant. Avery tried to absorb the late-afternoon sunshine that lit up her hometown. She'd missed Sweetwater and her mother, her best friend, their meddling, and this man who'd never once pitied her. If she was going to get better, she had to do it here.

"Two more pies coming up." Avery stood and wished she could run and tumble across the lawn like she had at seventeen, a wild, happy girl who never once worried what people thought of her or what the future might hold. For now, she would be glad that walking that far didn't seem impossible. "Then let's head back to the park, get the car. We can come up with some awesome prank to play on the mothers." She spun as Sam stood. "Remember that time we convinced them that we were planning to join the army together?"

"Yeah," Sam said as he massaged his arm. "When she figured out we were joking, my mother poked my arm so hard that I can still feel the bruise."

Avery brushed his arm. "Yeah, we need a good one, one they don't figure out until you're gone. Save that delicate arm." She trotted away as he mimed a clumsy kick her direction, the chuckles bubbling through her a happy gift.

Whatever happened, she would be okay. Putting one foot in front of the other was going to be a breeze. It was good to be home, and Sam was a big part of that.

She should figure out how she felt about that.

Later. After pie.

CHAPTER SEVEN

THERE WAS SOMETHING about walking into kids' story time dressed in full battle gear that made a man feel invincible. Sam never had completely gotten over the thrill of slapping on the helmet, even if he was only marching forward to stand in front of seven first-graders. The way their eyes lit up matched what he thought might happen if a superhero landed between the storybooks and the encyclopedias for young readers.

The opportunity to impress Avery while wearing his cape? Really sweet. She'd be impressed, no doubt.

The fact that he was already counting the days since he'd seen her worried him, but it was easy to tell himself it was because they were still catching up. And he was concerned about her health and well-being and so forth.

Forget about how well she'd distracted him

from his obsession with his email for an entire afternoon.

The restless energy always hit before he launched into his presentation. Today he paused outside the small meeting room, where Astrid had set up a ring of kiddie-sized chairs. Avery was standing in front of the whiteboard, a picture book open in one hand while she tried to turn the pages with the other. Since the other was covered in what appeared to be a wizard puppet, turning the pages was a complicated, clumsy process.

Her audience? They were over it. One little boy was drooping as if she'd already put him to sleep.

"'And then Princess Kijai escaped through the window,'" Avery read as she bobbled the book, "'and—'" The book fell and landed with a hard slap on the polished concrete floor. "Oh, sorry about that." She scrambled to pick the book up, but her puppet-covered hand knocked it under a chair and Sam had to save her again.

"Who wants to be a firefighter? Who wants to have the best, most exciting, most important job in the whole world?" Sam bellowed as he entered the library's children's area on Saturday afternoon. He'd learned the hard way that hesitation was a tell that let them know he was nervous. And once kids learned he was nervous, things got boring fast. They got quiet. Then he did, too.

The cheers accompanying his entry were due to both an excitement to see him and relief that Avery was done. She hovered as if she intended to insist that she finish her story, but he motioned to the door with his head. When she walked away, the kids cheered again and Sam cupped his hands around his mouth to shout, "Let's talk about firefighting."

His hyping skills had improved significantly. The way Noah Hawkins jumped up and down made him smile. He never missed one of Sam's days. In about twenty years, Noah Hawkins would be gunning for Sam's job.

If he hadn't made the jump to Colorado and the Highland fire crew by then, he should give the kid his chance.

"Come on, Noah. Let's tell them a story." Sam held up the fire ax he'd gotten special permission from his captain, Astrid, the town's mayor and Noah Hawkins's mother to carry into story time.

"The one with the collapsed bridge, Sam," Noah said as he clapped his hands. "It's my favorite."

Sam had told this particular story so many times it had the same feeling as making a grocery list, but kids loved it.

That had something to do with the bear cubs.

Sam eased down on the stool and pointed to Noah. "Only if you'll help me tell it." Noah's eyes grew and he nodded wildly before he raced to the small pile of toys to yank a bedraggled teddy out of the jumble. Sam began, "It was a regular August afternoon. The fire module was out fighting a routine lightning strike. It was a small blaze in one of the remote areas of the reserve, up toward Dogwood Gap near one of the backcountry campsites."

Sam studied his audience and knew every kid there was hanging on his every word.

"We'd dug a firebreak and were watching the fire burn itself out. Why do we do that, Noah?"

"To make sure the fire doesn't jump the

line." Noah thrust the bear in the air for added emphasis.

"Right," Sam said as he gently rescued the stuffed animal that Noah was now slowly and surely strangling. "Fire almost always follows the rules we understand, but sometimes it changes course, even after we've studied the weather and the surrounding land carefully. We'd already had a long day of digging and working to contain the blaze, but none of us were quitting." The small movement of air in the cramped room drew his attention to the doorway. Astrid was blocking the entrance, shifting her weight from side to side as if she was crossing things off her mental to-do list.

And Avery had joined her. She was seated on the low desk inside the door, one long leg extended to brace herself. If the kids were excited he was there, her face was completely serious. Surely she had to be relieved her disaster of a story was over. Was she always that bad?

If there was a story-time contest, he'd totally take the title. That felt good.

"And they had to hike in because the helicopter couldn't drop them off that day on account of bad scheduling," Noah added with a nod.

Sam was certain he should explain away that comment, but he wasn't exactly sure how to do it. The kid had a way of shouting the truth.

Sam cleared his throat. "This one almost got away from us because the lightning struck a spot with heavy, old growth. That makes it difficult to reach and means there's lots to burn in every single direction. Crews have to split up instead of forming a solid front, but we'd managed to contain it. The sun was going down, though, and we were ready to go home. At the end of a long day in the heat and smoke, fatigue makes it hard to stand sometimes."

"Did the fire jump the break or not?" the lone little girl in the front row asked, her impatient tone reminding him a bit of Avery every time she'd ordered him around as a kid.

"No, but he met a bear," Noah yelled with bloodthirsty glee. "A mama bear."

Everyone in the room was silent. Since he and Avery had climbed Yanu Falls a hundred different times and remembered each time they saw a bear as a special occasion, he'd expected her to be jealous. Instead, the lines on her forehead deepened. Why? She couldn't be worried. He'd obviously met the bear and come out on the other side. He was sitting on a stool in the library.

"Actually, we found the babies," Sam said, "and we were concerned about leaving them in the burn zone. She had two small cubs. They were tangled in old brush." Sam raised his hand. "Everyone put up your hand if you know what to do when you run into a bear in the woods." A few tiny hands shot up. "What do we do?"

Noah thrust a fist in the air. "We run like—"

"Running is not the first answer, but you aren't far off track." Sam cleared his throat and watched Astrid's shoulders shake. "If the bear doesn't see you, back away slowly, but don't turn around. If the bear sees you and starts to come toward you, make yourself as big as you can. Create as much noise as you can. Bears want to get as far away from the threat as possible."

Noah pointed at Sam. "Unless you got their babies."

"Yeah, if you're too close to their babies," Sam said with a sigh, "quick retreat is the best option. This time, we hiked back to the engine so we could live to fight another day. A smart firefighter knows when to take a break. We could come back later to make sure the fire was out, after Mama Bear and her babies had found safer space."

"But the bridge was out," Noah shouted, "and they had to call for rescue." He jumped up and down. "Firemen had to call other firemen to save their—"

"That's why we're all part of teams," Sam interrupted again. He should introduce himself to Noah's father. The kid's mother didn't strike him as the type to make her speech more colorful through the use of four-letter words, but Noah was picking it up somewhere. He'd already fit in around a firehouse dinner table.

The little girl in the front row thrust her hand in the air.

Mentally bracing himself, Sam said, "Yes, Miranda?" She had attended the last story time and managed to argue persuasively that every firefighting team should have a dalmatian on the payroll as a kind of rallying mascot to build morale and be a symbol of loyalty to the lands they served. Her passion had almost convinced him to broach the subject with the crew superintendent.

Then he realized he'd be the one responsible for the dog.

"My father says that, while firefighters are heroes—" Miranda pushed her glasses up her nose "—it's teachers who have the most important job in the world. Plus, you don't have to die. I'm glad my daddy is a teacher. I don't want him to die." She tipped her head to the side, ready for whatever his response would be. A beat of silence followed her words.

"But *nearly* dying is awesome!" Noah punched a fist in the air. "Like a superhero."

Confused over the correct path, hype or honesty, Sam searched the room for help. He understood Noah's enthusiasm. Testing his limits and winning was awesome, but telling a small crowd of impressionable children that seemed unwise. Even nearly dying *was* bad.

Astrid shrugged. Avery was frowning, her concern clear. She wasn't sure how he was going to get himself out of this, either.

Sam took a knee in front of Miranda. "It's hard to argue with your daddy, Miss Miranda. Teachers are heroes, no two ways about that." He bent closer. "And here's a secret. I'd be a pure disaster trying to teach you how to spell."

"That's okay, Sam," Miranda said as she patted his arm. "I already know how to spell."

Sam nodded seriously. "Right, because of your daddy. But I wanted to be a hero, too. This is how I found my way. I love the forests and the animals and I want to work to keep them safe, even when it's dangerous." He turned to look straight at Noah. "And the nearly dying? It doesn't happen often enough to keep things exciting, because I work with some strong, smart firefighters."

"So, you're both right?" Miranda said slowly, clearly puzzled how that could possibly be. "Both of them are the greatest jobs in the world?"

"I guess so, and whatever you decide you want to do should be the greatest job in the world." Sam glanced at Avery. "That's what we all need to find, the job that convinces us it's the best one ever."

He raised both eyebrows at Miranda. "Does the prosecutor rest?"

"You think I don't know what that means, but my daddy tells me all the time he's not on trial." Miranda sighed. "I don't have to be a lawyer if I don't want to. That's what my mommy says and she's never wrong. I would be good at it, though, possibly the greatest in the world." Her mouth curled slowly.

Again, her logic was impossible to defeat, so Sam offered her his hand. She shook it firmly.

"Who wants to try on the helmet?" Sam asked as he stood. As he'd expected, every hand in the room shot up. He waved it at Avery. "How about you, Miss Avery?" Instead of jumping at the chance to slap it on and take the fire ax for a bonus swing, Avery held up a hand and then stood. She bent to whisper something to Astrid and left the room.

Disappointed that she didn't hang around to listen to him, explore the gear he'd brought in or wonder at his amazing way with children, Sam refocused on making his career talk memorable. He'd done this a dozen times. Coming up with something new to keep everyone interested was getting harder and harder, but showing off the equipment on the truck never got stale.

"Let's go check out the engine," he said as he headed for the side door leading to the tiny parking lot, a pack of lively kids hot on his heels.

LEAVING HER CHARGES in the hands of Astrid and Sam was not the best way to finish off her second week at the Sweetwater Library. Did anyone miss her? No, but she'd never skipped out on a job. She'd worked through college, carried a full load to finish a double major in English and history, and managed to make the dean's list more often than not.

She'd been exhausted but too overworked to spend much time finding a better balance.

That was why Robert's insistence that cutting back to spend more time together had made absolute sense.

Now this part-time job working with kids was beating her.

At some point, she and Astrid were going to have to have a serious talk about what a disaster she was with the kids, but not today. Sam was in control and she could hear the excited voices all the way out here.

Sam Blackburn was better at story time than she was.

It annoyed her, irritated the winner inside her, but it was impossible to ignore.

She might have hung around, tried to pick up some pointers, but watching Sam celebrate taking risks had hit her hard. His eyes had lit up with excitement at retelling a story where he could have died in at least three different ways. Avery sat down in the chair behind the large polished desk and willed someone to call or to approach her with a book to check out.

She didn't want to think about Sam in danger.

And she didn't want to again experience the crushing weight of losing someone she loved. Her father had been the first man who'd died too soon. Then Robert, the man she'd planned to raise a family with.

Sam's pleasure at cheating death was too scary to watch. In her head, she'd imagined he stood behind a hose and aimed water at a bonfire. Controlled burns took up most of his time. *Controlled.* Widespread fire, angry, frightened bears, destroyed bridges…none of that was under control.

Pippi raised her head with a soft meow as Avery shifted back and forth in the rolling chair, discreet squeaks annoying enough to disturb a library cat.

"And you have nerves of steel, don't you, Pippi?" Avery murmured as she ran a hand down the cat's back. Pippi licked her lips and settled back to sleep, one suspicious eye slowly sliding shut.

"You okay?" Astrid said as she stopped in front of the desk, the noise from the children's area proof that Sam's time was up. Soon there would be a flood of easy readers and middle-grade books stacked on this desk.

"Fine." Avery stood, ready to relinquish her spot. "I needed a minute. Sorry to bail."

"Well, it was story time, but you weren't technically in charge at that point, so…" Astrid braced her hands on the desk. "I'll insist you convince me you're really okay."

Avery rubbed her forehead as she tried to come up with a good answer for something she wasn't sure she understood herself. "I used to be him. I used to be like Sam, ready for adventure and certain that life on the edge was the only way to live. But now…" Avery checked her khaki skirt and the short-sleeved sweater she'd put on without much thought. "Hiking boots. Jeans with enough holes in them to be comfortable. A messy ponytail. And I was so happy. Alive. Like Sam is."

That had to be what was bothering her. She'd attempted the climb up to Yanu Falls and failed, while Sam was charging at every adventure put in his path.

"And cheating death sometimes," Astrid said as she picked up Pippi and gave the cat a quick scratch on the chest. "Sure that doesn't have something to do with it? The death part?"

Avery dropped down in the seat behind the desk, her knees weak suddenly.

"Because you've already seen how some people aren't able to outrun it." Astrid put the cat back on the desk. "Until my mother died, I was nearly certain she'd live forever. So would I and nothing would change. But it did, and now, because of that, I can't ever see this world or time or the days we have with the people we love the same." Astrid took a deep breath. "You know?"

Avery squeezed her eyes shut, desperate to figure everything out. "Yeah, but he's…a friend, a guy I knew years ago who's planning to move on soon. We need firefighters. He's a good one. Why does listening to him talk about doing his job make it hard to breathe?"

Astrid seemed to struggle with whether or not to answer. "Because he's the person you used to be, the one you want to be now? And he's not invincible. You're not invincible." She held up both hands in surrender. "Sorry. Thinking out loud." Then she turned on one heel to go and referee a fight over the most popular beanbag chair.

"Not invincible," Avery murmured as she traced one finger down Pippi's tail. "But so alive and in love with his job. Maybe she's right."

Avery smiled at the disorderly line forming at the doorway to the children's area. In half a second, she'd have clamoring readers in front of her, library cards waving in the air. That was one of the most rewarding half hours of her job, when story time was over and kids were desperate for their books. The little girl who'd been ready to correct Sam over the greatest job in the world had elbowed her way to the front of the line, and the determined jut of her chin suggested no one was going to make her move.

Avery admired her, could see bits of herself in the girl.

At seventeen, Avery had gone after whatever it was she wanted.

Now? She was existing, making it through the day, and that was an improvement, but what would it take to get back to who she used to be?

Sam, cleared of gear and equipment, poked his head back inside the library. "You get a break?" he asked Avery. "I want to talk."

"Yep, in twenty," Astrid said as she led the short parade of kids bursting with energy through the lobby. "And she's going to need it."

Avery took the card Miranda slapped down on the desk and started scanning the bar codes on her impressive stack of books. She wasn't sure she'd figured anything out, but if what she wanted was more life in her days, she knew a guy who could give her some pointers.

CHAPTER EIGHT

THIS TIME, WHEN Avery found Sam, he was seated on top of the fire engine, like a bird perched on the highest branch to take in the view. "What are you doing up there?" she asked, one hand shielding her eyes from the late-afternoon sunshine. "Is that seat reserve approved?"

Sam pointed out three different steps for her to take in order to reach him, before he held up one hand with the paper bag and offered her the other. "You aren't afraid, are you? Do I have to dare you, AA?"

This was what he'd always done, using that same sly tone and the slightly disapproving frown to goad her into movement.

Today, she loved him for it. She wanted a closer look at the engine. She wanted to sit on the very top. And she was ready for a snack. He could give her all three.

Wishing yet again that she'd gone with

something other than a khaki skirt, Avery climbed as gracefully as she could until she reached Sam's hand. With one swift yank, she was seated next to him, her heart hammering with exertion and goofy exhilaration that she'd made it.

"Is that pie for me?" Avery asked as she snatched it from his hand.

Sam whistled long and loud. "I thought I might need a bribe. You didn't seem too happy inside. Out here, though, you've got real nice color in your cheeks. Inside, you sorta took on the gray tint you had on the trail at Yanu."

"There's no way you could see gray. It was night." Avery snorted and took a bite of the pie.

Sam folded his hands together and kicked his boots out once or twice, like he had when they'd managed to call a truce long enough to share the tree house shell in the old oak.

Avery devoured the peach pie and tried to ignore the heavy atmosphere of gloating. If she didn't mention story time, maybe he'd let it go.

"So, you're terrible at talking to kids. The worst." Sam held up his hands. "I never would have guessed that. I like it, but I wouldn't have guessed it. Avery Abernathy was good at everything."

Avery sighed loudly. "It's Montague now, not that anyone remembers that, and it's not that I'm bad at talking with children. I don't have a theatrical flair like the guy who stands in the center of the ring before a wrestling match. I'm perfectly fine with that."

"Uh-huh," Sam said slowly, his disbelief crystal clear.

"No, I can talk to kids. I can talk books and even television shows and characters." Avery yanked her skirt down to cover the bruise on her knee. "I don't have much experience performing."

Sam was quiet as he stared out over the shady streets of Sweetwater. "How in the world were you going to control a courtroom, counselor?"

Avery glared at him. "I wasn't planning to. I'm not a criminal defense lawyer on a television show who has to pull Hail Mary moves to win the day. In the real world, all a good lawyer needs is solid research and the ability to win any argument. I've got that."

She raised an eyebrow at him, willing him to argue. She was ready to demonstrate.

Sam held up both hands in surrender. "Fine. I'll be the first to say the world has lost a first-class argument winner. If you don't go back to law school and fix that, who will terrorize the unprepared?"

Her lips were twitching as she said, "Well, if Astrid fires me like she should, maybe I will go back to law school." This time when she said it, the hard pit in her stomach that had accompanied every conversation about returning to school for anything was absent. More time could be the solution.

Everyone else seemed to think it was the right choice.

Sam cleared his throat. "It's a matter of *when* Astrid fires you, not if at this point. You had a kid asleep, AA."

At that, Avery had to laugh. "I was hoping he had his eyes closed so he could listen better." They both chuckled. "You, on the other hand, had them jumping up and down. That's a skill."

Sam shrugged. "I know."

At his cocky answer, Avery bumped his

shoulder with hers. "Too bad you missed out on the modesty."

"When you're as good as I am at talking about what I do, there's no sense in being humble." Sam took a deep, satisfied breath. "No one would believe that."

Avery rolled her eyes. "What are you going to do when you move away? Can you do remote story times?"

She watched some of the grin fade before he said, "I will miss that. I like talking to kids. Because I'm so good at it. You should have hung around to watch me work." He turned away so it was impossible to read any emotion on his face. Were his feelings hurt that she'd left before he finished?

"If it's any consolation," Avery said softly, "I did want to put on the helmet." She waited for him to laugh but he turned back to her, his eyes serious.

"You gonna tell me why you were so worried?" Sam asked. "Or should I skip to the favor I'd like to ask?"

Avery chewed and pointed at her mouth to show that she was too busy for talking until he pretended to snatch the treat out of her hand. "Fine. To hear you talking about cheating death…" She shook her head. "I spent so long begging for one more minute with Robert that I…"

Sam sighed. "Yeah. Sorry. I didn't mean to bring up bad memories of the perfect love of your life." Sam stared in the other direction while Avery finished her pie.

"He was the love of my life." Avery crumpled the bag. "I miss him every day, but that doesn't mean he was perfect, Sam. He's gone, so it's easy to forget that. But neither of us was perfect." As she sat here with him, staring out over the town, that lack of perfection bothered her less than it had for years. She had a list of things she should have done better, ways she should have taken care of Robert, words she should have said, but that list was harder to remember this afternoon.

She should be thanking Sam for that.

"Think you'll ever find another?" Sam asked. "Love of your life? I'm wondering, since I can't seem to find a love of my *this week*." He bumped her shoulder.

If she knew the answer to that, Avery had a feeling her optimism might take a sharp upturn. Falling for Robert had seemed inevitable. The first day she'd seen him striding across campus, late for whatever meeting he'd set himself, she knew he was the man who could change her life. Had she imagined that meant dropping out of school, becoming a faculty wife and learning how to fill her days with volunteer work? Not really. Avery Abernathy had never thought that way.

"What's the favor?" Avery asked.

Instead of pushing the conversation, Sam said, "I got a call. From the Highland crew recruiter. They want me to fly out for a *conversation*. Not an interview, but a *conversation*. They'll also be doing fitness testing."

The sugar buzz she'd been enjoying evaporated in an instant. "Hey, that's great." She'd just realized how much she needed his help, but it seemed he really was going to be moving on. "When?"

"This week. I cleared it at the reserve, so I'm going to go." He ran a hand down his nape. "Haven't told my mother yet."

He met her stare and then shrugged. "Don't guess you'd want to do that for me?" Avery pretended to punch him, but he held up both hands. "I'm kidding. Mostly."

"Who was it who was bragging—" Avery leaned close enough to see the gold flecks in his hazel eyes "—*bragging* about escaping fire, destruction and angry mama bears ten minutes ago? That was you."

"Yeah, but now we're talking about hurting my mother." Sam rubbed the center of his chest. "How did you do it?"

"How did I break my mother's heart?" Avery drawled slowly. "Well, the first time, it was to go away to school, something we both wanted. Then I dropped out of law school, married a man she never approved of because he was almost twelve years older than me, and nearly killed myself watching him die from cancer." Avery squeezed the balled-up bag hard. "After you do it the first time, hurt them, it gets easier."

"No, it doesn't." Sam wrapped his arm around her shoulders and squeezed.

"No, it doesn't." Avery had to clear her throat before she could continue. "But you should go for it, Sam, live your own life. I had to. I have the scars now, but you have to go for what you want. Your mother knows you're hoping for this. She'll support you."

"Yeah." Sam waved as Noah and Miranda came tromping out of the library. They seemed to be arguing over something, but it was hard to make out their words.

"They remind me of us," Sam said. "He's going to charge out into the world, and she's going to change it. Passionately." He shivered. "I would not want to face her in a criminal trial. She's a baby shark right now. When she grows into her teeth, the world better look out."

"It's okay for her to be passionate and smart, Sam," Avery said, stung at his description of Miranda and her. "That doesn't make her a shark, or only cut out to be a lawyer. Imagine that passion aimed at curing cancer." Someday there would be a cure. There had to be. Too many people's lives were ravaged by it. Someone would find the answer. Why couldn't it be Miranda, the argumentative little girl who wanted to be right?

Sam studied her face. "You've got me wrong. I admire both the passion and the smarts. Noah and I can be brave, sometimes foolish, too, but I'll never cure cancer or finish law school or…a million other things that Miranda will do. The world needs her."

This was the perfect opening to ask him to

help her get her feet back under her, but he was watching her so closely that the words dried up on her lips. "And the world needs firefighters, Sam. Promise me you'll be more careful." She gave him the threatening stare she'd perfected at twelve.

"I'm always careful, AA," he said as he rolled his eyes. "It's like you don't know me anymore."

Did she? Settling into their old pattern had been easy, but she hadn't spent much time considering that Sam might be any different from the boy she'd known. Had he changed at all?

At seventeen, the future had been something to worry about the day after tomorrow, not on sunny days when there was adventure around the corner. This goal to join a regional crew could meld the two, going for the adventure with an eye to the future.

Sam checked his watch. "I have the best timing. You need to get back to work. We don't want to give your boss any other reason to fire you, other than poor performance, I mean. What do you think? About the favor? Can you distract my mother until I get back?"

Good. A ticking clock. She'd always been

more impulsive when she could hear time running out. Adding that to trash talk and she was ready to slam-dunk his favor. "When are you leaving?"

"Tuesday morning. Should be back Thursday. Prepare yourself for a great deal of Regina Blackburn." Sam blew out a breath. "I'm so glad you're back. If you could manage to appear punier, less flushed with fried dough and sugar, that would be great. They can nurse you, and before anyone knows I'm gone, I'll be back."

Avery stared straight at him. "I'm supposed to fake a decline. That is what you mean, right? Not that I'm so weak I'll be happy to have nurses."

Sam shook his head. "You are sitting on top of a fire engine. Get a grip." He snorted. "Weak. I can't even…"

Relieved, Avery said, "All right. I'll keep the mothers busy, but I need some help when you get back, too." She wanted to believe he hadn't changed, and she wanted to prove to him and to herself that she *could* change, could get some of the old Avery back.

Sam was already nodding as he eased around her and stepped down to the ground in a graceful, athletic move that there was no way she'd be able to replicate. Maybe if she had her jeans and boots.

"Whatever it is you need from me, you've got it. Step here, and then I'll help you down." He held out both hands and made grabbing motions, almost like she was a bag of cement he was prepared to catch. Flattering.

Instead of studying how far it was to the ground, Avery followed his direction. With one quick step, she was falling, but Sam guided her down, his hands solid on her hips, with a soft, steady landing.

Avery could feel the muscles in his shoulders shift under her hands. In his official navy T-shirt and olive cargo pants, Sam was strong and handsome but a regular guy, not a man who could be gone in the second when a fire leaped out of control. He was Sam, the kid who'd made her mad enough to spit and laugh so hard she cried, but he was more. It was tempting to stand there with him until the warm sunshine disappeared.

"You okay, AA?" Sam asked as he bent to stare into her eyes. "Do I need to check your pulse again?"

"I had to catch my breath," Avery grumbled. "What good does checking my pulse do, anyway?" She shoved back from him and ran both hands down her skirt, annoyed at herself and him.

"When your eyes are that fiery? It's overkill. It's clear you're alive and breathing at this point." Sam crossed his arms over his wide chest and Avery wanted to smack herself on the forehead. His chest *was* wide. He was tall and strong and so alive. And that was the part she wanted most.

"In exchange for distracting the mothers, I need you to help me—" Avery still wasn't sure what to call it "—take more chances. Do more things. Get out there."

Sam raised an eyebrow.

"I want to be more like the old me, the one who would scoff at the idea of needing someone to push her to chase adventure." Avery waved at Astrid, who was watching from the door. Break time was long over. "Can you do that? Dare me?"

"Only if you'll call me your life coach." Sam sighed heavily. "Or an expert, a life *expert*, something that shows my value. I could put that on my résumé."

Avery shook her finger. "You'll do it or

else. I'll convince the mothers you broke my heart and woe unto you." Then she marched toward the door.

"Hey, AA," Sam called, "thanks for the help. I needed it. Got any advice for me? A pep talk to send me on my way?" He held both hands out, like he was ready and waiting for the encouraging part of their conversation.

Avery stopped, amazed that he'd admit such a thing. As a kid, he'd never admit to needing her help with anything. This time, it was easy to find the right words.

"This interview? You've got it. They'd be foolish not to pick you." Standing there in his uniform, the park's engine behind him, Sam was calendar material, but more important, he had zero ability to give up. A heavy weight settled over Avery's shoulders at the realization that she couldn't say the same thing about herself. She had quit, but that didn't mean it was permanent. "Call me to let me know how it goes. I'll be the one languishing on the couch, asking for my robe and slippers."

Before he could answer, she ducked back inside the library, where Astrid was seated at the desk, Pippi curled in a ball in her arms. Avery had a job, of sorts. She had a way to get some of herself back, of sorts. When Sam returned, things would get interesting.

And when he left, she'd be strong enough to continue on her own.

As SAM BRAKED in the unloading zone at the Knoxville airport, he said a quick prayer that Avery was ready for a rough couple of days. His mother's first few quiet sniffles had made tiny cuts across his heart, but he'd reached the point where he was numb. If she'd ever asked him once not to go or implied that he was hurting her by going, he'd have canceled everything, called off the shot he'd been day-dreaming of for weeks.

Instead, she kept up a cheerful stream of chatter about all the wonders of the Rocky Mountains and how much fun he would have learning the trails there. She was doing her best to encourage him while clutching a ragged tissue in one hand.

"Mom," Sam said as he took her hand in his, "don't worry. I'm sure they're talking to a dozen candidates. This is a…test. That's all. I'll be home before the weekend."

His mother sighed, a long sound that mixed a gasp for air and a sob. "They'll be fools not to hire you."

"Avery said the same thing. It's good to know I've got my fans." He pulled his mother close. "Keep an eye on her while I'm gone."

His mother jerked. "An eye on Avery? She's a *fan*?" He could see the calculations start in her eyes and said another quick prayer for Avery. "You talked to her about your plans?"

She didn't say it, but it was on the tip of her tongue: *"You talked to her about your dream?"*

"You asked me to check on her, so I did. She's, well, working at the library." He didn't mention the way she'd folded when he'd celebrated the dangers of his job or how terrible she was at hers. His mother wouldn't welcome the reminder that sometimes nature and fire were both unpredictable. "You could talk to her about her investments, make sure she's thinking of her future."

His mother had retired from investment planning the year before. He'd assumed a hobby other than cards with her friends and worrying about him would appear. She and Janet had been working on projects here and there in Sweetwater, but he didn't know much about what occupied their days. They never called him for bail money, so he figured they were doing fine.

She eased back against the Cadillac's plush leather seat. "I could do that, polish up my rusty skills. Janet and I've had to slow down since Avery got back to town, but we can pick up a new project, too."

Rusty skills. She hadn't lost a step that he could see.

And if she and Janet found a new project, Avery would be dragged along once they saw through her faked decline.

He might owe Avery an apology when he got back home, but he'd wait to find out what the mothers cooked up.

Satisfied he'd stirred the pot well enough to leave for a couple of days without it boiling over, Sam opened the driver's-side door, got out and pulled his duffel from the back seat. When they met at the trunk, he kissed his mother's cheek. "Love you, Mom." The hug she gave him convinced him she was hale and hearty and would be fine without him. Some of the tension that had been a knot in his stomach eased.

"Knock 'em dead, son. You want it? You get it." She tapped his chest and then eased around him. Sam followed her and opened the door to close it softly behind her as she buckled herself in.

"Be careful driving home." He wasn't sure he'd gotten the last word out before she raised a hand in a jaunty wave and hit the gas.

The hustle of making it through airport check-in and security distracted him from the loop of worry that had made it impossible to sleep, but when Sam sat down at the gate twenty minutes before boarding, everything came flooding back.

The nagging question about whether he'd be able to make the move even if he got the job offer was so annoying. Of course he would. How often in his life had he worried like this? This was no time to start second-guessing.

The buzz of his phone in his pocket snapped him out of the angry pro-and-con conversation in his head. He shifted to pull his phone out of his cargoes.

You got this. His mother's emoji game was growing stronger. After the short message, she'd included multiple flexed biceps, a few mountains and a blue ribbon.

"Emoji answer or should I use my words?" Sam muttered. "A stern word about texting and driving is definitely required." Then he checked the time and realized his mother was exactly twenty minutes away. The time matched the distance to her favorite outlet mall. "Retail therapy, huh?"

He sent back, Take care of yourself, with a string of emojis she'd love. The dancing woman in the red dress was one of her favorites.

Before he shoved the phone back in his pocket, another text dinged. This one was from Ash. Heard about the interview. Don't blow it, sweetheart.

Sam was still searching through the emojis for the proper answer when the gate crew called his group for boarding. He settled on the little yellow guy blowing kisses and hit Send, certain Ash would understand his meaning.

"You got this," Sam muttered as he grabbed his duffel and joined the queue. He had less than twenty-four hours to get his head screwed on straight before the interview. Any lingering doubts would have to wait their turn.

CHAPTER NINE

A FEW TIMES in her life Avery had made promises that she regretted. Keeping the mothers preoccupied had sounded easy enough, but she'd underestimated them. Instead of worrying over Sam, they'd turned their attention to plotting a no-fail way to keep him in Sweetwater.

Romance appeared to be their favorite option. Avery sipped her plain black coffee and made herself as puny as possible.

"I think it's got to be a girl," Janet suggested as she studied the list she and Regina had been drawing up over dinner while Avery attempted different versions of "sickly and withdrawn." The hour she'd spent walking the downtown of Sweetwater between the end of her library shift and this meet-up might have negated the effect. Her cheeks were still red from the windy afternoon, which was not conducive to faking a weak constitution. The satisfaction of being able to walk that long without gasping for air or collapsing in fatigue on the nearest bench made it easier to sit through the plotting session taking place over the red-and-white-checked vinyl tablecloth in a cramped corner of Smoky Joe's, Sweetwater's original and only coffee shop. If the national chain sweeping the nation like kudzu wanted to add a Sweetwater location, they'd have a town of outraged locals and a few loyal tourists who hated the busyness of other local tourist towns up in arms.

Unfortunately, Smoky Joe's had opened approximately sixty years ago and the furnishings had gone from current to kitsch to "what is going on in this place?" Cookie jars lined the walls. All of the walls. So many cookie jars. Avery stared up at a bear peeking over the top of an outhouse and wondered who would want to put their cookies inside.

It was definitely a conversation piece.

Still, a single sip of the strong black coffee was enough to convince her that she'd missed this place and would have to be a regular visitor. Since her mother and Regina

Blackburn were busy, she had plenty of time to enjoy each sip.

Until she remembered her promise to Sam.

So, she tried sighing. Loudly. Both mothers glanced up, but there was little concern in either one's expression.

"We'll have to do some searching since we aren't getting any help," Regina said with a pointed glance at Avery. "Astrid over at the library is cute and bubbly. Sam could use fun in his life." She tapped the notepad. "I *should* also fall and break something as a safety net." Her slight frown convinced Avery that Sam's mother was completely serious.

Avery clapped a hand over her forehead, the sound loud enough to cause the diners at the next table to turn. "You have got to be kidding me. That's it, right? This is you, pranking me?" Avery held up her coffee cup and looked around, anxious for another shot of caffeine. "You both need to get a grip. I cannot be pranked, and the option to 'accidentally' break something in the effort to keep Sam in town had better be one lousy joke."

Before either could answer, the diner's owner, a woman named Odella who had been ancient the last time Avery ate here, tottered over, a coffeepot in her hand. She was a tiny woman, but tough. One look was all it took to see years of hard work in the lines on her face and the wispy knot of white hair on top of her head, but she moved quickly enough to serve her entire coffee shop single-handedly. "You girls need a refill?" Before anyone could answer, she was pouring. "When you gonna come in to help me redecorate the place, Janet? Last time I checked, you was all booked up. Don't trust nobody but you."

Avery straightened in her chair, surprised and excited…and deflated when she watched her mother laugh like it was the funniest question in the world. The furtive look she exchanged with Regina immediately caught Avery's attention. What were they hiding?

"Now, Odella, you know I don't know anything about decorating restaurants." Her mother pointed at the shelves of cookie jars lining the walls. "Besides, what would people think if they come into Smoky Joe's and don't see your collection?"

Who could say? They wouldn't be trying to calculate the last time all of them were dusted, though. Avery leaned forward. "Come on, Mama. This is a new challenge. It could be fun. Miss Regina, wouldn't you like to help?" Getting them out of the house and occupying them with something other than Sam's possible move and her own meltdown would give them all some breathing room.

Her mother's wrinkled brow was an indication of how serious this conversation was. She didn't do frown lines if she could help it.

Sam's mother raised one eyebrow. "Help with what? I do not do manual labor." She flashed her manicure.

Avery laughed, thinking she might be joking. No one else laughed. "But you could hire out that part, right?"

"You been working with Ethan Pace, ain't you?" Odella said as she scooped up the trash on the table. "His daddy's been in, looking for thermos refills, since they work sunup to sundown right about now. Kid does good work, although I'll allow he's as busy as you been."

"I *like* the manual-labor part," her mother said, one hand over her heart. "I purely love to paint. I mean, when this world fades, my house will still be standing, held together by years of new paint colors. That doesn't mean a project this size is for me."

"Who's Ethan Pace, Mama?" Avery asked as she added a dash of milk and stirred her hot coffee with a spoon. Something wasn't adding up. What had been keeping Janet Abernathy too busy to help with the redesign of Smoky Joe's?

And why did her eyes brighten at the mention of the Misters Pace? Either Ethan, or more likely his father, was a handsome man. That had to be the explanation, and Avery needed a few more tidbits to track them down.

"Ethan's her contractor. The one who did all the renovation on the house," Regina blurted with a quick glance at Janet. If that wasn't enough to set Avery's alarms blaring, then she deserved to be out of the loop. Getting them to confess to the truth was going to take some work, though. She could see that in the speed with which her mother nodded in a "good answer, good answer" kind of way.

"And his father?" Avery asked before sipping her coffee oh so innocently.

Regina raised her hands to her mouth to stage-whisper, "Has got the bluest blue eyes you ever saw and they are locked on your mama." Regina batted her eyelashes innocently.

Avery felt the zing of renewed energy as she watched her mother squirm in her seat. In a town this size, finding two Paces who did construction should be easy enough. Figuring out what else her mother was up to was a bigger puzzle.

"I could pay you." Odella slipped the handwritten ticket on the table under their empty plates.

The buttermilk pie had been delicious, but Avery was wishing for brain food at that second. The answer to her question was right there, on the edge of her mind, but she couldn't come up with the answer to two plus two. It was too bad Sam wasn't seated next to her. They'd always been good at solving mysteries together.

"I couldn't pay you *much*, but you could hang out a sign for advertising." Odella turned in a slow half circle. "I do love this place, but time's come to get it ready to sell, you know? I want to retire to a beach. Get me a two-piece and a sunny spot."

Avery's eyebrows shot up. Miss Odella on

a beach… It might not be the most relaxing sight for other beachgoers, but good for her.

"And the clock's ticking. Life's short. This girl here knows what I mean," Odella said as she pointed at Avery. "Once we know what we want, we got to go after it. New paint, floors, some way to display Smoky Joe's fine collection of rustic artwork, but fresh and clean. Then I sell, the new owner takes over, and Smoky Joe's is still a part of Sweetwater's square. That's how it should be."

"Have you already listed the restaurant?" Regina said as she eyed the large square room. Avery wondered what sort of calculations she was doing, but then she realized this powerful distraction was successfully derailing their plot against Sam.

"Naw, I want to get top dollar and all them decorating shows say you gotta spend some money to make money." Odella tipped her head to the side. "But if the right buyer was to come along, I could be persuaded. Ticking clock and all that. I'd say this place was ripe to be flipped, wouldn't you, Regina?"

Regina gave a big, fake chuckle. "How would I know?"

Avery was trying to come up with the

right questions to keep the conversation rolling when another customer hailed Odella and she tottered off.

"I can't believe you two," Avery said and snatched the notepad that they'd been studying out from under their noses. "This is a waste of time. Sam is going to do whatever Sam wants to do, and he doesn't need the pressure of two mothers working against him."

She shoved the notepad in her purse. "Whether he goes or stays, the two of you need to find a new obsession. And not me, either." She pointed her finger. "I'm going to get myself together. Sam has agreed to help. You two need to work on yourselves." Avery leaned out of the cracked red leather booth and waved at Odella.

"Mama's going to have some plans for you in two weeks—" Avery checked over her shoulder and took her mother's weak nod as agreement "—and Regina would like to help you find investors for this property. She needs to do some figuring to determine the correct price first." Sam's mother cleared her throat. Avery took that as her agreement. "Does two weeks work for you, Odella?"

Avery did not glance back at Regina Blackburn. She was already pressing her luck with her own mother.

"Well, Miss Avery, that sounds fine," Odella said, "and I'm gonna box you up a brownie to go for your help facilitatin'."

Since Odella had won blue ribbons for her brownies before she'd decided to give the rest of the competition a fighting chance and stopped entering, it was a pretty good reward.

Pleased with herself, Avery turned back around to see two angry women, one blonde and one brunette, with their crossed arms braced on the table.

"Now, what did you go and do that for?" her mother snapped. "I don't have the time for a project like this, never mind the training."

"If you stop fussing over me, you'll have a few extra hours every day," Avery said sweetly. "You work three days a week at the school. On the other four, you and Regina better get to researching." Hearing the old familiar speech patterns coming out of her own mouth took adjustment. As soon as she said *cain't* without thinking about it, she'd know she'd settled back home.

"Research? What research?" Regina asked suspiciously.

"We're going to need to study the competition, and not here in Sweetwater." Janet Abernathy thumped back against the booth. "Visit some other restaurants. Find out what's workin' for 'em. Then we take the best, bring it back home. That's how we know we're on the right track, since we've *never done this before*." Watching her mother raise her eyebrows at Regina was all it took to turn the light bulb on. They *had* done this before. Why was it a secret?

"All I need to do is set a price. I could do that with some quick computer searches." Regina waved a hand. "Not that I'm saying no to traveling to Knoxville to eat at some good restaurants."

"You could find the investor, broker the deal and earn a commission." Avery watched as Regina straightened in her seat. If they were flipping properties, her mother had the vision and Regina had the hard-nosed business experience. Everything was so clear that it was hard not to yell "aha" and point an accusing finger. "If it's such a good opportunity, you should think about going into business yourself. What do I know about these things? I never finished law school." Avery shot a quick look at her mother to see the corner of her mouth turn up in a reluctant smile.

"Me? In business? A restaurant?" Regina studied the flow of customers and the view out the window. "It does sit nicely on the square. I could add some souvenirs, play up the history of Smoky Joe's." She tapped bright red nails on the table. "But I'm *retired*."

Janet chuckled. "And you hate almost every minute of it."

"I like playing cards, Janet." Regina shot her a pointed stare. "I'm not the one who's picking out paint chips for a perfectly lovely living room."

Avery watched them frown at each other, speaking volumes without a single sound.

"Already, Mama?" Avery leaned forward. "You gotta spread your wings. Try this. You can spend less time watching me as carefully as a vulture watches the oldest, slowest mouse in the field. I can cook my own breakfast. I lived all on my own for quite some time."

"If you'd eat some of those breakfasts, you might be strong enough to sass me, girl." Her mother tapped her chin. "Restaurant fixtures," she said slowly. "I'm going to have to get some catalogs, that's for sure."

Avery wondered if she should give the post office a warning. They were about to experience an uptick in mail headed to Hickory Lane and fast.

Then she realized both ladies across from her were watching her closely.

"You think this will keep us from worrying about our children, do you?" Janet said slowly.

Avery reached across the table to wrap her hands around her mother's. "Maybe this will help your children stop worrying about you."

Janet and Regina exchanged a look of pure exasperation. Janet was the first to speak. "Worried about us, living the good life over here while one races off to fight fires and the other..."

"...nearly grieves herself to death," Avery said. "Yeah, but I'm better. These jeans? They fit again. They don't hang off my hips, thanks to Miss Rachel's pies. I walked for a full hour while I waited for you two. I have a job…for now. And when Sam gets back, I'm going to learn to keep up with him again, give him a run for his money."

Her mother wasn't convinced, so Avery added, "You'll see, Mama. I'm okay. Thanks to you, I'm okay, and all I want is for you to find something you love." She turned to Regina. "I won't tell you everything Sam said in his career-day talk because…" Avery shivered. "But he said something really smart. Everyone deserves to work at whatever they think is the greatest job in the world. Maybe it's not owning a restaurant, but you've got the time to do some looking around."

Regina pursed her lips. "What if I want to retire to a beach?" She glanced at the small elderly woman who was toting a heavy tray of empty dishes. "A different beach than the one Odella's going to be sunbathing at, obviously, but somewhere with fruity drinks and umbrellas."

"Sam would be the first person to say do it." Avery had no doubt about that.

Janet turned to Sam's mother. "You busy tomorrow? We could go to Asheville, check out some restaurants. Might have a kitchen supply store over there I could wander around in for inspiration."

Avery's off-the-cuff plan was working. She was a genius. With digging, she could find out more about Janet and Regina's covert business operation, too, and then spring that knowledge on them when they least expected it. If they brought up the matchmaking again, she'd lean heavily on the betrayal of her mother keeping a secret. Her mother's acting skills were so good that Avery had managed to pick up a few pointers along the way.

"I could join you in Asheville. Tonight, I'll go home and do some searching." Regina shook her head. "So much I don't know about investors, girl. It's like you tried to find the biggest challenge and then pointed me at it."

Avery smiled sweetly. "It always worked with Sam. It might work with you, too."

Regina's rolled eyes so perfectly matched her son's exasperated expression that it was hard not to miss him. If he'd been at that table, he'd have ruined any chance she had of making it all work out through enthusiasm and the inability to bite his tongue, but if he was here, their celebration would have been twice as satisfying.

"Here you go, missy," Odella said as she plopped a plastic container on the table. "One brownie. Now, when you come back, make sure you got a good contract for your mama." Odella shook a finger. "Wouldn't want to go into business without one, don'tcha know?"

"A contract," Avery repeated slowly. "But I'm not a lawyer." She studied the smug smiles on the women across from her. "You could find something good and basic on the web."

Odella wagged her head from side to side, wispy white hair flying as she did so. "Could, but wouldn't it be better to have you do that? Make any adjustments we might need." She nodded at Avery's mother. "Janet and I, we think you're close enough to a real lawyer for this business, don't we?"

With a sinking feeling, Avery watched her mother nod slowly, her smug grin hard to swallow. Regina was stirring cream into her coffee as if salvation had all sunk to the bottom of the cup.

"Fine. I'll see what I can come up with."

She gave her mother a big fake smile. "Hope you can afford my fee."

"Another brownie. That's all I'm paying," Odella snapped as she hustled away.

"I couldn't have planned that better myself," Avery's mother said slowly. "What's that saying? Hoist by your own petard? I don't know what that means, but I do recognize it happening."

Avery's reluctant chuckle was strangled, but it felt good. "Collateral damage, but I can deal with it. A boilerplate contract is all I have to come up with. It's the two of you who'll be working."

"Sure, sure," her mother agreed easily. "You might have forgotten, but I have not, that time you called me fresh out of your first contract law class. Remember what you told me?"

Avery studied her own coffee, desperate to stir up some distraction.

"'Mama, I've found it, the thing I was meant to do.'" Janet Abernathy turned to Regina and repeated, "'Meant to do.' I thought she meant drawing up contracts, but no."

"Well, what in the world, then?" Regina drawled.

"It was an employment contract, unfairly written." Avery sighed. "I named three different defenses to any attempt to terminate employment. My first contract class, and I was ready to take the case to court and win."

Regina reached over to cover Avery's hand, which was slowly shredding a napkin. "What happened to that calling, hon?"

"She fell in love," her mother said softly. "This girl always did do things out of order. Degree, job, husband, kids. That's what we always talked about."

"But she fell in love." Regina pursed her lips. "I know one or two other ladies who might have gotten their plans shaken up by love, too."

Janet nodded. "Yep. You can't let it pass you by when you find it, that's for certain."

"But when you get a chance, you make new plans." Regina dipped her head. "Or you let other people, nosy kids and such, make them for you."

Avery wanted to feel guilty about pushing them into this experiment with Smoky Joe's. But she so did not feel guilty at all. In fact, even with the minor hiccup of being dragged into it in their wake, she felt clever. So clever.

As Odella hustled past, Avery held out her hand. "Miss Odella, I changed my fee."

The small woman's frown was scary enough that Avery pressed back against her seat. "Ain't made of money, missy."

Avery gulped. "No. Sure. I just…" After she cleared her throat, she added, "I'll come up with the contract if you can send one of the Pace men over to meet me at the library." Avery smiled sweetly. "I think we have something important to talk about."

Odella tipped her head to the side and shot Avery's mother a shrewd look. "Happy to do that for free, girl." Then she was gone and Avery's mother was fuming in her seat. Regina's expression was set on "cat that ate the canary," so Avery knew she was on the right track.

"I have to go to the ladies' to put on my lipstick. Avery, are you coming?" her mother asked, her purse already hooked on one arm, her lips a tight, disapproving line.

"No, ma'am, I don't have any lipstick." Avery was still laughing when both ladies scrambled up out of the booth.

"Replace the booths with chairs, for starters," her mother muttered as she walked past on her way to the restroom.

Avery pulled out her phone and scrolled through her contacts. She realized she'd never gotten Sam's cell number, so she couldn't text him, not without drawing the mothers' attention back to them. Besides that, he was under the impression that she was taking one for the team by suffering a setback. He didn't do guilt well, but he'd always repaid every favor and kindness generously.

When Sam returned, he'd keep his promise to get her moving.

And he'd have the pleasant experience of watching his mother tackle something new.

Maybe he'd call her a genius, maybe not, but Avery would always know she had what it took to mastermind with the best.

CHAPTER TEN

WHEN SAM REALIZED he was staring down at his phone again, he cursed and shoved it back in his pocket. Instead of flight delays and late arrivals, his plane had managed to land ahead of schedule, so he was pacing outside baggage claim, waiting for his mother.

Nothing explained this restless urge to get back home.

He'd talked to his mother twice since the interview. Neither time had she mentioned she might be late. She had talked excitedly for at least fifteen minutes about the new project she and Janet had started. Revamping and brokering a sale of Smoky Joe's would be a good thing for the town of Sweetwater, but if he had to listen one more time about the gift show in Atlanta that they'd managed to shoehorn admission to, he'd... Nothing.

He'd listen even if he could repeat every word she said from memory.

Did his mother need a new project? Definitely. If it meant listening to her plotting and planning how to get a Sweetwater brand to splash on souvenirs for the rest of forever, he'd…endure. That was what he'd do.

He was anxious to hug his mother, but even more than that, he wanted to talk to Avery. Going away without getting her cell number had been a miscalculation. If he'd been able to call her before the interview, he might not have been stuttering nervous when the team leader had come out to shake his hand. A nervous firefighter didn't inspire much faith.

And after he'd managed to collect his nerves and get through the interview, he could have celebrated the invitation to the crew's fitness evaluation. Was he worried about completing the hike, carrying all the equipment, at a new altitude?

Maybe, but Avery would have handled those nerves.

He'd endured the hike, although it had been a bigger struggle than he'd anticipated. The gear was what he'd expected. The impossibility of taking a deep breath would take some adjustment, but he'd held his own in the group and helped carry one guy down when chest pains had stopped him.

He should have slept like a confident guy who was going to get a shot at doing what he wanted, because Sam was nearly certain he'd get an offer to join the Highland team.

Instead, after a sleepless night of staring up at the ceiling, he'd had to come to grips with the fact that he was thinking about Avery Abernathy Montague entirely too much for her to be an old friend. She was a new friend, too, and possibly something even more special.

She might be the kind of woman a man never forgot.

A short horn beep drew his attention. Instead of his mother's Caddy, Janet Abernathy's SUV was slicing through the traffic to slam to a stop at the curb. Avery rolled down the window. "Sorry I'm late. I had to wait for story time to finish."

The shot of adrenaline that raced through him was a complete surprise. While he'd been muttering to himself about his mother's tardiness, it had seemed nearly impossible to remain standing for one minute longer. The cramped seats of the plane, the constant noise of the terminals and the endless "what if" loop in his head had made it impossible to sleep.

But seeing Avery, her mirrored aviator sunglasses such a blast from the past, filled him with energy. Sunshine shot through the driver's-side window, highlighting her gold curls and driving away the years. This Avery? She was healthy and bright, and her wide smile replaced images of nursing her back to health with the weird thought that kissing her would spread that smile from her to him.

"Nice glasses, Maverick," Sam said as he dropped his duffel in the back. "To what do I owe the honor?"

Avery checked over her shoulder, her curls flapping in the breeze. It wasn't quite a sloppy ponytail, but at some point, her hair had relaxed. How long had he been gone? Sweetwater was working wonders already. "You owe this honor to my pure genius, that's all." She hit the gas hard and shot out into traffic, one arm dangling over the door, the cool October breeze lifting her curls again.

"Pure genius," Sam said slowly. "That's what brought on this sudden fit of investing fever?" Sam stretched his legs out and checked to make sure his seat belt was secure. The wheels squeaked as Avery took the ramp to the freeway too fast. "And are you in a hurry?"

Avery glanced over at him. "Am I making you nervous, Sam?" She accelerated to merge into traffic. "It's been way too long since I drove a car regularly, and I remember how much I love it." She tightened her grip on the steering wheel. "These curves? It's a blast."

"I bet you're glad I decided against becoming a commissioned ranger. Imagine me as law enforcement." Sam smiled at her double take. "We were both pretty sure I'd be the one who needed a good lawyer first. Fighting fire is definitely more my speed."

"Right. You were going to be my first case as a criminal defense attorney, as I recall." Avery grinned. "How long were you prepared to wait to start your life of crime? Because that would have taken some time." She toyed with the radio before turning it off. "Tell me about the interview or...*conversation.*"

Sam thought about refusing to drop the law thread, but decided he could come back to it. When she could concentrate. He was afraid to distract her too much as he glanced over the guardrail at a long drop. "It went pretty well. I think they were impressed with all my volunteer search-and-rescue hours, my continuing education." Talking to her about everything increased his confidence. He was going to get a shot at making the move to Colorado. "I made it to the next step. They're doing a fast track since several crews are short, so they did a quick physical fitness evaluation. I made it near the top of the pack." Sam sighed. "But my conditioning at high altitude can use some work."

Avery smiled at him. "As if I ever doubted you'd knock them out. Since you've been gone, my mother and your mother have been regaling me with tales of your heroism and bravery. All those volunteer hours, Sam? *Of course* they were impressed. Who wouldn't be? You work in one of the busiest areas in the state. It's not like you have no background."

Some part of him knew that she was saying what he wanted to hear, but he did want to believe everything she said. If they offered the job, he wasn't sure what he'd do, but he would like the chance to make that decision.

"They'll have a lot of guys with good experience," Sam said, "but I did everything I could. I must have mentioned half a dozen times that I was single."

Avery dipped her chin to stare at him over her sunglasses. "They can't ask you that information."

"I volunteered it. It should help," he said. He shrugged. "Every web search I've done brings up stories of families who are devastated when a wildfire fighter dies. Since I'm single, I should be a solid choice."

Avery's quiet might be the result of concentration, but Sam was immediately sorry he'd been the one to bring up the danger of the job. No one had forgotten it. Was he trying to talk her into talking him into changing his mind? Could she do it?

He'd like to say he knew the answer, but he wasn't sure.

"Sam, whatever your family situation, you will be thinking of the people you love, and you better be sure the people who love you will be devastated if anything happens to you, so don't even mention that to your mother again." Her sound of disgust carried loud and clear even over the wind whipping her hair.

Did she count herself in that number? Sam had no trouble recalling the way she'd left his talk at the library. Avery worried about his safety.

"Seriously, your training makes you a solid choice. I know for certain that when you go out into danger, you won't be fool-hardy. You called in a favor, built a debt that you'll have to repay, to keep your mother from fretting for two nights. If you ever once step out into the fire without seeing her face in your head, I'll be shocked."

Sam watched her confidently take the turns that would lead them up to Sweetwater. "Two days has made a difference in you, I have to say."

Avery made tight fists on the steering wheel. "It has, but I'm glad you're back. I'm not sure how much longer your mother could be distracted. Did you know they've been flipping houses? I mean, that's my guess. No one has told me that." The glare she shot him made it clear he was at the top of her list of people to set straight.

"They've done two houses. I'm not sure that's a business," Sam said as he tried to recall anything else they might have gotten into. "I don't know about this restaurant thing. How big is the market of buyers for a run-down coffee shop in a town way off the beaten path?"

"If anyone can figure that out, it's your mother. And the run-down part? You would not believe how many ways there are to display cookie jars. My mother is going to work wonders on the decor of that place. All three of you will owe me for pushing them into it. You won't know when I'll come to collect, but I will." Avery's ominous growl sounded so much like the pirate's voice she'd used every time they'd battled in imaginary ships across her front yard that Sam laughed.

"Plus, I found out there's a romantic angle for my mother. I haven't met the senior Mr. Pace, but when I do, I'm going to flex my own matchmaking muscles," she said, smiling. "Now, when this is over, your mother is going to go back to making a list of ways to keep you in Sweetwater, so you'd do well to encourage her interest in the business and any new guy that draws her eye."

The weight of guilt curled in his stomach. "A list to keep me here? What's on it? Forewarning might help me prepare."

"A girl." Avery smiled. "And since they know I'm too stubborn to be persuaded, it isn't me. Then your mother is plotting to break something. Like a leg."

Sam closed his eyes. "Seriously?"

"Hard to say." Avery made the turn that led into town. "I have a hard time reading them when they're together, your mother and mine, but it seemed sort of serious." She pointed over her shoulder into the back seat. "I have the list. Imagine my excitement when their number one candidate was scheduled for story time today. And she was awesome, by the way. If you are in the market for a beautiful date, I'd give my endorsement to Winter Kingfisher."

Sam groaned. "Ash's sister? My boss's boss's sister? That's who they think they can make me fall in love with so I'll stay in Sweetwater?"

Avery rolled to a stop at the four-way leading into the square. "She's gorgeous, Sam.

Young. Seems to have everything together." Her tone was teasing, but it was hard to tell what she really thought, thanks to the sunglasses.

"She's a year younger than us, Avery, not in pigtails." While she was distracted by traffic, Sam reached over to pull the glasses off. "Where did you find a pair of these, anyway? Everything old is new again, I guess."

"Those are mine. My mother boxed them up with all my awards." Avery's smile didn't quite reach her eyes. "They belonged to my father. Must have been on the dresser when she decided to wipe away my bedroom in one of the remodels." She took the glasses and folded them carefully. "I was glad to get them back. They are the perfect accessory for a sunny day."

She'd said the same sort of innocent comment to him more than once when they'd been running the roads or jumping into creeks or doing a million other things that kids do because they think nothing can hurt them.

"Yeah. Perfect." Sam rolled his eyes. "Dating Ash's sister, though? Career suicide." He grunted. "The guy's not anyone I'd want to tangle with, not without backup, even with the bum leg."

"What's wrong with his leg?" Avery asked as she hit the road out of town.

"Accident. Doctors weren't sure they could fix it, but Ash insisted. The guy is hard to argue with." Sam tried to imagine what would happen the first time he had a fight with Winter. "Doesn't slow him down much."

Whatever bits and pieces Winter left behind, Ash would incinerate. Sam might be strong enough to handle one Kingfisher. Two? He shivered at the thought. "It's like they don't even know me. I want someone sweet. Fun. Not nearly as intense as Winter."

Avery snorted as she pulled into the parking lot of the apartment complex some Otter Lake rangers used. "Right. Because you are so easygoing."

Sam shrugged. She might have a good point. "Want to come up? Tour my luxurious digs? I'll let you carry my duffel."

Avery slid out of the SUV. "Get your own bag. I'll carry the leftovers."

Sam's heart lurched in his chest. "You

didn't cook, did you?" He reached inside to grab his bag. "Or have you gotten better?"

"No, I haven't gotten any better. In Chicago, I mastered ordering in like a champ." As she marched around the end of the SUV, Avery was shaking her head. "But it's not too late for me to climb back in the car with the food *your mother* sent along." Avery motioned with her chin. "Show me your place while I'm deciding."

The energy that hit as soon as he saw Avery made it easy to trot up the steps. She was breathing harder when she made it to the top, but she wasn't in any distress. She noticed him cataloging her responses. "I've been walking every day. Made it up to the top of Yanu this morning before I went to work. It still took almost an hour and a half, but that's better than a couple of weeks ago."

Sam whistled. "Still, I beat you easy peasy, AA. Better not challenge me to a race."

She was still grumbling as he opened the apartment door. Since he'd never been much into clutter, he wasn't too worried about the state of the place.

At least, he wasn't until she turned in a

slow circle and said, "So, you're a monk, too? What's with the furnishings, Sam?"

He propped his hands on his hips and studied his living room. Sure, it held only a couch and a plasma television with every gaming system he could buy, but it was comfortable enough. The carpet was soft. What more did he need?

"At least you have a decent view." Avery set the containers she'd carried on the tiny bar between the kitchen and living room and bent to stare out his window at the forest surrounding the small complex. "All the rangers live here?"

"No, a few, single people who spend a lot of time on call, mainly." All the married types had set up real homes in Sweetwater. Sam had never been jealous until he realized it might be nice to have a dining table to offer a seat to his guest. "You want to have a bite? I'm not sure what she sent, but I know it's good."

"Nah, that's all for you. Your mother missed you." Avery wandered closer to the door before she stopped, a curious frown wrinkling her brow. "You picture that girl, the sweet, easygoing one, being happy waiting for news while you're off, enjoying your dangerous job?"

Avery wrapped her hand around the doorknob. "I mean, come on, Sam. Get real."

"An even better reason not to put anyone through that. I'm happy single." That wasn't exactly true. It was hard to imagine being so content half a country away from the people who loved him and did things like drive an hour to pick him up from the airport. "But I don't have any trouble imagining some woman happy enough to welcome me home with a hug and a kiss. What does that mean, AA?" He rubbed his hand down his jaw, the rustle of whiskers reminding him he hadn't shaved before heading to the airport.

"That you're normal, Sam. It's *normal* to want someone to be happy to see you. Believe me, after you find it, you miss it when it's gone." Avery twirled her sunglasses. "If one tough trip up to the falls taught me anything, it's that everyone needs people. And when you go away to Colorado, you're going to find that out." Then she shrugged. "But it's possible you need Winter, someone who will take those challenges with you."

Sam was quiet as he stared at his perfectly

fine, empty apartment. "Yeah, it's funny you should say that, AA." The more they talked, the clearer it became why he'd missed her so much while he was in Colorado, why seeing her face filled him with energy.

"I've got to get back, because I haven't finished my part of the project yet. Your mother and my mother have been cramming in extra meals at other restaurants, doing 'research' in order to meet Odella's deadline." She tapped her chest. "The one I roped them into—" she brushed off both shoulders, proud of her cleverness "—though they all but dragged me under by signing me up to provide a contract. Which I can do, even though I never finished law school."

Sam smiled at her irritated singsong. Avery was getting fed up with the reminders.

"I should hide some law-school pamphlets around the house," she said. "That would further throw my mother off my tracks." Then she waved her hands. "Except I told her over and over as a kid that Chicago was the only school for me. My plan might backfire."

"Unless you consider a different law school," Sam said, his eyebrows raised. "There are others."

Avery fiddled with her sunglasses.

She was so clever. She'd never not push the boundaries. When he left to fight fires, she'd rearrange the house, do everything he'd said they shouldn't and generally plot mayhem. He'd never know what to expect if Avery was the other half of his people, the one who made coming home worthwhile.

Why did that sound exciting?

Because he was an idiot, maybe.

"What was Winter doing at the library exactly?" Sam asked, unwilling to let her leave if he could find a way to make her stay.

"Once a quarter, she comes to tell Cherokee legends. She had a big group. It was great." Avery shook her head. "The difference between her story times and mine is embarrassing. The kids were mesmerized. She's like that. You can't look away."

In his work at the park, he'd run across Winter, one of the public information officers, once or twice. She was good at her job. People trailed behind her, ready to listen. "What stories did she tell?"

Avery stretched. "First, it was the one where the warrior finds a secret lake and promises not to hunt there. Then he does, and now it stays hidden."

"Look for a rush of kids climbing to the top of The Eagle Nest, searching for smoke. Remember when we did that?" Sam laughed. "My grandfather was thrilled to have two eight-year-olds demand to see that mist."

"But we never did." Avery sighed. "And he never stopped trooping up there with us. He was a good man, your Gee."

He was. Sam had never missed the man who'd left his mother before his third birthday because his grandfather had stepped in, helped raise him and the girl next door, after her father died too soon.

Sam nodded. "Yeah. I owe him a lot."

"Then she told the two-wolves story, with the disclaimer that even she wasn't sure it was a Cherokee story from way back." Avery nodded. "I like her. She said the Cherokee know a good story when they hear it."

The two-wolves story. Sam had heard it more times than he could count.

"I get it now, too." Avery ruffled messy curls. "If I have two wolves inside me, they aren't hate or love. They're fear and…bravery or…whatever word that means you do what you want to do even if you're scared."

Sam understood Avery in a way he hadn't since she'd returned home, so different from the girl he remembered. "If the job offer comes, I'm facing the same decision."

Avery didn't argue with him or explain that her own grief and pain were bigger than his career decision, because she was better than that. She reached over and took his hand. "Which wolf is going to win?"

Sam tangled his fingers in hers. "The one I feed. The one you feed." He dipped his chin. "So we're going to have to come up with a better name for that wolf, because you know that's the one we're picking. How about *courage*?"

"Good name." Avery squeezed. "I need your phone number."

Off balance, Sam stumbled a step. "Why?"

"I wanted to call you or text you to celebrate my stealth victory with the mothers, but I couldn't, not without pulling them back on our tracks." Avery shifted around to pull her phone out of her pocket. "And now, more than ever, I need you to help me feed Courage."

Sam pulled his own phone out. "Are you going to do the same for me?"

Avery rolled her eyes. "Of course I am. If I have to do this, you do, too."

Sam punched in the number she read off and then typed a text. "Feed Courage. When I send that, you'll know what I mean?"

Avery nodded. "I will."

Sam slowly untangled his fingers, already missing this connection that made it so much easier to believe that he was going to do what he wanted instead of playing it safe. The idea that he'd ever back away from a challenge was irritating.

"You don't have a job offer yet, do you?" Avery asked as she opened the door. "I need more time with you."

Her words landed like a punch to the abdomen, but the warmth spread quickly. "Not yet, but that doesn't mean that's the only decision I'm facing."

She frowned. "You thinking about asking Winter out?"

Sam shivered. "No. Way."

Avery laughed. "Fine. I've gotta get the car back before they make it home from Asheville. My mother's got about a hundred packages to pick up at the post office before it closes. All catalogs."

Sam rested one shoulder on the doorjamb. "Thanks for picking me up."

"I'm glad you're home. I've missed having a partner in crime." Avery slipped her sunglasses on, and it was like the past and present melded in a comfortable but completely new, overwhelming way.

"Yeah, me, too, AA." Sam eased up to walk her back down to the car, but Avery slipped her arm around his waist and went up on tiptoe to press a kiss against his jaw. He managed to get his arm around her shoulders to stop her immediate retreat. "What was that for?"

He slipped her sunglasses off. This close, her eyes were clear, a deep green that he'd never find again and never be able to forget. "I'm welcoming you home. I've missed you." Before his befuddled mind cleared enough to wrap the other arm around her, Avery had stepped away.

"Now, don't you fall for me, Sam Blackburn. I can't be the girl with the firefighter husband who's always taking chances, risking everything." Avery slipped her sunglasses on again, her teasing smile firmly in place. "If I ever become someone's person, the other half, he's going to be so boring that even his guardian angel hits the snooze button now and then. You do not fit the bill."

She raised a hand and trotted back down the steps. Sam braced his hands on the railing and watched as she rolled out of the parking lot. "Boring, huh?" It was easy to imagine Avery's easy life with that guy.

Then Sam realized he was picturing her first husband, Robert, in the boring role. A college professor who wore tweed to work. That was the guy whose death had nearly destroyed her.

Instead of focusing on the fact that this was the first time Avery had even considered that there would be another man, her second other half, Sam stepped back inside his apartment and walked over to inspect the leftovers.

He hadn't realized how much he'd missed Avery's blend of sweet support and hard-nosed dare until she'd landed back in Sweetwater, so different from before. Now that he'd remembered how much better he was when she was around, leaving would be that much harder.

"You don't have the job yet. Get a grip." Sam opened one of his mother's containers of leftovers and then closed it again, dissatisfied with his options now that Avery had left the building.

When his phone rang, Sam sighed with relief. A distraction. Perfect.

"You back to the mountain yet?" Ash said as soon as Sam had the phone to his ear.

"Just dropped my duffel in the middle of the floor. I'm ready to go." Sam crossed his fingers. "Got an emergency you need help with?" That would be the best way to handle his nerves: a battle.

"Meet me at the ranger station." Ash hung up before Sam could ask any questions.

Which was just as well. He wasn't going to say no.

By the time he rolled to a stop in front of the small building that served as the visitor information center for the Otter Lake area and the rangers' offices, Sam had convinced himself that Ash was in some kind of existential crisis.

Finding his friend tangled in a knot of

electrical cords and lights in the small shed at the edge of the visitor center's parking lot was not what he'd expected.

"I decided to try to organize Macy's storage building. That was a horrible mistake." Ash muttered something under his breath. "How can she find anything in this mess?"

"This is the emergency?" Sam drawled as he watched strong, silent Ash string together a long line of curses.

"You said 'emergency,' not me." Ash winced as he stepped out of the tangle and reached up to hang a strand of lights on a hook.

Sam shook his head as he reached for the first loose end he could find. "I don't know how she does it. And yet if we asked her to find a set of lights, she'd be gone five minutes and come back with three different options, all perfect in different ways. Could be she's magic, part witch or something."

Ash nodded. "I did pretty good until I hit these. Chased a king snake out that would have had Macy swinging a hoe and yelling about no-good snakes." Ash wiped the sweat off his brow. "Not a bad way to spend an afternoon, anyway."

"An afternoon when you were supposed

to be away from this place? An afternoon off?" Sam asked with as innocent a tone as he could manage.

"Shut up and untangle."

They worked silently until all the strands were wrapped in smooth coils and hanging on the hooks that Ash had put up for such a purpose. "Now, all that's left is threatening to fire her if she messes up all my hard work."

Sam didn't answer. He crossed his arms over his chest and raised a single eyebrow. They both knew there was no way Ash would fire Macy Gentry. She managed to keep the ranger station running smoothly and with as little trouble for the rangers as possible.

"So, I know you aced the interview and somehow managed to pass the physical," Ash said as he led Sam through the door into the rustic station. A rough rock wall formed one side of the lobby, while gleaming wood paneling finished off the room. Macy was deep in conversation with someone at the campground and only narrowed her eyes at Ash as they passed. Sam winked and grinned, and Macy winked back.

When they made it to Ash's cramped but spotless office, Ash pulled two bottles of water out of the small fridge hidden under a table. "Already had a phone call from the recruiter. He'd like to come out to the park to meet with me and the incident commanders who've worked search and rescue with you." Ash chugged half the bottle of water while Sam tried to process that. "Seems like you might be getting a job offer." Then he stretched in his chair, clearly happy to have the chance to surprise Sam.

"Already?" That was all Sam could come up with as an answer.

Ash grunted. "Already. We talked about next week."

Shock made it hard for Sam to think. "They add to the crews in the spring. Why come out here now? And do you think they visit the work sites of all the candidates?" No way. There was no need to do that. But why make an exception in his case?

"Nah, something else is going on. Might not even involve you. Maybe they're scouting more recruits or…" Ash shrugged. "Doesn't matter. They're serious about you. Why aren't you celebrating?"

That was a good question. Why did he want to throw on the brakes and insist everyone take their time to sort through this?

This was what he'd been waiting for. He wanted them to be interested in him, and he should have been plotting ways to impress whoever made the trip to his park to watch him work. Really.

So why was he wondering what Avery would say about how quickly this was unfolding?

Was he going to be ready to say goodbye?

"Oh, man, are you having doubts now?" Ash asked. "You've done the hard part. I thought for sure you'd fail the physical, big softy like you." When Sam had no answer, Ash tipped his head to the side. "Seriously. What's wrong?"

Sam scrubbed both hands over his face. "Wish I knew."

They were both quiet long enough that it got weird, so Sam exhaled loudly. "The trails. I gotta get some perspective. It's time to climb." He stood and waited for Ash to follow. "You coming?"

Ash squeezed his nearly empty water bottle. "Why do I get the feeling you aren't weighing job opportunities?" He stared out the tiny window with a view of old forest and a small patch of green grass. "What else could tie a young man in knots?"

"Oh, do tell, wise one." Sam crossed his arms over his chest. Ash was about to give him a hard time, but he couldn't deny he valued his friend's opinion.

"Glad you recognize my leadership ability." Ash tossed his water bottle toward the recycling can and cursed when it missed. "I can still guess this might have something to do with a girl, like the one you carried down from Yanu a couple of weeks ago?"

"I meant 'wise' in a completely different context, Ash. Any wisdom you have comes from old age, anyway." Sam grinned at Ash's scowl. "And the girl…" He wasn't sure what to say to that. Was Avery the one who was making it difficult to get his head wrapped around making this jump? "What does it mean when you want to talk over the big things with someone to understand how you feel about them?"

"Are we talking about an old man who knows a thing or two?" Ash put both hands on his chest for illustration. "Or a *differ-*

ent friend who helps you think clearly?" He sighed. "Or it could be the person you've been waiting for your whole life and she showed up at exactly the right time or the worst time ever. Hard to say."

Their eyes met. Ash didn't have any answers for him, but there was some comfort in knowing the guy understood how confused Sam was.

"Let's head up Yanu. Easy climb. The fresh air will help your brain function. Don't expect me to tell you what to do about a woman. I got nothing." Ash winced as he stood. "All I know is nothing is going to be solved by talking about it. You're going to have to *do* something."

A weight settled on Sam's shoulders.

"Luckily, you have a few days to decide what that is." Ash clapped a hand on his shoulder. "Today, let's climb."

CHAPTER ELEVEN

"I SHOULD LOOK at this as a sign of progress," Avery muttered as she smacked the stack of quilts and sheets her mother insisted she had to have on her bed. Lying under them while trying to toss and turn was a real workout. That and staring up at the ceiling all night long had taken a toll on her optimism. "From sleeping sixteen hours a day to apparently…" She turned her head to study the display of the antique digital alarm clock her mother had dug out of whatever closet it had been buried in. "None. Zero hours of sleep. That can't be good."

Listening to Janet and Regina babble excitedly about their trip to Asheville had kept her up later than she'd meant to be, but after she'd finally managed to escape the planning session for Smoky Joe's, complete with whiteboard and large, long to-do lists, Avery had settled into her nest, certain she'd rest well after a long, busy week.

And then she'd watched the shadows on the ceiling grow longer. Her mother had finally quieted, and now all Avery could hear was her own breathing.

This was when the memories started and the tears arrived. She hated nights like this. One innocent thought about the missing University of Chicago pennant she'd hung over her bed as soon as she'd decided law school was her destiny led to memories of the campus and the first time she'd seen Robert Montague striding down the sidewalk, his eyes hidden because he was checking his phone.

She'd never been one of his students, mainly because his specialty was intellectual property and she'd hated every taste of that she'd gotten in her lower-level classes, but floppy brown hair and a total disinterest in college girls had apparently been her type back then. Pursuing Robert had been such a fun game, and catching him had been so satisfying that when he suggested they get married, she'd been ready for their next step immediately. Both of them had dreamed of a family.

But first there was tenure and their future income to secure. Avery had done her best to fill her days with enough volunteer work that it still seemed that leaving school was a good decision. They'd had such a comfortable city life with great restaurants and smart friends. Settling in had been simple.

And then cancer struck, and whatever she and Robert had planned was out the window because survival took precedence. First he'd continued to work until fatigue and sickness had taken their toll. The floppy brown hair had thinned until it was gone. So had the friends and acquaintances, leaving Avery alone to carry the weight of all their decisions.

Robert had never hesitated to give her his opinion, on her hair, her clothes, her goals or what to do next. It would be nice to have advice right now. Working at the library was no solution, and she needed something to challenge her brain.

Otherwise, she'd be spending more nights like this one. Alone. Thinking.

As long as she lived, she'd never forget struggling to breathe while a man in a dark suit walked her through all the options for a funeral service. Robert had joked that he wanted to send out invitations with RSVPs so he'd have an estimate of the attendance, but Avery had been too afraid to laugh.

The memory of Robert's pale face flashed through her mind and the old familiar panic hit. Avery lurched up to lean against the headboard.

"Calm down, Avery. There's no need to panic." Her voice was steady, as it had been every time she'd spoken to her husband as he died slowly in front of her. "He's already gone. Nothing to be done." She closed her eyes and focused on her breathing until her pounding heartbeat slowed.

The quiet *tink* of something hitting her window caught her attention, but it had to be a bug or something. Desperate for distraction, Avery picked up her phone and scrolled through her contacts until her thumb hovered over Sam's number. This had been prime sneaking-out time when they were in high school. Both of their mothers had slept so soundly, only the end of the world would have rolled them out of bed. That meant plenty of time to climb trails they shouldn't be on or meet people they shouldn't waste time with.

But Sam had worked a long day. There was no sense waking him. Morning would be soon enough to talk.

Why did she have this urge to hear his voice tonight? He wouldn't have any answers for her.

But she'd feel safer because he was near. If she wasn't careful, letting Sam rescue her would become a habit. She would see him in the morning, so she could talk him into doing something physical. She was having trouble sleeping because she'd been following her mother around instead of pushing her body. If he was busy, she'd… She wasn't sure what she'd do to occupy her time, but her mother was only half a step away from sending her on a reconnaissance mission to the next "new Southern" restaurant she'd read about in her stack of magazines, wherever that might be. Apparently, Smoky Joe's was going to move away from home-cooked desserts and hot, hot coffee to fine, "new Southern" dining.

As far as Avery could tell, that meant cornmeal was used in *everything*.

She could see if Brett Hendrix had a favorite trail to show her. "Any port in a storm, Avery?"

Her phone vibrated. Avery picked it up to read a text from Sam. Feed Courage. Climb out the window.

Relief made her dizzy for a second. Avery thrust her quilts away and raced over to the window. She raised it carefully.

"Pebbles on the window. That was our sign," Sam called. "Have you forgotten?"

"I thought I was imagining things. Besides that…technology…hello?" Avery waved her phone. "And the tree's gone. Can I use the stairs?"

The night was clear and the moonlight was bright enough that she could see Sam's grin. "Whatever. Get down here." He looked so much like the old Sam, his shoulders hunched against the cool air.

"Give me five," Avery said as she stepped back, her heart thumping hard again. Whatever he had in mind, it had to be better than letting the memories swamp her. She yanked her jeans off the floor and slipped into them before grabbing her sweatshirt off the dresser. "This is when never learning to put away your clothes pays, Mama." Avery was grinning big enough to make her ears hurt as she quietly opened the bedroom door. Her mother's room was dark, and Avery had a flash of wonder. She was a grown woman. There was no need to sneak out.

But it was definitely more fun.

Avery tiptoed down the stairs and grabbed the hiking boots she'd left by the door. They hadn't seen much hiking lately, but the town square had been covered thoroughly.

She had the door unlocked and was turning the knob when her mother said from the top of the stairs, "Think you'll be home for breakfast?"

Avery straightened and felt the blush cover her cheeks. Which was silly. "I don't know, Mama. There's no need to scramble an egg for me. I'll get my own this time."

"Uh-huh. I don't know whether to hug that boy for getting you out of the house, to explain to him that the middle of the night is not suitable or to wish you could find another love interest that makes you beam that way." When Avery started to protest the "love interest" part, her mother crossed her arms over her familiar Tennessee Titans sweatshirt. Whatever Avery said would prolong the conversation, could change it into an argument, so she opened the door. "You and Sam be careful."

"Always, Mama." Avery was relieved when she stepped out on the porch. Sam was propped against the railing. "Sorry it took so long. I was busted on the way out."

He groaned softly. "Matchmaking, phase two, is about to commence, right?"

"Who cares?" Avery said as she laced her boots. "We know it's crazy. They'll figure that out soon enough."

Sam shoved his hands in his pockets but didn't answer. Did he not agree? It *was* crazy. Even if the two of them had enough in common to make anything work, he was leaving and she was…running away from memories.

"How did you know I was awake?" Avery moved to follow him to the truck he'd parked at the end of the drive that led to his mother's house.

"I didn't. I'm glad you were." Sam, in a weird, weird move, stopped to open the truck door for her to slide inside. He'd never done that, not once, when they were growing up and partners in whatever scheme they could come up with to run wild.

She stared hard at him before getting in the truck. He didn't say anything as he quietly closed the door. Instead of running around the hood, a goofy grin on his face, Sam walked steadily, one hand tracing the metal. He didn't say much as he started up the truck and put it in Drive.

"Where are we headed?" Avery asked with a happy sigh. "I can make it up to the top of the falls and back if you want to give it a shot. Or The Eagle Nest? That's not far. We could get there by sunrise. Lucky you can get us into the park." The clouds had a bright pink tinge. Sunrise wasn't too far off.

"I was thinking Otter Lake. You want to visit the otters? They're still moving around at this time." Sam rolled the window down, a cool breeze drifting in as he meandered toward the highway leading up to the park.

What was with his mood? He never drove this way, preferring, as she did, to make it a challenge. Tonight, everything seemed different, more dreamlike, and now they might as well be the only people in the world.

"I'll follow you." Avery leaned back, content with that decision. She trusted Sam. She wasn't staring up at her ceiling, mourning what was lost and wondering if she'd done everything she could or wishing she could change something that she had done. She was living her life. That was worth something.

Sam didn't answer, but he did accelerate on the roads leading to the ranger station. The Otter Lake rangers maintained the lands around Otter Lake, one of the Smokies' most popular lakes. Fishermen loved it because it had plenty of secluded coves. The otters loved it for the same reason.

They passed the Otter Lake Campground, a large area with spots for RVs and primitive camping along with a combination gas station, bait shop and restaurant. The windows were already lit. Did it ever close?

Avery turned to ask Sam about the restaurant, but it seemed wrong to disturb the silence in the cab of the truck. The question could wait. She reached over to touch Sam's leg. Instead of answering, he covered her hand with his. Which was so strange in this friendship, but Avery couldn't argue with how right it felt. If she had a chance, she might stop sleeping altogether. She and Sam could explore the wonders of the Great Smoky Mountains and she'd never have to think again.

AFTER A LONG night of considering the question of Avery and who she was to him now, Sam had been forced to do something. Ash's words had kept running through his brain. Thinking wasn't going to change anything. Talking wouldn't do much, either. If he wanted to figure out what to do about Avery, which apparently had something to do with how he felt about the Colorado job, he had to do something.

And Avery hadn't called. She hadn't texted. That meant it was up to him to continue this conversation, the one about making a choice about how they'd live. He was having a difficult time with the courageous part of the pact. A brave man would have asked her on her front porch if she spent too much time obsessing over him, too.

Not *obsessing*. That was the wrong word choice.

Wasn't it?

"Are you afraid you'll get in trouble?

Should we be here?" Avery asked as he stopped in front of the gate blocking entrance to Otter Lake's most successful otter cove. The population here was hard to track, but when the rangers wanted to show off the park's repopulation program, they brought visitors here. This morning, he wanted to show off.

"With a civilian, too?" Avery pointed at the No Trespassing sign they were about to climb over.

Sam hopped over the gate and reached back to offer Avery a hand. He was less than surprised when she brushed the offer away and clambered over on her own. Disappointed, maybe, but not surprised.

"Nah, I don't think anyone would be shocked to find me here." Sam switched on the flashlight he'd brought only because of Avery. He knew the path so well that light, especially on a clear night like this, wasn't necessary. The first time she tripped over an exposed tree root, Sam stopped. "Want the flashlight?" He wasn't going to offer her his hand again. At some point, she'd ask him what was going on with that, and he didn't have an answer.

"Sure." Avery took it from him, turned it off and shoved it in her pocket. "It's hurting more than helping, actually. Gee would be appalled."

She was right. Of course she was. His grandfather had insisted they had everything they needed on them to negotiate these mountains whether it was day or night. Over the years of fighting fires and search and rescue, Sam had decided his grandfather had been almost right. If you included the pocketknife he'd used to cut himself out of numerous bad spots and a good supply of water, then he was equipped with everything he needed.

"Remember the time Gee brought us up to Yanu to show us the difference between cloudy nights and clear?" Avery said, her breathing labored but steady. "That scared me. A lot. I'm not sure I'm meant to be in the dark woods at night."

Surprised, Sam stopped. "But…here we are."

Avery slammed into his back with a grunt. "Alone. I meant *alone*. If I'd known *you* were the one who was going to cause me to break my nose, though, I might have rethought this." She rubbed the bridge of her nose, and Sam wished he could do the same to his shoulder blade, the one that would have a nose-shaped bruise in the morning.

"Sorry." Sam turned and resumed his careful steps. After a minute, he could hear her follow, the occasional grumble under her breath enough to make him smile. He'd been in such a weird mood while he stared up at the bland ceiling of his boring apartment. All he could imagine was talking things out with Avery, like they had more than once as kids. When her father had died, they'd sneaked out after dark to sit on the edge of the tree house platform to talk about death and what happens next.

Neither one of them had a good grasp, but he'd never forget Avery staring up at the stars like there might be an answer there.

"Clear tonight. We should be able to see the stars," he murmured and reached behind him to help her over a log. "Otters. Stars. It's like a nature double feature."

Avery laughed breathlessly. "Are we getting close? Because…" She bent to brace her hands on her knees to catch her breath. "If you give me a hard time about this, I totally deserve it, but I will plot my revenge nevertheless."

"You're doing great. We're almost there." He took her hand to guide her along the path that was almost impossible to see in the shadows of the woods lining Otter Lake. From there, he could make out occasional splashes and one chittering mother who was lecturing her children not to go out into the dark. Because mothers everywhere were the same.

Out of nowhere, Sam could imagine Avery leading her little girl out into the starry night so they could see what there was to see. She'd be the kind of mother who would raise confident kids.

Unsettled, Sam moved too quickly and pulled Avery with him. She stumbled on the rocks and bounced up against his shoulders. "I hope you are a better guide when the lights are turned back on because…" She brushed her shoulder off and then bumped him lightly. "Kidding. I kid. This is awesome. Thank you for coming to get me."

He wanted to promise he'd always come to her rescue.

But he'd failed to do that when she needed

a friend the most. He'd let her disappear completely from his life.

Sam also wanted to make it clear that she was saving him, too, but he didn't know how to put his emotions into words. Instead, he pointed at the rock he'd decided was the best place to think. "Have a seat."

Avery paused for a minute to stare up at him. "Are you okay? You've been in a weird mood ever since I met you on the porch."

Sam eased past her to sit down on the rock. "I needed not to be alone and the first person I thought of was you. That's the reason for my weird mood."

He couldn't see her eyes but her lips were twitching as she plopped down beside him. "You flatterer. I give good advice. I might not have finished law school, but no one can doubt my ability to argue either side of any question."

If all he'd needed was advice, he'd had his shot with Ash, but nothing of the weird dissatisfaction he'd felt ever since he'd come home had come together into any good question. Today, or rather yesterday, he and Ash had climbed Obed in silence. Sam had been thinking again, but Ash was impossible to read. If still waters ran deep, Ash was a bottomless well.

"Think you'll go back?" Sam asked as he pointed at a lively group of otters. In the gloaming of presunrise, they were hard to make out from their vantage point, but it was nice to watch a healthy group diving. "Sun'll be up soon."

"To law school? Or Chicago?" Avery asked as she knelt closer to the edge of the rock outcropping to see better. "No."

"To which one?" Sam wasn't sure why he imagined her coming to her senses and heading back to the city, especially in a moment like this when Avery was chasing a better view of otters instead of worrying over dark woods, muddy knees or whatever else might be in the dark with them.

"Neither." She sighed. "You know, it's easy to tell myself that all the noise and convenience of city living is worth the trade-off, but when I'm out here, I wonder how in the world I managed to stay gone for so long." She turned to face him, her face lit by the pink of sunrise. "Thanks, Sam. I needed this to stop my mind from…running away with me."

He got that. His mind was doing its best

to confuse him. "So, no Chicago, but you shouldn't dismiss law school altogether. You know you'd be an awesome lawyer."

"When I decided I was going to become a lawyer, I methodically researched law schools at the library. The University of Chicago is one of the finest schools in the country and I had this idea that it would be easy and not too expensive to travel home from there. Then I rarely did it." Avery eased back down on the rock. "Now I can't imagine being so far away from home, from places like this, again. I can't even explain it, but that first day, even as ragged as I was, when I made it to the top of Yanu it was like I'd been holding my breath for years and I could finally breathe deep. It's like...that was a previous life. I don't want to go back to that Avery. She worked hard and she still ended up...alone, with nothing to show for it. New Avery is doing life differently."

Sam frowned and then pointed out a small group of floating otters. "Mamas and babies. See? They're holding hands." Avery made the *aww* sound he'd expected. He heard it from females of all ages when he pointed it out. "What was wrong with that old Avery?"

Since they hadn't kept in touch after she went away to college first in Knoxville, then Chicago, he had no idea who that Avery had become. What was the reason the Avery he'd met at the top of Yanu had been so miserable?

"That Avery was necessary, at least to get me to this point, but I think of how easy it was to leave, to turn my back. Robert asked me to marry him and I…stopped. Now, sitting here, it makes no sense. I gave up me to be *us*. I hope that was because I was young and he offered everything I wanted. Now I know I've got to find something I love so much that no man will be able to convince me to leave it behind." Avery wrapped her arms around her legs. "I want to find the greatest job in the world. A wise man once said we all deserve to find the job that makes us feel that way, and I believe he was right."

Sam rubbed his jaw. "Wise? That's the first time you've ever called me that."

She frowned. "I'm sure I've used it before, but in combination with another word or two. In any event, it was less complimentary. Now I mean it as the highest compliment to you. I needed this. You knew that."

She stretched out her arms. "I needed these mountains and this air and the sound of happy otters."

"Well, what if Chicago is the problem? There are law schools in all kinds of places." Sam had no idea if there was a law school in the entire state of Colorado, but he was certain there were lawyers. They had to come from somewhere. "Will you be happy at the library?" Why was he pushing this? Did he want some of her planning to rub off on him?

"You and my mother," Avery grumbled. "Why can't I *be* for a while? I went through some hard stuff. Do you know what it's like to be told someone you love has weeks to live? That there's nothing to be done?" She shook her head. "I'm sorry. I'm not angry at you. I…"

"You're angry. You have a right to be angry. You loved him." Sam took a chance and put his hand on the middle of her back. Some of the tension eased as he rubbed small circles. "Anger at losing someone you love is right. I'll never forget when Gee died. We nearly tore the tree house down, one angry kick at a time."

"Yeah, I learned when my dad died, anger

is so much easier to turn on and off than tears." She was silent as she watched the otters. As the sun rose higher, it was easier to make out the playful dashes and tumbles of happy animals secure in their environment.

"Tell me about Robert." Sam stared out over the lake, determined to rip off the bandage in one yank. When she confirmed her husband was the kind of guy no other man could measure up to, it would be easier to put her right back in the friend box instead of…whatever she might be someday.

"He was older. So smart. He knew minutiae about intellectual property and talked about it so often that I sometimes wanted to pull my hair out." Avery rocked slowly. "He would have made a good father, one who came home at the end of the day instead of dying in a crash because he refused to pull his truck over and rest." Avery didn't turn to Sam but he squeezed her shoulder. Losing her father in an instant had shaped her as a girl. Now, as a woman, she'd had to deal with losing someone she'd loved one day at a time. "But he had opinions, so many of them. We could fight over what to have for dinner like it was life and death."

"Did he actually win?" Sam asked, determined to lighten the mood.

"Sometimes I let him. He wasn't a gracious loser." Avery tucked her hands at her sides. "Not like you. I taught you early how to lose properly. Robert never had that, so he...he was pretty good with the silent treatment." She turned back to stare out over the water as golden sunshine highlighted the gentle waves hitting the shore. "That family we were planning? Yeah, can you even imagine what the kids would have been like?"

Sam could. They would have been so smart, courageous, and kind at the same time. Avery might tease about sore losers, but she'd always been such a likable winner because, deep down, she didn't take it too seriously.

Sam wanted to ask about her hopes for the future. Would she ever change her mind about dating and return to her plans for a family?

Probably not with a guy who took risks with his life every day on the job.

"When we were growing up, we never got to see anything like this." Avery shook her head. "There are too many otters to count."

"Yeah, sometimes reintroducing animals

works. River otters in the Smokies are a success story." Sam thought about rolling a few of the facts he had memorized for speaking engagements, but it wasn't necessary.

"Do you know how hard it is to figure out what you want to be for the rest of your life?" Avery asked, her voice quiet in the pink light.

"That's why we're here. I don't even have a job offer yet and I've almost convinced myself that leaving here would be the worst decision I could make. My family. My memories. My friends. Why would I leave that?" Sam didn't look at Avery but knew the second her eyes landed on his face.

"What?" she asked too loudly in the silence. "All the trouble you gave me for leaving, and now you're too chicken to even consider it?"

Sam didn't answer. There was nothing to say.

"Listen, Sam," Avery said, then paused. "I can't believe I have to say this to you, but none of that will change. Your family will still be your family, even if you're in Colorado. These mountains? They will stand tall after you leave and be waiting whenever you want to come back. Whatever you do, it's not forever. You can go and decide it was a terrible decision. That's okay. I thought, of the two of us, you would understand so much better than I do that being afraid to take a step is unacceptable. Decide what you want most and go for it."

Then she stood up to pace. "Now I get it. This isn't about me needing you. It's about you needing me. And I can do that. That's so much easier than figuring out what I want to do for the rest of my life."

Sam laughed. "Could you do both? Help me get it in gear and figure out what will make you happy?"

She braced her hands on her hips as she stared down at him. "We'll see. Here's what I know. You set me on the first path, the one to becoming a lawyer. My husband was the fork in the road that led to…this mess that I'm in. When I figure out the next phase, it'll all be on me. Win or lose, this is my choice this time."

Sam rubbed his chest. The notion that something he'd said mattered enough to her to set a course by was a sweet encouragement.

If he didn't get his mind off how much he

liked Avery, he was going to do something stupid, the stupid thing he'd been chasing away every single time it floated up to the surface of his tangled thoughts.

One kiss could settle everything.

"What did you do in Chicago? After law school and before your husband got sick?" Sam stretched his legs out. If she didn't like his question, she could give him one hard shove and he'd go rolling right into Otter Lake. He wanted to be ready to swim if it came to that.

"I volunteered, provided legal aid." Avery wrapped her arms tightly over her chest. "Actually, I filed, answered phones and tried to comfort people who were desperate for help. I loved it. All the help I gave, none of the pressure of law school or passing the bar or dealing with a husband who deserved my time. If I'd known how little we were going to have, I might have spent more days at home."

"You feel guilty for doing something you loved, that helped people who needed it, because your husband, a grown man who ought to have enough to keep him occupied…" Sam grunted. "I never would have seen that coming from Avery Abernathy, the girl who insisted she could climb the face of Yanu and would have done it if I hadn't called her mother."

"Yeah, me, either. It's depressing." She turned to stare back out over the lake. "I wouldn't have guessed I'd need my mother to rescue me from my own grief, either, or that a hike to see these otters would have made it clear that I don't care what anyone else thinks. Not anymore. If I'm happy working at a library doing story time…" Avery waved her hands wildly. "Okay, so I'm not good at it, but if I'm happy, then who cares that I never finished law school or live at home with my mother or feel…?"

Sam waited for her to finish her thought. How did she feel?

Then he sighed and stood up next to her. "You know who cares you didn't finish law school? Those people you were helping at Legal Aid, the ones that made you happy. That's it. That's all."

He ignored her ugly glare. "You want to get closer to the otters? Pretty soon, they'll head for quieter spots for the day."

For half a minute, tense silence nearly convinced him that she wasn't going to let it go.

"When the time comes and you get that job offer?" Avery said in a mean voice. "Don't you dare expect me to pull my punches, either. Got it?"

Sam offered her his hand and then led the way down the rocky shore to the lake. They both squatted near the water to watch the otters frolic around the fallen logs that framed their cozy cove.

"I'm going to find what makes me happy, Sam. And then I'm going to do it." Avery tipped her chin up and met his stare. "Dare me."

She might as well have been seventeen again, but the feelings he had were so different. Instead of wanting to beat her in whatever race they cooked up, he wanted to help her, to encourage her. A breeze sent one curl over her forehead to land across her eyes. Before she could brush it away, he smoothed it aside, happy to see the spark of determination in her eyes. "Do it, AA. You're the only one who can."

Sam knew there was never going to be another moment to try it, the kiss that could settle everything. The woods were quiet. The water was turning golden with sunrise. The two of them belonged in that spot at that time.

So he slowly pressed his mouth against hers, the sweet taste of her lips completing the most perfect moment in time.

And instead of shoving him headfirst in the water, Avery wrapped her hands in the loose sleeves of his sweatshirt and held on, so Sam deepened the kiss. He pulled her closer, hands solid on her hips, and tried to memorize the wonder of holding Avery Abernathy in his arms.

When he ended the kiss, Avery pressed her forehead against his shoulder and held on tight, so Sam crossed his arms around her back, content to stand there as long as it took for one of them to come up with something to say.

She won that race. "Sam, I can't believe you…that we did that." She eased back, her fingers pressed over her mouth, the concern on her face enough to worry Sam.

Sam shoved his hands in his pockets. "I wanted to. It's all I could think of ever since you picked me up at the airport, how nice it would be to have a greeting like this every time I came home."

Avery shook her head. "I'm not that sweet girl, though. The two of us together? We're no good. You have to do this job, Sam, and I can't…" She inhaled slowly. "I nearly had a panic attack before you picked me up because I was reliving losing my husband. Two of those nightmares to ambush me every night? I can't. I won't." She grabbed his hand. "But I love you so much, Sam. You're the friend I've needed forever. Please, don't doubt that I *need* you."

The desperate plea on her face was impossible to ignore. She believed what she was saying. He wanted to argue that there were no guarantees to life, that he might outlive her by decades but that was a risk he'd take. Instead, he held out both hands. "Listen, it was the…atmosphere. Otters are so romantic, am I right?"

Avery wanted to argue, but she nodded. "Yeah. Romantic." They both knew they were lying but the friendship depended on going with the lie.

"I couldn't ever fall for a girl who couldn't

beat my time to the top of Yanu," Sam said, "even if she should be a lawyer but gave up."

"Wise words from a chicken who wants to back out on his dream?" She waggled her eyebrows at him and shoved his shoulder so quickly he bobbled in response. She was going to play along.

If that didn't say enough about his stupid assumption of what they might be to each other if only she weren't grieving and he weren't hoping to move across the country, nothing would. They both needed this friendship too badly to let anything, even attraction, mess it up.

To shake off his disappointment, Sam said, "Last one to the truck is the chicken and gets to explain why we're here when the park's closed." Then he took off in a mad scramble up the hill.

Her angry "You cheater!" was followed by loud hoots that scared away every wild animal in a half-mile radius along with all the otters. Sam was still chuckling when he turned to help her up the steep incline. Avery, true to form, accepted his help and then sat him down on the rock with a hard shove and took off at a dead run.

Sam stood slowly and stared out over the lake. Whatever happened, this was his home. Avery was right. It would still be here when he came back. And she would be...somewhere in the world. He wouldn't lose touch with her again, no matter where the two of them lived. Some of the anxiety that had been slowly building in his chest at the idea of saying goodbye to Sweetwater eased.

Wherever he went, Avery could still be a part of his life.

Now he knew enough not to let that go. Time was all they needed to make this work. With no other choice, he could wait.

"You're losing!" Avery's voice was farther away than he'd expected, so Sam turned on a heel and poured on the speed. Win or lose, he had to give it his best shot.

CHAPTER TWELVE

"YOUR STORY TIMES are getting better, Avery," Astrid lied as she waved at Miranda, who was marching out the library door with a backpack filled with books. "I mean, you almost managed to keep everyone's attention for the whole thirty minutes this time. Only Justin nodded off. It was a good thing that you knocked that chair over. Loud noises make it harder to sleep."

Avery lifted her head from the circulation desk and propped her chin on one hand. "At what point do we decide that I do not have what it takes for this job?"

"Listen, that's on you, not me. I'm glad to have the help." Astrid scooted up on the desk and picked up Pippi. "Still, I'm going to guess 'soon' is the answer."

"A book about pirates should be exciting. I tried the voices. I even wore an eye patch."

Avery popped the patch that had landed somewhere over her right ear.

"But you didn't prepare for Miranda." Astrid patted Avery's arm. "It's okay. I'm not sure anyone can prepare for Miranda."

"Yeah, I mean, that defense of the pirates and their way of life as a direct reflection on how society has failed them?" Avery rubbed her hand over her forehead in the vain hope that she could iron out the "what is happening here?" wrinkles. "How old is she, again?"

"You did a good job of defending the justice system, but I'm pretty sure that's where you lost the rest of the room." Astrid sighed as Pippi stretched out in her arms, a long, orange feline statement of "don't care, keep scratching" that was cute and as good an answer as any.

"I ought to start looking for my next job," Avery said slowly, "even though the choices here in Sweetwater are limited."

"What about Knoxville? I guess it might be hard to make that commute every day." Astrid motioned with a shoulder. "We have the paper if you want to check it."

"Thanks, Boss," Avery said as her lips

twitched. "Nothing like your current employer encouraging you to find other work."

"You'll be much more interesting when you come back for a career day. Once you find something that you can talk about passionately, other than the reason our legal system fails innocent people, then you will have those kids hooked." Astrid smiled sweetly, a dimple winking in her left cheek. "Did you see what I did there?"

"Yeah, arguing passionately about our legal system… What kind of job would *that* be?"

She'd discarded a dozen different careers in her plotting of what to do with the next three or four decades of her life.

Librarian was out, and while she was at it, Avery crossed off teacher. Being able to command a room of kids was beyond her, and both professions depended heavily on the skill.

Her mother still hadn't confessed to her budding business redecorating and flipping homes, so that left out joining the family company. Which was just as well since the threat of looking at one more paint chip, shoved under her nose by her mother, made her feel vaguely violent.

No matter where she went, she always returned to law school.

Was it going to come back to that? After all these years?

Avery closed her eyes. The only thing that had caught her interest, especially since Sam had dropped off the face of the earth, was researching boilerplate contracts for her mother.

Which no one really needed her to do. It wasn't like either Odella or Janet would charge into court to demand recompense if their business relationship stalled. Her mother was operating well enough on her own without a personal corporate attorney, so for fun Avery had been thumbing through the old law-school books she'd shipped home before she'd gotten married.

And it was fun, reading through her notes, remembering the way counterarguments flowed for her.

Avery picked up the folder she'd been carrying everywhere, as if contract law might have a sudden new development that would require her immediate attention, and slipped it in the tote bag she'd slung over the back of the chair.

"Seen Sam lately?" Astrid asked, an innocent blink her only other comment.

"Not since the weekend." Even as she said it, Avery still had a hard time believing Sam had kissed her. No matter how many times she turned it over in her head, it made no sense.

Even more unbelievably, she'd kissed him back.

And apparently that had been enough to push Sam back a step. The only communication she'd had with him directly had been a text. He'd taken a selfie at the top of Yanu Falls. Under thirty minutes to the top. Not my best, but nothing to be ashamed of. His broad grin had been so typically Sam that Avery had to smile through her irritation.

She hadn't had a chance to get back up to the trail, which was fine. She was nowhere near his time. Not yet, anyway.

From his mother, she'd heard today was his day off. And he hadn't invited her to go climbing at Obed, even though he'd threatened more than once to take her. Since she'd had to be rescued from an easy hike from

Yanu, there was no way she'd be ready for a climb straight up.

"Why? Did you need to talk to him about his next story time?" Avery asked.

"You two are thick as thieves," Astrid said as she pointed at Avery's eye patch, "another group of people who've been forgotten by the justice system, no doubt."

Avery smiled. "Have you been talking to my mother? She asks oh so casually about what Sam and I are up to. That's her sly way of checking to see whether anything is coming of this friendship."

"Yeah, mothers are pretty much the same the world over. I sure do miss mine, but not the matchmaking." Astrid stood. "I was wondering if you might want to go out with this guy I know. He's awesome. You could set me up with Sam. I'm talking double date." Her singsong was cute, but the immediate shock that swept over Avery wiped away any amusement.

"Sam's…busy this week, some assignment at one of the weather stations the engine crew monitors. He's also meeting with the hotshot recruiter because he's planning a move. Remember?" She'd learned all that from eavesdropping on her mother's conversations with Regina Blackburn, a fact that was starting to move from irritating her to hurting her feelings.

Their new old friendship would survive a kiss.

Wouldn't it?

Avery wasn't sure why it was important to make it clear that she knew more about Sam's life than Astrid ever could, but the urge to snap was strong. They'd planned a climb somewhere, to be determined by Sam, but Avery was afraid Sam would cancel it.

If he did, she was going to give him a piece of her mind. They were stronger than one kiss.

She needed him too much to let that end a friendship.

Astrid sighed. "Sure, sure, his new job. You know, I get that the move is a big, exciting thing, but he's a great guy." She waved her hand at the small building they were in. "Leaving all this could be a struggle, but there are libraries in Colorado. And universities that could lead to any number of exciting new careers."

Avery tightened her grip on her tote. "Really? You aren't even dating but you could see moving across the country. Because of Sam?"

"If he was the right guy, I could. Could you?"

Avery studied Astrid, confused by the whole conversation. Then the realization that she'd messed up crossed Astrid's face and she waved her hands. "I went too far. Don't tell your mother."

Amused but annoyed at her mother's never-say-die attitude, Avery rolled her eyes. "No way. She's roped you in? I thought she was done with the matchmaking. Sam and I are friends. I'm hardly enough to keep him here. For the past two decades, we lived pretty successfully a thousand miles apart." Avery had no idea if that distance was correct but it sounded right.

"And yet your mama is certain he's the one who's been bringing you back to life." Astrid tilted her head and peered at her. "She's not wrong, is she?"

No, she wasn't wrong, but why did that have to mean romance?

And why, when she'd made a new friend for the first time in years after being deserted by her old friends, had her mother been able to turn Astrid to her side?

"I can't believe she's pushing like this. I lost a husband. She should understand how that's changed me." Avery slung her tote bag over her shoulder and watched it settle.

For some reason, dragging that old University of Chicago bag out of the closet had been satisfying.

She'd never forget the first day she'd picked it up at one of those mixers for new students.

"Honey, she does understand how it changed you. That's why she's worried." Astrid set Pippi down. "Did I tell you about the dog I'm going to go visit at the shelter in Knoxville? He's a mutt, but the name Jem suits him perfectly. Want to go with me to meet him?" Astrid relaxed, relieved to have done the job she'd been given, even if it had gone sideways.

"Have you already got permission to add a library dog?" Avery asked, grateful for the change in subject. She didn't want to blast Astrid, but this whole lecture about loyalty and what friends do for each other was rumbling around in her head.

"Naw, but the mayor? He's an easy touch. One look in Jem's eyes and that guy'll be wrapped around his little paw." Astrid motioned with her head. "Pippi's approval's the one that's got me worried."

Astrid had a unique point of view. The guy who signed her paycheck was no threat, but her sleeping orange cat could derail everything. "I'll think about your offer. For the double date." Then she shook her head. "Actually, no, I won't. I'm not ready to be dating."

"Then you could set me up with Sam for a single date, I guess." Astrid watched her closely as she swung a leg back and forth. "Couldn't you?"

Uneasy, Avery marched around the desk and stopped. "You and Sam?" Was Astrid pushing buttons again?

Astrid shrugged. "Why not?"

She had a good point.

"He's out there for who knows how long," Avery said, "pretty much out of touch when he's fighting fires. Wait—you know what he wants to do, right? These crews jump into out-of-control fires. It's a scary, unpredictable job. Why would you sign up to be the woman worrying about whether he was coming home again?" Avery asked. If anyone had been able to convince her to get serious about her and Sam, this was the argument she had ready to trot out. She'd been working on it ever since their shared sunrise at Otter Lake. That kiss? It had been good, the kind of first kiss a woman dreams about before it happens and finds impossible to forget.

But Sam was her friend, a lifeline to the new Avery. She could continue their friendship long-distance, but falling for him would be too risky.

She'd given her heart to the most stable guy she'd ever met.

And it had almost killed her.

Losing Sam? The kid who'd pushed her and the man who'd helped bring her back to life? There would be no coming back from that.

"Sounds like you've already examined the downside to Sam Blackburn." Astrid shifted her weight back and forth. Avery had learned that was a sign she was deep in thought. "Only a woman who can see the real potential in a man is going to spend her valuable time doing that. Well, she sees the potential *and* she's scared to death of it."

Avery propped her hands on her hips. "Scared to death of what? Sam?"

"Dating Sam. Losing Sam. Loving Sam." Astrid's face was solemn and Avery was surprised how the quiet words slammed through her.

"You aren't afraid of those things?" Avery snapped. "Because let me tell you, as the voice of experience, you should be terrified. You will never be the same."

Astrid reached over to squeeze her hand. "And what about if you lose out on the love of your life the second time around? I mean, imagine that, never changing, never growing, never becoming who you were meant to be because you were afraid of the changes." Then she held up both hands. "Honestly, if you don't make me shut my mouth, I'm going to be spouting off who knows what nonsense, and all I promised to do was suggest a double date and catalog your responses." She mimed turning the key on the lock of her mouth and tossing it away.

"How much is my mother paying you for this?" Avery asked, as confused as ever about what she wanted and wishing her mother would tell her the answer.

"No payment," Astrid said as she swung her knotted hands back and forth, "but she did move me up on her waiting list of clients, so that's something. A full year is too long to wait to get my living room spruced up, you know?"

At the reminder that she still hadn't confronted her mother about whatever side business she'd been working on without telling Avery one thing about it, Avery changed her mind about her destination. She'd been prepared to head for the fried-pie place and then hand over the contract she'd enjoyed drafting for Odella entirely too much.

But now, finding her mother and demanding to know the details about her "new" business were at the top of her list.

"'Bye, Astrid. I'll make sure my mother knows you've done your job." Avery ignored Astrid's token protests and stepped out onto the curb. One slow survey of the main street showed Regina's car parked in front of Smoky Joe's. Since the women rarely went anywhere separately, it was easy enough to guess where her mother might be.

Before Avery determinedly jaywalked across the street, her phone vibrated. She dug it out of her pocket to see a message from Sam. Need a rain check on the climb up to Yanu. Call you when I get back.

Discouraged, Avery stopped and thought about how to answer. The short beep of a small car's horn got her moving out of the street with a guilty wave. As soon as she was back on the sidewalk, she typed, Afraid I'll beat your time? Fine. Feed Courage. Her lips were twitching as she imagined his scowl when he read the text.

She waited there in the shadows of the hardware store's awning until a cold breeze surprised a shiver out of her. She glanced up at the mountains, where heavy black clouds hung low. Off in the distance, thunder rumbled. As warm as it had been, they needed the rain, even if the thunderstorm brewing made her uneasy. Avery tugged the ugly scarf she'd given her mother as a high school senior out of her coat pocket and wrapped it twice around her neck.

As she dropped her phone back in her pocket, she realized the scarf would be another weapon in the upcoming showdown with her mother. Bolstered by her powerful indignation over her mother's secret business and the way she'd found the knit scarf she'd worked on for weeks shoved inside a box in the top of her closet, Avery straightened her shoulders and marched right inside Smoky Joe's.

Odella, Janet and Regina were all staring at the design board that had been spread out on her mother's kitchen table for two weeks. Each one of them was frowning, and Odella was tapping her chin.

"Nope. This wasn't what I had in mind." She waved a hand in the air and snatched up her coffeepot. "Fine dining. In Sweetwater? The place'll be out of business in two months. We ain't so much about fine as home and comfort and good." Then she stomped off, shaking her head as if she couldn't believe she'd wasted her time on such nonsense. "You come back to me when you got a plan for the heart of *this* place, not whatever you're dreaming of somewhere else."

Stunned at Odella's response, Avery watched Janet and Regina stare after the older woman, both of their mouths hanging open.

Some of Avery's fury drained away as she memorized the sight of her perky mother caught off guard…and surrounded by kitschy, dusty cookie jars.

"Well, I never." Her mother folded gracefully into one of the red booths in front of the door and propped her elbow on the table. Her head hit her hand with a thump.

"Me, either," Regina said as she turned in a slow circle. "Seriously? I could do it, make this place a go. I know it." Then she gave Janet a gentle shove and eased down beside her.

Avery slid across from them, confused now that her plan to attack was shot in the foot.

"Well, this is disappointing," Avery said as she pulled the file out of her tote and slipped it under her mother's elbow. "I had planned to spike the ball, which is really a basic contract that absolutely no one could disagree with. And now, that would be totally overkill."

Regina yanked the folder out from below Janet's arm and slipped her glasses on. She perused the document quickly. "I'm impressed anyway, hon." Then she closed the folder and plopped her hands on top. "I guess if Odella won't hire us to renovate the place, we'll just have to buy it as is." Regina paused and she and Janet studied each other carefully. "I've crunched these numbers, and they don't lie. We can't let a good plan go to waste."

Sam's mother raised an eyebrow.

Avery's mother sighed. "Well, now, I guess we can't." Then she offered Regina her hand.

After their giggling handshake, Regina said, "Your next contract can be an offer to purchase Smoky Joe's. Then we'll need you to review the agreement we have with our contractor. It's time we flipped some real estate for long-term investment."

Janet slowly turned her head and her eyes were bugged out at Regina.

"Mama," Avery said softly. "Come on."

"Ain't no way she hasn't figured all this out," Regina said, "and that's assuming there was any figuring to do. She and Sam are thick as thieves. He's the one who introduced us to Ethan."

Avery waited for her mother to meet her stare. "Why couldn't you tell me that you and Miss Regina were in business together?"

Her mother sighed. "Listen, baby…" She fussed with her bangs. "The first time Reggie and I bought a house? It was the day Robert was rushed to the hospital because he couldn't breathe. Remember that day?"

Of course she did. Avery would never forget the way he'd clawed at her arm, desperate for help, or how long it had taken the ambulance to arrive.

"I called that evening, completely clueless about everything you were going through, ready to celebrate." Janet closed her eyes. "I couldn't believe you hadn't called me."

Avery shifted in her seat, uneasy at the tone of her mother's voice. Was she angry that Avery had done her best to handle every crisis?

"I don't remember that." And she felt vaguely guilty because of it. "I had a lot on my mind. They put that tube in and I just… I couldn't leave him because every time he woke up, he was in a panic. If his eyes even fluttered, I was there."

Her mother reached across the table and squeezed her hand. "Of course. You were doing what you had to do, and no one can fault you for that."

She said it, but did she mean it? It would be easy to say the words to smooth things over now.

"Okay, but Robert's been gone for more

than two years." Avery wanted to understand, but it made no sense.

"And you, you've been juggling insurance companies and settlements and selling the house and getting rid of all his things and..." Her mother gulped. "I've been there. You remember that, don't you?"

Avery could see the suffering in her mother's eyes. They had that in common. If Robert's slow exit had made it simpler by giving her plenty of time to plan, her mother had been thrust into the deep end without any life preserver and with an angry little girl clinging to the edge of the world by her fingernails. And she'd managed so well that Avery had never once had to wonder if she was on the verge of an eternal, terrible solution to all her problems.

She was so much stronger than Avery had ever been.

"I do remember, Mama." Avery rubbed her throbbing temple. "I did this all wrong. I got it so wrong. If there's anyone in the world who could talk to me about how I felt, it was you."

Her mother's grim expression was enough of a confirmation of her hurt feelings, her frustration and worry, that Avery wanted to bang her head on the table. "I wanted to get control."

Regina tapped the table. "Uh-huh. I have heard that one before."

The three of them were quiet as the bustle of the late-afternoon crowd flowed around them.

"Listen, now I know and I'm so happy to know." Avery slid the folder back and forth. "And we have options here. If Odella won't sell and you want to do the restaurant, we'll find a new place. There are other spots here on the square with real historical charm. We can renovate and go from there."

Neither of the women across from her brightened at the suggestion.

"Or…" Avery shook her head. "Seriously, the two of you are already so busy. Astrid sold herself out by pretending to be interested in setting me up on a double date in order to interrogate me on my feelings for Sam so she could report back to you in the hopes of moving up on your list of clients."

Her mother tilted her chin up, the pride at the business she was building clear on her face.

"I've told her, if she'll come up with the

deposit, we'll work her in sooner than next year," Regina said with a roll of her eyes. "She gets the friends and family scheduling advantage, no double agenting required." She leaned forward. "Who was she going to set you up with?"

Janet wrinkled her nose. "Gotta be the mayor. The two of them are either friends or enemies depending on the day. You and him, her and Sam."

Regina considered the matchup. "She's a nice girl."

Avery waited for her to disqualify Astrid from the running. Instead, Regina nodded slowly. "I could see it. I expected him to be interested in more of an adventurous woman." She waggled her eyebrows at Avery. "But that isn't working and a mother is not the best judge of her boy's love life."

The urge to argue was hard to squash, but Avery knew nothing good would come from presenting the case that Astrid was all wrong for Sam. Making a case for anyone as acceptable or unacceptable for him was an indication that she'd spent entirely too much time thinking about him and what he needed.

Unexpected kisses could do that.

Not that anyone else knew about the kiss.

Or that Sam would ever get within a lip's width of her again.

"I can't imagine a girl like Astrid being happy waiting for Sam to come home." Avery bit her lip, mad at herself for letting anything loose. And as soon as her mother's lips curled in a smug half smile, she knew she'd been played. Again.

"Thing is, no woman's going to be too happy with the waiting." Regina cleared her throat. "I'm saying, as a mother, I worry about him even if he's nowhere near a fire. He does crazy things, pushes himself as hard as he can because..." She shrugged. His mother didn't understand why Sam did what he did. "But I love him. I don't want to change him. And instead of nagging or worrying so much over him, I've got to find my own things."

She turned to Avery's mom. "This might not be the best use of your skills, Janet. I mean, we like flipping houses. Where would we come up with enough money to build a restaurant? They fold at the drop of a hat. It's not a good use of time or money or... our skills."

Avery cleared her throat. "Well, I was thinking…this is what I've been looking for, a new business."

Her mother frowned, an ugly scowl marring her brow. "A new business? You want to become a decorator?"

No. No, no, no. She had no desire to become a decorator. Following her mother around the hardware store had made her long for being stuck on Yanu Falls again. At some point, she'd decided she'd rather sleep out in the dark woods than choose between this blue paint chip and that blue paint chip.

But she couldn't go back to thinking life at the library was ever going to be long-term.

"I have to find something to do. When Sam goes…" Avery swallowed hard. Maybe she was the one who would have the hardest time letting him go.

If he'd never kissed her, would she feel the same way?

"You are going to find a way to build the life you want, not follow along in my wake. We've done that long enough." Her mother crossed her arms and rested them on the table. "Besides that, it's your money."

"It's Robert's money, his retirement, his insurance." They'd never imagined they would need any insurance on her, but he'd always had enough to cover a year in their house. Selling the house in Chicago had added to a nice nest egg, enough for her to invest in a business if she wanted.

Her mother shook her head slowly. "Nope. We will do this on our own. Regina is good with money. I promise you we've got this under control."

"So you didn't tell me because you didn't have to. No, wait… Because you didn't want to, didn't want me to be a part of this thing that you love." Avery nodded. "Got it." She grabbed her tote, prepared to slide out of the booth so she could stomp off the way teenage Avery had frequently done.

Instead, her mother blocked her escape. "Now, wait a minute."

When her mother took that tone, Avery had no choice but to listen.

"You were drowning," her mother snapped before raising a hand to whatever Regina planned to say to calm the waters. "How in the world was I supposed to ramble on about my fun new hobby while you were buried? You didn't want me to come, so I couldn't figure out what to do to help." She sighed. "I called. I listened to you talk about the weather and... I waited." She cleared her throat. "I'm so sorry if that's not good enough, but you could help a person out by giving them a hint or two on how to help."

Then she crossed her arms over her chest, her hurt and irritation written clearly on her face.

Avery was ashamed and angry and amused that they'd struck the same battle poses.

Regina, looking like the deer caught in on-coming traffic, stared from Janet to Avery and back until her face brightened. She waved enthusiastically. "Ethan! Over here!"

Avery held her mother's stare until a tall guy dressed head to work-boot toe in denim stopped by their booth. "Ladies. I was directed this way by the librarian." Avery shot a glance up at the movie-star-handsome lumberjack looming over her.

Avery knew her mouth was dangling open, but she wasn't sure what to say in response.

The guy squinted and stared at them

around the table. "Am I interrupting something?"

Regina nodded. "Yes, thank goodness. Ethan, we're going to have to postpone our plans for this place."

With the beard, it was hard to guess his emotions, but the guy merely shrugged. "That's fine. Got enough work to keep us busy through the winter as it is. That's why I'm here."

When Avery met his stare, she had to admit that if the father's eyes were anything like the son's, they were the bluest blue that ever blued. Then he said, "I need your help."

Avery nodded slowly and realized she had no idea what she was agreeing to. "With what?" The weird squeak was embarrassing, but he didn't seem to notice.

"We're going to be adding at least one guy to the crew, maybe two," Ethan said, "and since we've always been a family business, we need some advice and employment contracts if that's the best option, to protect everyone involved."

Avery straightened the edge of the folder that had the document she'd labored over for

Odella. She had enjoyed it… "You know I'm not really a lawyer."

"I'm not really a businessman, but the two of us, we're awfully close." Ethan offered her his hand. "If you can give me some help, I'll be happy to hire you, law degree or no."

Avery was on the verge of shaking his hand, the realization that the law was going to follow her whether she wanted it to or not settling deep in her bones.

It was becoming clear a return trip to law school was the only solution.

Before she could frame her answer, Regina's phone rang. She pulled it out and frowned. "What in the world is Ash Kingfisher doing, calling me? Is he hunting Sam?" She answered the call. "Hello?"

Avery stared at her mother because it was clear something wasn't right. Ash Kingfisher would know the assignments of the Otter Lake rangers and fire team. Sam was supposed to be working.

Goose bumps erupted down her arms, the fear immediate. Was Sam injured?

Ethan tapped his business card on the table and mouthed "call me" before he faded away. Avery absentmindedly picked up the card and clutched it in her hand as she watched Regina.

"Lost communication. Okay. That happens," she said slowly, one hand covering her heart. "Should I be worried?"

Whatever Ash said was meant to comfort, because Regina said, "Fine. I'll wait for your call? An hour? Thanks, Ash." Then she ended the call and squeezed the phone tightly with both hands. "Ash wanted to let me know, in case I heard it from someone else in town, that there was a fire burning near the weather station north of the Otter Lake range. He can't get in contact with Sam's crew, so he's headed that direction and he will call with an update." She swallowed hard. "It's all routine."

Avery's mother wrapped her arm around her best friend's shoulders. "An hour should give us plenty of time to brainstorm for the new project. Then, when we know Sam is safe, we'll have dinner to celebrate."

Regina nodded and Avery scanned the room. Half the diners were watching Regina Blackburn closely. She couldn't tell if they were locals or tourists because the faces had changed since she'd been away, but she recognized the look.

She'd seen it enough in the hospital to last a lifetime. They were morbidly curious. They were listening intently to pick up every crumb. The people from Sweetwater would do whatever they could to help Regina Blackburn when the time came, but until then, they'd chew over the story, and whoever had the rarest details would be the most popular one in town.

"Let's wait at home. I've been dying for a cooking lesson, Miss Regina. Now would be a good time. Could you teach me to make lasagna?" Avery tried to sound as if she had no other motive but enthusiasm, but the two women across the booth exchanged a look. No one believed her, and for good reason.

Janet Abernathy didn't cook unless she had no other choice and she'd passed this philosophy down to her daughter.

Right now, they had no choice. Distraction was the name of the game.

As soon as they knew Sam and his crew were safe, the charade would be over. They'd all laugh about it and then head out for pizza.

Until then, they were going to occupy their minds with something else.

Avery had a feeling she was getting a lesson in the best way to cope with loving Sam Blackburn.

CHAPTER THIRTEEN

"THIS LATE IN OCTOBER, we shouldn't be seeing conditions like this. The humidity was good, temps falling," the burn captain muttered as he marched back and forth, checking the equipment he'd set out to test humidity, wind speed and temperature. They hadn't planned to do any burning on this trip out to the weather station responsible for reporting the northeast quadrant of the park, but two different lightning strikes had started small blazes that afternoon.

Whether they let the fires go in order to clear out old growth or extinguished them because of the deteriorating conditions, Sam was glad to have some real work to do.

He'd already told his crew about his job offer and they'd been doing their best to batter his confidence into submission with enough trash-talking to fell a less secure man. All this waiting for the burn captain to give them a yea or nay left plenty of time to run their mouths, and he was enjoying himself until the first lightning strike on the hillside above the weather station snapped them all to attention. The dropping temperature meant cold blasts of wind. Thanks to the drought, everything was drier than it should be and ready to burn. If fire surrounded the weather station, it might be a loss before they could get in place.

"Extinguish the burn," the burn captain bellowed as he motioned above his head to wrap it up. "Then we'll ride out the storm." He pointed to the old wood plank building that served as a crude shelter. Inside, there was plenty of equipment to track the conditions on this side of the mountain range, but there were few creature comforts.

"Blackburn, take Rodriguez, Sutton and Jackson and come in from the north," McKesson, the crew chief, yelled. "Gotta make sure the firebreak is holding."

Sam raised a hand to indicate he'd heard the order and trotted up the path to reach a break in the flame as a hard, shrieking wind barreled up the side of the mountain, the push enough to fan the flames high. He noticed the nearest guy pause as the flames shot up old pines in an instant, racing to the canopy above them.

"Watch the station," Sam yelled through cupped hands. He and his smaller crew were on the station side, the only people who could move to intercept the fire if it turned. He got waves in response and then all four of them began wetting the area with the retardant they carried in case fires threatened to burn out of control. The trees engulfed in flames swayed with the hard wind. Sam hit the comm clipped to his shoulder. "Chief, come in."

He got nothing but static back. Since their equipment was intended for the challenges these mountains presented, it was unusual that any breakdown lasted long. They depended on the communication for safety. "Chief, come in. We have a situation, a possible threat to the station itself. We've begun spraying, but some response from the east to shut this down would be advised."

Sam cursed as he motioned the guys closer to the station. If they were going to protect the station, they'd have to do the best they could alone. The rest of the crew was on the other side of the flame. They'd notice the shift and anticipate the move as well as he had.

"Not much to burn," Sutton said as he motioned at the new growth carpeting the area around the weather station. The spot was remote, but clearing the area of fuel was a priority. Prescribed burns left room for healthy growth by clearing out dead limbs and dry leaves. Protecting the weather station was one of their main duties.

"Yeah, but we gotta watch those," Sam shouted and pointed up at the trees that were on fire.

Then the rain clouds opened, dousing the fire, the firefighters and the weather station in the rain that east Tennessee had needed since May. Sam drew in a deep breath, relieved to have some help from Mother Nature. The fire could be contained, but the threat to the station was not good. And the park had already lost hundreds of acres to fire over the dry summer and fall.

With rain like that, they were better off taking shelter. Another lightning strike convinced him.

Sam gave his own "wrap it up" motion

and watched the other three men trot back down toward the weather station. At some point, they'd all have a chance to come back this way to make sure the fire was either contained or dying. For now, they could get warmer and drier inside.

Sam checked the area one last time to be sure the fire was still acting as they expected.

Then he heard a howl of wind, a loud crack, and had only a split second to see the tall pine with its upper branches still on fire break in two.

Before he could yell for help, the trunk caught him and everything went dark.

Waking up in the middle of a fireman's carry, his head face down to the damp ground flashing between the yellow boots of... Sam had lost track of who was carrying him, but if he didn't get to where he was going and soon, whoever his rescuer was would have a pile of vomit at his feet.

"Hold," Sam said weakly. Then the throbbing pain in his head cleared for a split second and he shouted it again, his throat on fire. "Hold!" Every breath was torture, the pain in his side nearly unbearable.

The bobbing, throbbing torment paused. Firm hands pulled and shifted him until he was right side up, the ground and smoke and fire spinning around him in a kaleidoscope of bright orange, sullen gray and pitch black. At least the ground was solid underneath him. He wasn't spiraling away.

Sam held up one hand in warning and apology before he leaned over and threw up meals he could no longer remember eating. When he was certain he could do so without choking, Sam collapsed in the ground cover and old pine needles to gasp for clean air. Smoke made the air hazy but he could see three worried faces, and he was almost certain that he would eventually remember all their names.

At this point, his ears were ringing, his head needed to be removed so that he could replace it with a brand-new one, and all he could do was fight to regain his breath through a stabbing stitch in his side.

Before he was completely ready, the guys watching him with worried frowns lifted him again, this time by the shoulders and feet so that he could watch the smoke rise to meet the storm clouds as rain washed his face. As rescues went, he'd seen worse, but he'd never been a party to one himself. Ever.

And so far, he was not a fan.

The crew had cleared a break in the flames, and Sam breathed more comfortably when the rest of the engine crew and the crew chief rushed out of the weather station to meet them.

"What happened?" McKesson shouted.

"Tree. Heard a crack. When I made it over to Blackburn, he was on the ground, pinned." Rodriguez grunted as they reached the narrow doorway and he took the full burden of Sam's shoulders. "You ever wonder what two hundred pounds of firefighter feels like, Boss?"

The rest of the crew moved out of their way until Rodriguez set him down carefully in the only spot big enough, the cleared plank floor in the center of the room.

Sam held up a hand, determined to show them that he was fine, but he couldn't quite get his voice to work.

Eventually, he managed to croak, "Two twenty-five, thank you very much." He watched confusion flitter across Rodriguez's face and then waited for him to repeat it for the rest of the group.

Immediately, the tension in the small structure lightened.

Losing one of the crew was the worst thing that could happen to any team, so Sam understood why they watched him so closely, but he couldn't do anything else to reassure them. If he tried too many words, he'd scream as best his aching throat would let him.

McKesson knelt next to Sam. "Get me a lantern."

Before he could ask twice, every man in the room had thrust a flashlight or lantern or an illuminated cell phone the chief's way. "That'll do. Place is lit up like we're going to land a jet."

With careful hands, the chief traced Sam's head. Sam tried for a manly grunt when one gentle probe sent a shard of misery all the way to his toes, but it might have included a whimper at the end.

The chief muttered, "Bump." He pried Sam's eyelids open. "Nausea and vomiting. Think we're talking concussion."

Rodriguez cursed. "Sorry, man. We had to get you out of the fire zone."

Sam knew the kid was talking about his rough exit, but saving his life was more important than the indelicate way they'd pulled him out. He wanted to say that, but his throat was on fire. He tried a thumbs-up but couldn't move his left arm.

At his second grunt, the chief made quick work of all the buckles and fasteners securing his jacket, utility belt and the harness where he'd had a canister of retardant that was now apparently squashed under a fallen tree. "Could be the smoke. Besides, blame the tree for the bump."

Sam wanted to nod, but the dizzy urge to pass out again was difficult to fight off, even with the gentlest jostling he could expect. They needed to know how badly he was injured. For that matter, *he* needed to know how extensive the injuries were.

Was his career over, delayed due to a recovery period, or on a few days' mandatory rest and as-good-as-new status?

The chief worked methodically up both arms and across Sam's collarbone. When the pain level remained at "I want to die but I won't," Sam relaxed.

The chief turned to his legs and Sam was even more encouraged that he could feel the firm grip as McKesson removed his boots. The realization made him want to cry like a newborn.

If his legs were solid, *he* was solid.

Then, with one light sweep of the chief's hand over Sam's left side, the whole world went hazy. He might have lost consciousness for half a second because he missed everything but "…broken ribs. Could be bad bruises, but I think we've got fractures." Sam had to fight back more nausea as he watched the chief lean back. "You having trouble getting air in, Blackburn?"

Flail chest, or multiple broken ribs that detach and make it impossible to breathe, could be dangerous here. Sam tried to calm the panic in his mind, but each breath was a struggle.

"In through the nose. Out through the mouth," McKesson said in a low voice. "We aren't in any hurry here, Blackburn."

Sam focused on the chief's calm face and breathed every time he repeated the instructions. Eventually, the smothering sensation faded. Pain was bearable; dying because he couldn't get enough oxygen was not.

McKesson squeezed his shoulder. "Good man. You keep that up. Let's try some water for that throat. Want to?"

Sam wasn't sure whether he wanted to try water, because the nausea was clawing back up his throat, but he wanted to be able to speak for himself, so he raised a shaking right hand to take the thermos from Rodriguez. When he sipped it, sweet tea exploded on his tongue, the taste comforting and welcome and smooth as it slid down his burning throat. "That is not water."

Sam wasn't sure anyone would be able to understand his gravelly words, but Rodriguez shook the thermos. "My girl, sometimes she sends me with two. That's how I know she's with me. I got something sweet." He wiggled his eyebrows and Sam wanted to laugh but he knew it would hurt, so he nodded.

The chief's glare was intense as he shoved the thermos back at Rodriguez. "Drink the water, Blackburn." His canteen was old-school, but Sam was sure it held regulation tap water and nothing else. The chief was like that.

Now that some of the pain in his throat had eased, Sam was thirsty. He took the first swallow of tepid water and closed his eyes in relief. It should have worried him that it felt that good to breathe and sip water, but he was going to take the small victory.

"Now we know you're still with us, let's see if we can get the incident commander on the comms," the chief said. "There ought to be a satellite radio somewhere around, too."

When Sam tried to give the chief his water back, he was firmly held in place by one broad hand. "Stop moving." He reached over to click on the comms again. "Crew chief to commander. We've got a fire in progress, lightning strike in origin, but we also have an injured crew member. Respond with orders. Over."

Sam wanted to object to the need to get any direction from the fire crew incident commander. It was obvious they should contain the fire.

When there was no answer, the crew chief met his stare. "This station is currently out of the fire zone, but that doesn't mean it will stay that way, Blackburn. We can't leave you here."

Sam would have argued, but every slight shift stole his breath, so he did his best to relax and concentrate on the right words. He wanted them to do the job. He could get himself out of the station if things got worse.

Then he realized he couldn't get himself to the doorway without passing out.

If they moved him outside, near the engine…

Sure, when he regained consciousness, he could totally crawl up into the engine, start it up and crash into the flames to save his team.

Because that was as good a plan as any he could come up with at this point.

The blow to the head had rattled his brain.

"Whatever you think, Chief," he croaked as he settled down to wait out the verdict. He was part of the rescue at this point. He was no longer part of the team.

And that burned, but he knew when he was beat and he wasn't going to waste anyone's time pretending otherwise.

Even if it made him wonder how ready he was for bigger mountains and bigger fires.

"Anybody unearth the sat radio?" the chief said as he stood. "We're going to need a second crew." He raised the lantern that had been at his side to get a better look into the corners of the small, boxy room that had served as a weather station, albeit with equipment upgrades, for almost fifty years.

"Nothing, Chief," Rodriguez muttered as he stared hard at his cell phone. "And we've got no service."

"Of course we've got no service. When the comms don't work…" The chief held out both arms as if the rest of the sentence was completely common sense.

"We could find something to stabilize him and move him into the engine." Sutton, one of the older guys on the team, stared out the window. "Or we could take a shot at damping the fire. Rain's working, but we could add in some firebreaks. Two guys stay here with Blackburn, and the rest of us dig. Then we take him back down, radio when we can and send another crew back up."

The crew chief opened the door as a wild gust of wind tipped another pine down, the flames contained and burning slowly at this point. The canopy fire had fizzled out, which was good news. The ground fire was burning, but with a slow spread that the rain had not prevented. That wasn't terrible news, but it made leaving the area under these conditions a risky move. If the wind shifted the flames, they could lose the weather station or more. Few natural firebreaks existed in this remote area. And if the fire jumped the road, it could spread up the mountain without anything to stop it.

"Rodriguez, you and Sutton head back to the engine with Blackburn. The rest of you, grab shovels and start digging. We aren't going for containment, not here and not after this drought. We've got to extinguish it." McKesson urged one of the other guys out of the way. "They've got a transfer board. At least something is going right." The chief disappeared a minute before returning to slide a wood board alongside Sam.

Before Rodriguez could bend to lift him up by the shoulders to scoot him onto the board, the chief grabbed his jacket. "Before you go, you agree that you don't leave him behind."

"Sure thing, Chief," Rodriguez said easily. "We've got this."

The chief shook his head and turned to Sutton. "Nope. If we don't put this out in five minutes, Blackburn'll be fretting like a toddler. He'll insist you come back to help us and I do not want this injured man to be left alone. Do you understand?"

Sutton saluted. "Count on me, Chief."

Since Sam had been quietly plotting a way to do exactly that, he was disgruntled when the two men shifted in place to pick him up. Then Rodriguez grunted under his weight and he felt better. Holding his breath as they maneuvered him and the board through the narrow doorway was easy enough.

He mentally chanted "please don't drop me" in a continuous loop until they were outside again.

Watching the smoke and stormy clouds go by before he squeezed his eyes shut against the driving rain was something that Sam would never forget.

Was it humiliating? A little bit, but more than that, he understood now that the stories he'd been telling at the library weren't completely accurate. The bears? They hadn't been anywhere near hurting him. He hadn't cheated death, not really.

But tonight, if that tree had fallen differently, if the flames had shifted before they were ready, if the other members of his crew had missed his injury or been caught up in their own accidents, if his ribs were damaged further in the rescue, he could well have died. The twin forces of gravity and Mother Nature had been impossible for him to overcome.

"Almost there, Blackburn," Sutton muttered as he motioned with his chin over his shoulder. "We'll get you warm in two minutes or less."

The sarcastic reply that he'd like to know how they intended to accomplish that was on the tip of his tongue.

The burn of his throat and the noise of the storm convinced him no one needed his attempt at lightening the mood—not yet, anyway.

No matter how careful they were as they moved, each step the firefighters took was a sharp pain in Sam's side, so he'd given up on the hope the chief was wrong.

His ribs were broken.

But he was alive.

They deposited the board on the ground

next to the engine and carefully lifted him inside to sit in the driver's seat.

And as he caught his breath while Rodriguez and Sutton hunted for dry clothing or towels, he could see the faint glow of the light bar on a reserve vehicle headed in their direction. When Ash Kingfisher jumped out of the SUV, red, white and blue lights swirling in the rain, Sam rested his head back against the seat. However he'd done it, Ash Kingfisher was there with the rescue.

Sam opened the engine door and waved weakly. When Ash trotted over, one hand cupped over his eyes to assess the damage, Sam said, "Tell me you've got another engine coming."

Ash didn't react to Sam's croaking voice except to say, "Right behind me. What happened to you?" Then he waved his hand and trotted back to the rear of the engine.

Sam watched the three of them confer for half a second, then closed his eyes, relieved that another engine was on the way.

It didn't arrive with sirens blaring, but the flashes of light when the second engine eased up alongside the first sent a shot of energy through Sam. Everyone was going to make it out of this fine.

Both doors opened, a cold wind whistling across the seat as Sam jerked and then covered his rib with a wince.

"I'm going to take you into town. We don't have a medic with either company, but the chief's certain you have busted ribs and a possible concussion." Ash eased his shoulder under Sam's with a careful motion. "Sutton will help from here, and Rodriguez is waiting until we get you out to shift up and help." Ash's calm stare made it impossible to panic, even though Sam knew it was going to hurt.

"No fainting jokes," Sam muttered. He wasn't sure Ash heard him, and at the first shattering jolt through his midsection, Sam was beyond caring about anyone's opinion. He didn't yelp or whimper. Biting through his lip was a possibility, but it was the manly way to suffer. That had to be good enough.

"I've got you, Sam," Ash said quietly. As Rodriguez moved to lift Sam's legs, he shook his head. "Walk. Hurts less." His legs did still work. He could do this with help. Each step was painful, but nothing like hanging upside down over Rodriguez's shoulder or being jostled at both ends by two guys walking over rough ground.

"Passenger seat or back seat?" Ash asked as they approached his Expedition. "I could fold down the back if that's more stable and you lie down."

"Passenger." Sam might regret it, but he didn't want to roll around the back of the SUV like a bag of potatoes.

Ash nodded, reached in to lower the back of the seat so Sam would have a solid view of the ceiling upholstery and then helped Sam crawl inside. Before he closed the door, Ash pulled a shock blanket out of the glove box and spread it over Sam.

As soon as Sam was in, he knew he could relax. He'd done every bit of the hard part. When they made it to the hospital, passing out would be a good thing. They'd put him on a gurney, wheel him inside, and when he woke up again, everything would be better, thanks to X-rays and modern pharmaceuticals.

When Ash slammed the driver's door, Sam cursed. "Sorry. I forgot about your head."

Sam had, too, thanks to the pain in his

ribs. The throbbing picked back up. "No problem."

Ash started the SUV, eased over the humps of dirt marking the edge of the gravel road and handed Sam his phone. "I'll tell you when we're back in cell range. You need to call your mother."

Then Sam watched him wrap both hands tightly around the steering wheel and blessed Ash's grace under fire. The trip up here from Otter Lake had taken more than an hour, because the engines moved slowly on the curves, hills and unpaved roads. Ash was going to beat their time by a long shot. He was going to beat his best time, too. He turned up the frequency of the windshield wipers and then reached down to aim all the vents at Sam. Since the heat was already pouring out, Sam was sure he'd be covered in sweat by the time they made it to town, but that was fine. Shivers shook him now and then. They had little to do with the temperature.

"Don't you go into shock. I'll have to kill you." Ash's lips were grim as he slowed down enough to glance Sam's direction. "Then your mother will kill me and she'll go to jail. No one wants that because she's a nice lady."

Sam clenched his teeth until he was sure they weren't going to chatter. "How does my mother even know?" He had a difficult time understanding the words coming out of his own mouth even though he knew what he meant to say. It was proof of their friendship that Ash understood and answered him.

"I called her." Ash shrugged a shoulder. "Sorry. I figure you wish I hadn't, but Sweetwater's such a small place. I was afraid she'd hear about it and panic."

"So you told her and caused her to panic?" Sam wanted to sit up and frown so hard at Ash that he would remember it forever. Instead, he clenched the phone tightly in his hand and wondered if they were in range yet.

In his whole career, he'd never once had an injury that required a trip to the hospital. Sprains and bruises, definitely, but this would be the confirmation that his mother always expected that he was lucky to make it home alive.

A routine trip to perform maintenance at the weather station had turned into this, a rescue and a panicked mother.

If he got the job in Colorado, how could

he take it now, knowing that this was what his mother would remember? And Avery? She didn't need to step foot in another hospital ever again because she'd done her time.

"Tell me when I can make the call." That was all he could do at this point. "And find me some water to drink."

His throat was still coated in prickly thorns that speaking set on fire, but he was going to set everyone's mind at ease as fast as he could.

Ash reached down into the oversize glove compartment and pulled out a bottle of water. "Take it easy. No vomit on the upholstery, please." He took the lid off and held it out. "I thought I was doing the right thing, man."

"You definitely did." Sam carefully sipped as Ash returned his attention to the road. Ash was right. If his mother had heard about the engine crew losing communications, she would have worried.

And then if word of the fire burning at the weather station had made it back, she might have added up all the variables and come to the right conclusion, that Sam was in trouble.

Now he wasn't, so he could fix this. Then he'd go to the hospital, wake up with the good drugs in his system, and everything would be fine.

"Try to call." Ash didn't look away from the road, and Sam could tell that they'd reached top speed. Gravel was flying. It was hard to anticipate how close they were to the paved road until…

The hard thump jostled him, bouncing him against the seat and surprising a yelp out of him. Ash cursed and apologized in a long string, but Sam had managed to hold on to the phone. With one more stabilizing sip of water, he said, "Slow down. I'm going to make the call, and if she hears me whine like that, you're going to be dead anyway."

Ash didn't answer but eased his foot off the gas.

After Sam caught his breath, he hit Redial on Ash's phone. It had been two hours since he'd called Sam's mother, according to what it said on the screen.

Enough time for her to imagine the worst.

Since Ash had to have called from the same spot, the last spot his phone could make the call, Sam was relieved his friend had put off delivering the news as long as he could.

CHAPTER FOURTEEN

AVERY HAD DECIDED the only way to distract
Sam's mother from the fact that it had been
more than an hour since she'd talked to Ash
was to go ahead with the cooking lesson.
Desperate times, desperate measures, and all
that. Checking the clock on the microwave
without letting the other two know she was
doing so was frustrating, but the worry over
what was happening with Sam could escalate quickly.

Avery had to be strong for all of them.
"We should have started cooking lessons
sooner." That way, she could have been
depressed *and* miserable for the past two
years...but well fed.

Since her own mother used half of her cab-
inets to store fabric samples, things that she'd
been employing in her covert business, and
Avery had managed to miss since her mother
was shoving a plate of scrambled eggs at

her every time she turned around, Regina was forced to take the lead today. Avery had thought of the most time-consuming dish she could imagine that would also come in handy someday.

And after three trips back and forth to her own house for ingredients, Regina sighed with satisfaction as she bent to look in the oven window. "Lasagna. Sam's favorite." She straightened and checked the phone she'd had clutched in her hand. "Any reason you wanted to learn how to make Sam's favorite meal in the whole world?"

Avery folded the dish towel she'd been using to dry the dishes her mother had washed. "Are you kidding? Lasagna is *everyone's* favorite." She met her mother's stare and then snatched the cheese grater from her hand. "Did you even know you had one of these?" she asked as she opened the single drawer where her mother shoved all her cooking utensils. Another drawer held her flatware. The rest? Office supplies.

"Did you have to empty out an office to make a space for me?" Avery asked, amazed all over again at how self-absorbed she'd been. She'd missed her mother's business and it was right here under her nose.

Regina's phone rang as her mother said, "It was no burden. I do like to paint."

It was silly the things they'd never said to each other to make sure no one had to carry any extra *burden*.

"Ash? Is that you?" Regina eased down into a kitchen chair, her hands shaking as she propped an elbow on the table. "What have you found?"

Whatever Ash said, it was good news because Regina smiled at her and her mother before covering her eyes with one hand.

"I've been so worried. Are you hurt? What's wrong with your voice?" Regina listened intently. "The hospital? But you're okay?"

The line on her forehead deepened as she bent forward, intent on whatever Ash or Sam or whoever it was on the line was saying. Avery bent closer, desperate to know who was speaking and what the news was. If it was Sam and he'd had them all worried over nothing, she was going to use this as the perfect example to prove her argument. Colorado or Tennessee, she wasn't the right woman for him. No way was she going to spend the rest of her life on pins and needles like this for him to land on his feet, the proverbial cat with *all* the lives.

Then she realized, no matter who the right woman might be, Avery would never be able to stop worrying about Sam Blackburn. Not anymore, not since he'd helped put her back together. For better or worse, they were connected.

Her stomach hurt so badly that she might also never eat lasagna again.

Janet Abernathy mouthed silently, "Can you drive us to the hospital?"

Avery immediately nodded yes, although the thought of walking into an ER again made the hard knot in her stomach roll. Definitely no lasagna for her.

At the reminder that they had something baking, Avery pulled open the oven door and slipped two pot holders around the casserole dish. Regina had barked orders for almost an hour, but the final cook on this was going to have to come later. Her mother silently opened the refrigerator, and they'd gotten the pan inside when Regina ended the call and stood up so quickly her chair tipped over and landed with a crash.

Then she bent to pick it up at the same time Avery's mom did and they narrowly avoided another crash.

"Ladies," Avery said. "Forget the chair. I've got the keys. Are we headed to the hospital or the ranger station or Sam's apartment?" It didn't matter. She knew the way and it was clear that backing out of driving them to the hospital would be a bad idea.

You don't have to go in if you don't want to. Your mother will understand. So will Sam's mother.

But would Sam? That was harder to answer. He might understand. That didn't mean he wouldn't feel the hurt.

If she was in the hospital, she'd want a visit from Sam. In fact, he might be the only one to convince her that she'd be okay.

Giving him that much importance was a horrible mistake. He was leaving. And even if he stayed, this wouldn't be the last time he needed an ER. She was in so much trouble.

"Everyone load up." Avery made a sweeping motion with her hands. "We'll come back to this."

When Regina moved to leave the kitchen without her purse, Avery snatched it off the table and followed her mother through the small hallway to the front door.

No one said anything as Avery made the short trip into Sweetwater. Regina was staring hard at her hands. Her mother was staring hard at Regina while she patted her back with enough force that Avery could hear the thumps in the front seat.

Avery didn't know whether to call attention to it. The silence was so tight with tension that the smallest sound or out-of-the-ordinary event could shatter it like a mirror, calling down years of bad luck on them all.

She braked easily in the ER's portico. "Go ahead. I'll find a parking spot."

Regina was out of the car before she even finished speaking, but her mother stuck her head between the seats. "You coming in?"

That was the question, wasn't it?

And the answer was she'd slowly go insane the longer she sat outside without the answers. Avery grimly nodded. "Yes, ma'am, as soon as I find a parking spot."

Her mother squeezed her shoulder. "You don't have to do it, you know. I can call you soon as I know something else. He'll understand." Her mother's concern was clear in her eyes. She didn't want Avery to do anything that would bring back the pain or set back her recovery.

And Avery could understand that. She'd scared them both for long enough. She could do this. "I'll be in soon."

Her mother swallowed whatever she'd intended to say and slid out the other side of the SUV. Avery was pulling into a parking spot as a reserve SUV roared up and somehow managed to brake on a dime without squeaking or rocking. A tall guy with dark hair jumped out of the driver's side, and Avery slowly slid out of her mother's car. This was it. This would determine how much she could handle. If Sam was in one piece, she was strong enough to do this. But if he wasn't…

The dark-haired ranger trotted inside, and a small team followed him back out the sliding glass doors. She lost track of Sam in the surge of people, but when everyone dispersed, he was stretched out on a gurney, and Ash had stepped back on the sidewalk.

The crowd moved sedately back inside

the hospital, which Avery took as a good sign. He wasn't in critical condition or they'd be running. She'd seen that often enough. Pushing the code-blue button had given her a firsthand view of how quickly doctors and nurses responded to life-and-death calls. Whatever was wrong with Sam, they could fix it. And they had the time they needed.

She didn't realize how hard she was struggling to breathe until the big guy turned to ask, "Do you need help, miss? I can call for a wheelchair." He didn't hesitate. It was clear Ash Kingfisher was a man of action, especially in a crisis. How lucky they were that he hadn't waited for more information before heading up to the weather station.

The thought of Sam waiting, suffering, while his team battled a flame that might be a threat to all of them hurt. Avery winced at the pain in her stomach but waved a hand.

"No, I'm okay, but I was worried that Sam was in bad shape. Is he all right?" Avery asked before she brought one hand up to chew on her fingernail.

"You must be Avery." Ash Kingfisher offered her his hand to shake. "Sam mentioned you shared that bad habit." He shrugged. "And that you were back in town."

Avery tried not to give too much credence to Ash's words. Sam had talked about her, no doubt as the thorn in his side.

She wanted to ask so many questions that they tumbled in her brain and only one made it to the top. "Is he…okay? Really?" She cleared her throat. "His mother didn't say anything about what happened."

Ash gently touched her, his hand a reassuring weight in the center of her back, and some of the fear eased. "He's got a concussion and broken ribs. Considering what might have happened, though, he's already ahead of the game." Ash wrapped his arm around her shoulders. "Can I get you a chair? Should we go inside?"

Avery inhaled slowly and held the breath before she forced herself to mindfully exhale. "The hospital portion of this evening *really* isn't helping me, but…" She repeated the breathing exercise. Ash was watching her so closely that Avery started to feel sorry for him. He was a man who had no idea what to do to help her but was incapable of leaving her there while she was shaky on her feet.

"Let's go inside." Avery could do this. "I can't go home without seeing him for myself."

Ash nodded. "And he wants to see you, I have no doubt."

Avery studied his face, even more questions bubbling up.

Ash cleared his throat. "I mean, I'm guessing." Then he held out one hand. "A guy like Sam, one who doesn't hesitate, has got to have some reason to waver on a decision he's already made his mind up to go for."

"He's wavering?" Avery asked softly. "On heading out to Colorado? Did he get a job offer?" And had he turned it down? Why did that fill her with such a giddy wave of joy? He shouldn't have to quit his dreams because of her...and whatever they might have someday if she ever decided she was ready for something new.

"I'll let him answer that, but he's anxious. Haven't ever seen that." Ash ran a hand down his nape. "Smart man's gotta figure there's something that changed in the meantime. Only one thing I can think of."

Avery squeezed her eyes shut. She didn't want to be the thing that derailed his life.

She'd been there and had been afraid she was never going to find her way back.

With a flash, Avery got mad about it, too.

Why would a man ask her to change her life so drastically? How could Robert have made it so easy for her to give up what she'd been working toward?

And how in the world could she convince Sam to go for what he wanted? She refused to be that person for Sam, the one who changed the course he'd set.

Friends. They were *friends.* They could be friends while he was in Colorado. That would give her time to get her head on straight.

All she had to do was march into the hospital, take a page from Sam's own book and give him enough grief that he convinced her he was fine.

"Listen, Ash," Avery said as she wrapped her hand around his forearm, "I'm going in there. I have a long, complicated history with hospitals. I need you to get me to Sam. You can do that, right?"

The corners of his mouth twitched but Ash nodded. "Yes, ma'am. Thank you for giving me a job. That's what I needed."

Avery sighed. "Okay, I'll continue to give you jobs. Together, the two of us will make it through this. Feed Courage, Ash."

"You've got a deal," Ash said quietly and motioned her toward the door.

The smell hit her first. There must have been some general supplier who had a bargain on cleaning products, because the Sweetwater hospital smelled like all the places she'd spent months in with Robert. Her stomach lurched and Ash squeezed her hand where it rested against his.

"You can do this," he said. "This place is not that one."

Avery nodded wildly in the hopes that the nausea would be swept away. She waited patiently while Ash asked for directions to Sam and his family. At first, she wasn't sure the nurse running the information desk would let them through. There were laws against sharing that info, but Ash flashed her what Avery was certain was a rare smile. The nurse fluttered until he tapped the reserve badge, and then she motioned him on.

Avery breathed slowly through her mouth. "Did I tell you I've met your sister? She's amazing."

Ash didn't glance her way, but he snorted. "Yeah, if I had a quarter for every time I've heard that in this lifetime." He cursed as he lurched. "Sorry, leg gives me trouble." They stopped and Ash stretched his leg. "Winter is one of those people everyone thinks is awesome. If they knew how mean she is before her coffee, they might change their opinion."

Avery gave him a quiet chuckle. He needed it. Some of the grimness faded. Then, as some of the devil in her kicked up, she leaned forward to say, "I tried to set Sam up with Winter. She's that awesome."

Ash whistled. "Yeah, I know how well that went over. If she was the last woman on earth, Sam still wouldn't go out with her, not if I was alive and kicking." He straightened. "Sam's the kind of friend who doesn't let anything derail a friendship. That makes him rare."

Not even a kiss that Avery had shut down?

Avery considered that as Ash took her arm again. He was absolutely right. No matter how long they were separated, she and Sam would always settle into the familiar patterns. He could go a thousand miles away. His next visit home might be a year in the future, but when he walked over to the fence separating his home from hers, Avery would meet him there and the conversation would resume like it had never ended.

Sam might have wanted more. There might be a distance they couldn't bridge, but if she needed Sam, he would be there for her, kiss or no.

As they got closer to the curtained areas of the emergency room, Avery could see a crowd around one bed. Her mother and Regina were huddled together at the end of the hallway, hands clasped. Sam's ugly cursing made everyone gasp, but the doctor, in a completely matter-of-fact tone, said, "We know he's alive and kicking. Let's get an X-ray to confirm the fracture."

Avery stopped behind his mother. "How is he?"

Regina wiped a hand under both eyes. "No burns. That's what I was afraid of. Concussion. Possible broken ribs."

The garbled sounds coming from the curtained area were concerning until Regina added, "And some smoke inhalation has roughed up his throat. Makes him sound like he's been a smoker since before *I* was born."

Regina laughed, a gurgle like the tears were there, waiting for something to set them loose. The three of them watched them wheel the bed out to take him for X-rays.

"Ms. Blackburn, you're his mother, right?" The handsome doctor with salt-and-pepper curls shook Regina's hand. If the situation had been different, Avery would have called it a meet-cute because the two of them might as well have been the bride and groom on top of the cake, complete with lovesick expressions. "Your son, he's a lucky guy, but we're going to get him put back together. He's in some pain now, but he's stable. As soon as we know the extent of the damage, we'll give him a painkiller. He's young and strong, in good shape. I don't expect this will keep him down for long."

Regina patted his arm. "Thank you, Doctor. When will I be able to take him home?"

"We're going to keep him here for observation. I don't expect to see any new developments, because he is so healthy." The doctor squeezed Regina's shoulder. "You can check on him and head home. He'll be out of it, ready for some rest, as soon as we get him settled."

Avery noted Sam's mother nodding and wondered if she'd leave him alone in the hospital. How could she walk away with Sam lying there in an empty room?

Before Avery could shoulder her way into the conversation, a weird urge she couldn't even understand, Sam was being wheeled inside.

The doctor stepped back. "You guys keep the patient occupied. I'll return as quickly as possible." He stopped once to glance over his shoulder at their group and then he hurried away.

Regina's gaze followed him until he stepped through the swinging doors.

Avery wasn't sure what was going on until Janet murmured, "In the most unexpected places."

"Don't you start with me. My son has been injured." Regina tipped her chin up.

"And who was making kissy faces about me and Michael Pace in front of my poor heartbroken daughter?" Janet snapped.

"Ladies." Sam's croak stopped them in their tracks. "No fighting over men I can't intimidate now."

Regina hurried over to his bed and took

his hand between hers. "You lied to me. On the phone. I'll never trust you again."

Sam winced. "No shaking. Please."

Regina immediately froze, her mouth twisted. "I'm so sorry, baby." She tried to let go of his hand but Sam squeezed hers tightly.

"I'm okay, Mom." He tried to shift and winced again. "Soon as I get a pill, I'm going to be out of this world. Possibly literally."

"Bad jokes. Must mean he's going to pull through." Ash stood at the end of the bed, his feet braced and arms crossed as if he was ready for any problem.

Sam raised his right arm to point at him. "My hero. Right there. How'd you know?"

Ash shook his head. "No matter what you think, we aren't psychically connected. There was a big fire, lots of smoke. Couldn't get anyone to answer. What else was I supposed to do?"

"Wait. But you didn't. And I'm glad." Sam wrapped an arm over his ribs. "Really."

Ash grunted. "Part of the job. I better get back to it." He held his hands out. "Ladies, if there's nothing else I can do to help, I'm going to head back to the mountain."

"Of course. There's still a fire to put out."

Regina eased around the bed and wrapped her arms around Ash's neck. After an awkward pause, he returned her hug.

"Well, I don't put out fires. I'm headed back to base. The incident commander will update me." Ash's cheeks had a bit of color, as if he was embarrassed by the attention. "I only leave my office for the easy rescues."

"Thanks, sweetheart," Sam growled. "I owe you."

Ash nodded. "Don't you forget it." Then he turned on a heel and marched back out through the double doors. Avery was sorry he was leaving. While Ash was there, their group had been a collection of family and friends. Now? She wasn't sure whether she still counted as one because the other was in jeopardy.

Then Regina Blackburn stared from her to Sam and back before turning to Janet. "I think it will be a long night, Janet. Should we go find some coffee?"

Avery's mother tilted her head to the side. "You know I don't drink the stuff. Never have."

Regina waved a hand. "Of course not. For me, silly. I'll be the one staying with Sam."

"No one's staying," he croaked, "because I'm fine."

Regina frowned at him and then led Janet away.

Suddenly too tired to stand, Avery eased down on the doctor's rolling chair. She wanted to be close enough to touch Sam, to watch and make sure that he had everything he needed, but she was so uncertain of what to say to him that she wished she had her own trouble speaking. When a nurse brought in a glass of water and said the doctor thought it was okay for Sam to drink since nausea didn't seem to be a problem, Avery forced herself to take it and lean over him on the bed. "Here. Drink."

Sam tried to reach for it, a wince wrinkling his lips before he could hide it. "No, let me." Avery offered him the straw and waited for him to sip. When he pulled back, she set the cup down and sat back on the stool. She was so tired. This always happened to her. She could hold up under crisis, but when everything was done, she turned to mush.

Avery bent her head forward to rest her forehead against the bed. The feeling of Sam's fingers brushing through the hair at her nape was comforting and so much more. She turned to face him. "I was so afraid."

He nodded. He didn't have to say he'd known she would be. They were friends, had been for a long time.

"I wasn't sure you'd come here." The last part of his words died off in a whisper but Avery could read his lips.

"I couldn't stay away." Then she grimaced. "But I only made it in because of Ash. I owe him a big thank-you. I might still be standing out on the sidewalk looking in otherwise."

"You didn't have to." Sam winced at the weakness of his voice and said slowly, "But I'm glad you did."

Before Avery could say anything to that, the doctor was back, his mother and hers bustled in, and everything was set in motion. Because of his concussion, the doctor was admitting him. A nurse brought in a small cup with ibuprofen.

"This time tomorrow, we'll release him." The doctor closed the clipboard he'd been writing on. "I expect him to be out of work at least four weeks, but more likely six given his occupation."

No one in the room could predict how Sam

would react to being out of work for that long, but no one was prepared to argue, either. Avery studied his face as he listened to the doctor outline the treatment plan and what came next.

If she'd had a million dollars to bet, she'd make the world's safest wager that Sam was already plotting to cut everything the doctor recommended in half.

By noon, he'd have demanded his release and be hounding the poor doctor to be allowed back to work in fourteen days or less.

But tonight, he was too tired to argue.

And Avery was glad.

By the time they had him settled in a room, Sam was drifting off now and then, the loud bursts of Regina and Janet's argument over who was staying with him provoking a restless shift of his legs and a frown now and then.

"We should both stay, Reggie," Janet said, her eyes narrowed in determination. "He's been practically a son to me, too. I don't mind sleeping in a chair. We can take turns."

Avery wasn't certain whether it was possible to have flash-forward visions, but suddenly, she could imagine the three of them locked in similar conversations while they hovered over Sam's hospital bed in the years to come.

Because she was certain that this would not be his only trip to the emergency room. That would be entirely too much to hope for. His job was dangerous and accidents happened, but when Avery realized that this was the first time his mother had gotten a call like this, ever, in Sam's career...or in his whole adrenaline-filled life, it said that he was strong and smart and did a good job of taking care of himself and others.

And whenever his mother snapped or her mother shushed her, his brow wrinkled.

If they woke up the patient in the desire to care for him, Avery would lose her cool. There had been an episode once, long after the doctors had said there was nothing to be done for Robert, when one of the night nurses had come to take his blood pressure, of all things. Of course she'd had orders, but Avery had dragged her out in the hall to make it clear that no one was waking up her husband unless they were carrying the cure for inoperable lung cancer. Not anymore.

There was no doubt Avery had been a mess that night, but her firm voice had worked.

Tonight, she was going to attempt reason. If that didn't work, she'd flip the switch to full-on avenging angel.

She wrapped her hands around her mother's arm and Regina's and urged them toward the door. Whatever the current state of their argument, they both got quiet. Surprise had a calming effect sometimes. At the doorway, Avery hit the light switch, casting the room into shadow except for the light over Sam's bed. She didn't want that one out. She needed to see his face.

Because she couldn't leave him there. Even knowing he was going to be strong again the next day, she couldn't leave him while he was weak.

"What are you doing, Avery?" Regina snapped as they stepped out into the noisy hallway. Avery never had figured out how anyone expected patients to heal with the constant hubbub in a hospital hallway. "You better take your mama on home," Regina said. "I'll stay with Sam and I'll give you a call when the doctor says he can go, although I would not expect it to be late in the day because there is no way my boy is going to be content in this place—"

"I'm not going. I'm staying." Janet would have stomped her foot. Her stubbornness was crystal clear, but she sent a quick look around and bent closer to whisper loudly, "You do not need to be spending your night alone here, Reggie. I won't have it."

Avery wrapped her arm around her mother's shoulders, happy the steel was back in her voice.

Regina didn't need to spend the night alone watching over her son. That would stay with her for the rest of her life.

And in that moment, Avery understood the long line of mistakes she'd made in caring for Robert. She'd insisted her friends go and told her mother she didn't need her. And it had seemed true in the moment. Regina no doubt wanted to be everything Sam needed.

But if they left her there alone, she'd bear the weight of that for the rest of her life. Sam would be fine, but Regina would remember the waiting and worrying at his bedside until she died.

She didn't need to carry that, not if Avery could help.

Coping with hospitals wasn't something she wanted to be an expert in, but she was. She would use it to help Regina Blackburn.

"None of us are going home." Avery held up her hand to interrupt Regina's exasperated response. "We wouldn't sleep anyway. Mama would be worried about you, and I would worry about…" *Sam*. She'd almost said it, but it was clear on their faces that they heard what she couldn't say. "I'd be worried about both of you. Here's what we're going to do. You two are going to go down to the cafeteria to have dinner." Avery shook her head as they started to argue again. "I'll go later. While you're gone, I'll watch Sam. I've got a few tricks up my sleeve, things I learned to make any night in a hospital room more comfortable. Get all your chatter out. You speculate on how long it'll be until we get married or cuss about where I get my nerve or whatever, but when you come back into Sam's room, you be quiet."

She watched them consider her orders. Neither one knew what to do with her sudden take-charge attitude.

Avery wasn't certain it was the right decision herself, but she did know a few things.

Head of that list? If they woke up Sam with chitchat, she would lose it.

Nobody needed to experience that.

Some of the brewing attitude must have shown on her face, because her mother nodded meekly.

They turned to go, but Avery stopped them with one hand on her mother's shoulder. "Before you go, in case anything happens…" She cleared her throat. "I don't know what could happen here, but in case I need to say this because I don't have another chance… I'm sorry, Mama. I should have asked you to come when Robert was sick. I see that now."

Her mother blinked, moisture welling up in her eyes. "Well, Avery, I'm not sure what to say."

"I made so many mistakes. I chased away my friends because I could tell it hurt them to stay. I told you I had everything under control because it hurt you that I was in pain. And I did." Avery smoothed her hair behind her ear. "But it took a toll, and I could be better off now if I'd asked for help. So I'm sorry."

Her mother's hugs had always smelled of clean laundry, her only perfume, and now the fragrance was a comfort and a reminder of how many times her mother had known what Avery needed. "There's my smart girl." Her hard squeeze was enough to set everything back in motion.

"Let's go for dinner, Reggie. Avery's got everything under control." Janet didn't hesitate as she slipped her arm through Regina Blackburn's and guided her down the hallway.

Relieved she'd gotten that off her chest, Avery turned a determined face toward the nurse's station. First, she'd be nice. Then she'd get tough.

The young girl behind the desk looked up the instant Avery stopped, a good sign.

"Y'all can head on out," she said. "Sam's in good hands and he'll be ready for breakfast early in the morning."

"No. We're all going to stay the night." When the girl immediately shook her head, Avery answered with a nod. "Yes, we will. And I'm going to need a couple of recliners for his room and at least three blankets, although more would be better."

Hospitals were always so cold. This one

was no different, and she'd left her house without her layers. Rookie mistake.

"Ma'am, we can't do that. Each room is equipped with one for good reason. Responding to an emergency around all that equipment would be dangerous, even critical."

The girl was clearly worried about how this was going to turn out, so Avery sighed. "A second recliner, then. We'll take turns. And if that won't work, the hospital administrator could explain to me why you can't accommodate a reasonable request."

The girl's eyebrows shot up. "Fine. I'll see what I can do. You can wait in the patient's room."

Avery pretended to consider that. "Or I can wait here." She crossed her arms. "That's what I'll do. And do you have anything to eat? I'm purely starving." Purely? That was east Tennessee through and through, even better than a *cain't*.

The young woman held up a finger to indicate that Avery should wait one minute. As she listened to the girl request help moving a recliner into Sam's room, Avery rolled her head from side to side to chase away some of the tension. It felt good to use her skills to get something done to help Regina. If she wasn't here, her mother and Regina's concern would escalate into a fight, wake Sam up, and everything would end in shouting and tears.

She wasn't sure which of them would be shouting and which would cry, but it had better not be Sam.

When the girl motioned over her shoulder for Avery to follow her back to a small kitchenette with an ice machine, a few canned drinks and bowls of soup ready for the microwave, Avery relaxed. She could have done battle but it was so much better not to have to. She picked a chicken noodle soup that would no doubt taste like nothing and chew like rubber tires, and squeezed the girl's hand. "You don't know how much this helps. It's been a long day, and even long nights are easier with warm soup."

Some of the annoyance melted from the girl's face. "The second chair is on its way." Then she was gone. Avery studied the instructions on the cup of soup and the buttons on the microwave before she filled the cup with water and hit Cook. It was foodish, much better than she'd expected. When her mother and Regina made it back, she'd consider leaving them alone to head down to the cafeteria.

She pointed out to herself that she'd successfully faced one of her fears in order to get to Sam.

That made her wonder if the need for him and his energy would be enough to help her overcome other hurdles.

Like…figuring out what she wanted to do next.

At some point, she was going to have to come to terms with the fact that fear was what was holding her back. She could do anything she wanted, and she couldn't make her mind up to quit the job she was so terrible at and move out of her mother's house? That made no sense, not unless there was an emotion she wouldn't even look in the face.

Fear. She was afraid to take a chance because she could make the wrong choice again. Or she could choose correctly and lose it all. Again. Would she recover from the second loss?

Avery sipped the hot soup until all that was left were the hard noodle-like things at the bottom of the cup.

Then she wandered back into Sam's quiet room. The second chair had arrived like magic. It was wedged tightly in the corner, which was a good thing. Avery had seen smaller sofas. The stack of blankets on top was impressive, too. She'd maintained the face that had gotten her at least one win in mock trials. She'd always been good at bluffing when she had to.

Avery picked up two blankets and stepped closer to the recliner beside Sam's bed. She should let Regina take it. She and her mother could comfortably fit in the second chair. None of them would be sleeping well, but they were certainly better off than before.

She eased down in the recliner as she studied Sam's face. Had the commotion of the moving furniture awakened him? If so, not for long. That was good. Avery fussed with the few items on the stand behind him and noticed a crumpled paper cup. They'd brought him a painkiller. His plastic glass of water was still pretty full, so she made sure he could reach it with his good arm if he needed it.

And then she forced herself to stop fussing. It was a habit she'd picked up during long nights. If her hands were busy, she didn't have to think too hard.

Avery stretched out in the recliner and told herself she'd wait until Regina and Janet made it back. Then she'd make sure they followed her orders and settled quietly before she tried to sleep.

Avery threaded her hand through the rail to cover Sam's good hand. When he tightened his fingers around hers, she relaxed against the recliner, pulled up the blanket and fell asleep.

CHAPTER FIFTEEN

SAM WASN'T SURE what time it was when his painkiller wore off, but it was the most reliable alarm clock in the world. Before he could figure out how much of a fuss to make, a nurse was hovering beside his bed in the shadowy darkness, a paper cup in one hand and his plastic glass of water in the other. Neither of them spoke as Sam swallowed the pills, so it might have been a dream. If he could stay awake long enough, he'd know, but his eyelids were already heavy.

Aware of the hard ache in his side, Sam slowly turned his head to see Avery's face. She was asleep, breathing softly, her curls wild. Over her shoulder, he could see the hazy forms of his mother and hers, cuddled up side by side in the world's biggest recliner.

He wanted to laugh, but it would hurt and he didn't want to disturb his guardian angels.

"They're so sweet like this, like cuddly

little puppies in a basket. And it's prime sneaking-out time. They'd sleep through an invasion." Avery was still blinking sleepily but her smile was wicked. "We could make a run for it. By the time they woke up, we could have you settled in your own place. They would be shocked."

Sam wrinkled his nose. "Yeah, I took more pills. I won't be much help for long." Then he nodded. "Let's do it anyway."

How pitiful was it that he was so relieved to have them there? He didn't think waking up alone would have been scary.

But after the night he'd had, the last thing he wanted to examine was loneliness.

Here, he didn't have to worry too much about it.

When he made the move, would he ever have another day without it?

"Glad you're here." The burn in his throat was better, but still there. Before he could ask her to hand him his water, Avery had sat up and was offering him the straw. "Nursing school. That's what you should do next. Good at it."

She rolled her eyes. "Nope, it's pretty clear to me I was on the right track before. Vague threats were all it took to get us all the comfort and style. Those I'm good at. Nursing would be a real chore for me. That I do out of love only." Her eyes met his and he was thankful for the light over his head.

He wanted to ask her so many things, but his voice wasn't up to it. Tonight, in this hospital room, they were close as ever and might as well have been the only people in the world. This was his chance to make a declaration or ask her for one.

Instead, he'd croak. She'd worry. And nothing would be solved.

So Sam squeezed her fingers. "Sorry you're spending another night in a hospital."

Avery glanced down at where their hands were joined. "Me, too." She squeezed her eyes shut. "I realized tonight how much harder I made things for myself and the people who loved me by shutting them out. I owed Robert that time and care and attention, but I needed help. I could have used someone to sleep beside my bed so I wouldn't be lonely when I woke up." She motioned with her head over her shoulder at their mothers and Sam knew what she meant.

"Sam," Avery said slowly, "this is going

to sound so strange but…" She stared at the darkness as she weighed her words.

"I got the job and I'm taking it." Sam had to repeat the last two words twice, but eventually he knew she understood him. "This might slow things down but I'm going to Colorado."

Her slow smile was reassuring. He wasn't sure what she was going to say, but he knew she was going to be his friend.

"You've had a bit of a day, haven't you? Did they call today?" Avery leaned over him to offer him the water again, even before he knew he wanted a drink. Seriously, she was so good at this. He should have felt like a real baby, but instead, he knew she cared. That was something he'd never experienced before, a woman other than his mother who cared.

"They did. I told the chief before we loaded up to head out." And then everything had fallen apart. He hoped that wasn't a sign, but if it was, he was going to turn it around.

"Learned something, too." Sam studied her face. He wanted her to get what he was saying but saying it would be a challenge. "Cheating death is nothing to celebrate. I've never really been there before, but now I know. If I was careful before, I'm going to be obsessed."

Avery frowned. "Well, it's not a bad lesson to learn."

"My crew could have been injured. That's nothing to mess around with." Sam would never have been able to live with himself if anything had happened to the rest of his crew, accident or not. He had to take care because the success of the rest of the team depended on all of them being safe.

But he couldn't say that, not that night. He should take up letter writing or something. Sure would come in handy.

Avery bent forward to press her lips to his. In his state of impending painkiller happiness, Sam was too slow to respond, so she was back in her seat before he knew she was kissing him. That was going to be his first complaint as soon as he got his voice back.

"Sam, I'm not ready for you. Not yet." Avery leaned closer so he could see her eyes. Whatever was coming, she wanted him to get how important it was. "You deserve a woman who faces fire head-on and I've been a runner, but I want to change that. I'm making my turn, getting ready to run forward instead of away. Give me some time to feed Courage."

Sam wanted to argue. He wanted this conversation, but even if he could have put all the words together, sleep was slipping up over him. And before he was ready, the pain faded and his eyes shut.

The next thing he knew, he was in the middle of a flurry of activity and three solemn faces were staring at him intently.

But none of them were Avery's.

Had he dreamed the night before?

Sam scrubbed the sleep away with his right hand and tried to sit up until the ache in his side convinced him he was fine as he was. "What'd I miss?" He hated being pinned center stage like this. Hospital beds were the worst prisons invented.

The doctor he vaguely recalled from the evening before checked his eyes. "How's the head today, Sam?"

If he'd had more than thirty seconds to take stock, Sam might have a better answer, but it didn't matter. He knew the right one. "Good, Doc."

His mother, wise to his ways, dipped her chin and waited.

"I mean, it's a dull ache. I've had worse." That much was true. Sam met her stare. "Really."

The doctor pursed his lips as he studied the chart that must contain whatever readings the nurses had managed to gather through the night. He couldn't recall details, but he remembered a blood-pressure cuff here and there. "Everything looks normal to me." The doctor closed the chart. "I'm ready to release you if you're ready to go."

Sam immediately nodded in the affirmative and eased up slowly to sit. "Ready."

"Right. I'll need you to walk to the end of the hallway and back. Need to check for coordination, make sure blood pressure remains level, no dizzy spells or renewed headache." He stepped back and stopped, clearly ready to observe Sam's dismount from the hospital bed with a critical eye.

Determined to seize his chance for early release, Sam eased his legs over the side of the bed and did his best to ignore his audience. Then he realized the dangers of the hospital gown and motioned his mother toward the door. "You guys wait outside."

Her immediate frown made it clear she disapproved of his order and his tone. "Sammy, I am your mother and I will—"

"Get a view you haven't seen in many, many years if you don't wait outside," the doctor interrupted. Sam rolled his eyes, irritated that he needed any interference because he was a grown man.

Then he watched his mother meet the doctor's stare and brush her hand through her hair.

As if she was worried about the state of her hair after a night of sleeping in a hospital chair.

Because the doctor was there?

"I'll step out for a second," his mother said with a sweet smile, "but if I hear one bit of a commotion, I am back in this room in a heartbeat. I have seen your birthday suit before, young man." Then she turned on a heel and ushered Janet Abernathy out ahead of her.

The doctor, instead of following or returning to the business at hand, watched her leave. Sam cleared his throat, ready to try standing, but he didn't want to take the man out like a toppled pine if it didn't work. "You might want to step back."

The doctor followed directions while he shook his head like a man coming up for air. "Your mother…"

Sam waited. He'd heard the beginning of that sentence a few times in his life, but there was no way to predict how it would end.

"She's single? Not dating anyone?" The doctor dropped his chart on the table beside the bed. "Seriously, at least?"

Sam froze on the side of the bed. Was this guy really asking for a date while he was about to demonstrate his ability to walk? Unprofessional. Sam wished Avery was around. She'd be able to set the guy straight with one lawyer-type stare.

As it was, he wanted the chance to go home more than shooting down the doctor's interest in his mother, so Sam slowly, painfully stood. "Yes. Single. All single." He took a cautious step, ready for his knees to buckle with pain or his head to swim, but he was steady. Sam straightened carefully, each centimeter a stretch that shifted the pain in his side, but he was able to keep it up until he could meet the doctor's stare head-on. "But that doesn't mean she's alone."

The doctor whistled. "Pretty tough words

for a guy who's going to be shaky and sweating by the time he walks two hundred feet and back." He tapped the bed's rail. "But I get the concept and I like it."

Sam frowned as he reached behind him to make sure his gown was covering all the important pieces and securely. Then he said, "Pretty brave words for a guy who thinks I'm the only guy who would protect my mother. I'm a firefighter, Doc. We stand together."

The doctor's lips curled in a reluctant smile. "Got it. Mess with her, your whole crew has your back." Then he bent forward. "Naval physician here. I get a brotherhood."

Sam studied his face and then turned for the door. "She's an adult. She makes her own decisions." He yanked the door open, uncertain how he felt that his mother had attracted the attention of this guy. He wanted Avery's opinion, but she'd bailed on him.

He tried not to blame her for that. She'd waited with him through the night. He was pretty sure about that. He was less certain that her promise that she'd eventually catch up to him was real.

His mother and Janet were gossiping in

the doorway to the empty room across the hall. He had no doubt he knew the subject.

Ready to put some distance between himself and this place, between his mother and the doctor, Sam turned to make the long trek down the hall that led to the elevators. He'd been in the Sweetwater hospital only a few times, to visit friends and their newborns most often, but he knew the basic layout. He could do this.

His breathing was labored by the time he made it to the nurse's station, a semicircular desk at the meeting of two hallways.

Then he saw Avery. She was standing next to three boxes of doughnuts, a grateful expression on her face. When she looked up, she raised her eyebrows. She hadn't expected to find him roaming the halls.

And she hadn't left.

The surge of optimistic energy made it easier to stop in front of the elevator. He waved at the couple getting on before the doors closed and then turned to make the long journey back to his room.

Before he passed the nurse's station, Sam checked once more to make sure he wasn't exposing more than he meant to and did his best to pick up the pace.

Unfortunately, the doctor was right, and by the time he eased back in his bed, Sam was clammy with sweat, his heart was racing and he needed a drink. Water would have to do.

Instead of the flirty doctor, Avery stepped back inside. She offered him his glass and waited until he drained it to put it back. "Good job, killer." Her lips were twitching. "How bad do you hurt?"

"It's excruciating," Sam grumbled, "but mainly my pride. The ribs are bad, but I can handle it." With ibuprofen, another day of bed rest and his own clothes, he'd manage.

Avery grinned. "I like seeing you like this."

"In pain? Sweet." Sam frowned at her.

"Humbled. It is sweet. Very sweet." Avery squeezed his hand. "I thought you might like to give putting on your clothes by yourself a shot." She reached into the tiny closet and pulled out a stack of clothing. "I left early this morning, rousted Ash up to meet me at your apartment and packed a duffel."

"Then you got doughnuts for the staff—"

"—that I terrorized last night in order to make sure your mother and mine were as comfortable as could be. It was the least I could do." Avery sniffed. "I feel guilty, but now they have doughnuts."

Sam laughed and then wrapped a hand over his ribs. "But only a little guilty."

"Right. Just doughnut guilty." She stepped back toward the door. "You don't push any harder than you can, Sam. If we need to call for someone, someone other than your mother, to help you get dressed, we will." She had more to say but she shut up quickly when he raised a hand.

"I won't forget this favor, Avery," Sam said as he patted the clothes. "You've proved yourself to be the best friend a man could have with this gesture."

She was grinning as she stepped outside. "I'll guard the door, tough guy."

Sam wanted to laugh, too, but that would hurt. Slipping on the loose T-shirt Avery had brought was almost enough to knock him out, so he had to conserve his energy, but by the time he'd slipped on the sweatpants and shoved his feet in the ragged running shoes, he knew he was losing steam fast. He was stretched back on the bed, breathing as evenly as he could, when she stuck her head in. "Are you decent?"

"As I'll ever be," Sam answered and coughed. His throat was better, less four-alarm fire and more hazy smoke. He had a feeling he'd have gravel in his voice for another day or two.

Avery hustled in, followed by the rest of his team, his mother's thunderous frown an indication of further storms. "We've got your discharge ready to go," the doctor said from the doorway. "If one of you will go pull your car around, we'll get a nurse to wheel him out."

"I can walk." Sam wanted it to be true. If they believed him, he'd have to prove it.

"Hospital policy," all four of them said like some fancy chorus who'd trained together for years.

"I'll get the SUV." Avery picked up her bag and waited for him to meet her stare. Her amusement at the situation was enough to lighten some of the black cloud over his head. She'd always been able to do that. If things got dark, Avery Abernathy could tease a smile out of him, and then he was strong enough to face whatever it was.

When Gee had died, he'd been almost certain his whole life was over. Then Avery had challenged him to a race up Yanu and she'd beaten him. Had she cheated? Of course. Did it matter? Not a bit. That run had been about grief and fear and anger. At the top, she'd been kicked back like it was all in a day's work. He'd never forget seeing her that way, the sunshine in her messy hair, her smile wicked and free, but her eyes so watchful.

All along, Avery had been watching out for him, like he'd done for her. Whatever happened next, Sam hoped that would never change. Not again. Now that he knew what he had, he didn't want to lose it.

CHAPTER SIXTEEN

SAM'S GLARE AS he stared from the doctor to his mother and back made Avery grin as she pulled to a stop under the hospital's pickup area. The day was full of sunshine, the skies blue and the cold air crisp after the storm, but Sam might as well have been sitting under his own rain cloud. Add that to the unnatural way he was posed in the wheelchair and it was clear Sam was over his stay at the Sweetwater hospital.

The doctor pulled open the passenger-side door and bent to offer Sam his hand.

Which was soundly rejected.

Sam eased up on his own and settled against the seat with a huff. He snatched the seat belt the doctor helpfully held out and shoved it at Avery. She didn't say anything but sent him a warning glare as she took the belt and clicked it in place.

Then they listened to Regina and the doctor share niceties back and forth until Sam had enough. He grumbled, "Regina Blackburn. Hickory Lane. Look her up in the phone book. We need to get this show on the road."

Avery wasn't certain but she thought she heard Regina's mouth close with a snap.

When everyone was seated and buckled, Avery eased away from the curb. "Tell me if I need to slow down."

Sam grunted and the silence inside the SUV was oppressive. She glanced in the rearview to meet her mother's stare. Her shrug showed she had as little understanding about how to proceed as Avery did.

When Avery made the turn down Hickory Lane, Regina said, "You didn't have to be so rude, Samuel." Her sniff was all about disapproval. "This new job of yours won't take you far enough away that I'll let you forget your manners."

Avery wasn't sure he was going to answer, but he closed his eyes. "You're right. When I go, you'll have plenty of time to fill. You need to find someone else to cook for."

Avery bit her tongue. While she and her mother had spent plenty of time going round and round over the years, sometimes loudly and with the intent to win, Sam and his mother had been peaceful neighbors. His mother doted on Sam, and he was careful to let her.

But Avery could feel the eruption building and set the car in Park as quietly as she could, aware the simplest thing could lead to a meltdown.

They were out of the car and following Sam slowly up the steps to his mother's porch when Regina stopped. She propped her hands on her hips. "You think I have nothing better to do than stack up leftovers, Samuel Blackburn? I ran my own business for more than thirty years. I've started a new business with Janet. You might not think much of my brains, but I can keep myself busy without you or any other man to cook for."

Sam's lips were tight as he sat down carefully on the porch swing that had hung on the Blackburn porch for as long as Avery could remember. They'd once spent an afternoon jumping from the swing as it swung back over the edge of the porch.

The fact that neither she nor Sam had any broken bones was a miracle.

Then he wrapped his arm over his ribs and she realized that she was the only one who'd never broken a bone. That was a nice competition to win.

"Mom, of course not, but I know you enjoy cooking and it's hard for one." He shook his head. "I would have told you this eventually, but I got the job offer yesterday. I can't believe how quickly they moved, but they're building a special team, one that splits duties with fire and search and rescue, a year-round on-call crew permanently stationed on Copper Mountain. They want to start training in January. Possibly the worst time for fires but the best for search and rescue." Sam closed his eyes. "I need your doctor friend to clear me to fly to Colorado in two weeks, so I can find a place to stay."

His eyes were serious as they met Avery's. They didn't have a psychic connection but she was nearly certain he wanted to say he wished he wasn't leaving so soon.

Or that was what she wanted to say.

"I was planning to give my notice and make the move, begin working on acclimatizing to the altitude. I didn't have too much trouble with the fitness test, but their search-and-rescue training could be a different story." Sam cleared his throat. "It would be nice to get some climbing in before the snow makes some trails impassable."

Avery crossed her arms over her chest, the threat of impassable trails something she'd never considered. Here in the Smokies, they got snow, but winter was as unpredictable as the rains. One day might be freezing, while the next week was full of sunshine and spring temperatures.

In the Rockies, the snow would be no minor inconvenience to the crews called to work it.

Something else to worry about. Great.

"You're talking about moving in weeks?" Regina asked as she sat down next to him. "Can't you wait until January?"

Sam took her hand in his. "I could, but I want to do this, Mom. I want to try this, and the longer I stay here, the harder it will be." No one looked at Avery at that point, but she could feel the weight of unspoken words.

Regina didn't say anything as she stared down at his hand. "Well." She licked her lips and blinked rapidly. "Don't you worry about me. I've got a business to build. We're about to buy Smoky Joe's, too. Avery still needs her head screwed on straight, so I can focus my efforts on her instead." She shook a finger at Sam. "And I will go out with that handsome doctor if he asks me. I can get by without cooking as long as I got plenty of other excitement in my life, right, Sammy?"

Her disgusted expression matched his so perfectly that it was impossible not to laugh.

Janet was shaking her head as she opened Regina's front door. "Y'all are discussing your business out here on the front porch for all the neighbors to enjoy, and wasting daylight. We've got things to do."

Regina snapped to attention and marched in behind Janet. "What neighbors? You're the only one who could listen in and you were standing right there. If we'd disappeared inside and slammed the door behind us, you would have wheedled everything he said out of me anyway. And what are you talking about, too much to do?"

"We've got to do some research on Copper Mountain, Reggie." Avery couldn't see her mother from the spot she'd taken on the porch swing, but her mom's tone made it easy to imagine her face. "He can't find his own place to live without our help. I also think you ought to check into plane tickets. He's injured. He doesn't need to fly across the country by himself. Who will carry his suitcase, and what happens if he misses a flight?"

Avery stood up to pull the door closed behind the two of them, their voices fading into a muffled jumble. "Let's give them a minute to settle. I imagine they're overtired." She studied Sam. "You are, too. Want to sneak into my mother's house? The sofa's pretty comfortable and you've got at least an hour before they know you're missing."

Sam took a deep breath. "Don't suppose you'd try to get me home? I want to go home."

She scooted over to rest her shoulder against his. "You're about to have a brand-new home. Maybe it's a good thing to say goodbye to this one."

"You promised it would still be here for me whenever I wanted to come back." The faint line on Sam's forehead could be fatigue, but Avery was nearly certain he was worried about the changes.

"It will be. Doesn't mean it will be exactly the same. You might as well soak it up. Staying here will please your mother to no end. I can bring you fruit pies and generally badger you off of your fainting couch, and when you leave, you'll miss us. That's the way it should be." Avery didn't want to be too sentimental. He'd handle it like a hero, but she'd be mad as a doused cat if she showed any tears. The afternoon was too pretty to fret over the future.

"Fine. I'll stay here. I'll take my mother to Copper Mountain with me on one condition." He leaned down. "You find something to occupy *your* mother. I cannot even imagine making it through a trip like this with them trailing me like ducklings."

Since Avery had recently had the experience of herding her mother through an airport, she could imagine the trouble the two of them would get up to.

"Deal. And I'll ask if the handsome contractor's father might like a home-cooked dinner." Avery sighed.

"You're going to set your mother up? Who's the handsome contractor?" Sam grumbled. "Pace. You have to be talking about Pace."

Avery nodded. "He's handsome. I'm guessing his father is, too. Regina said you connected them to the Paces for the reno work. I think it would be a good idea to distract my mother, because the time has come for me to get serious about whatever comes next."

"It's not Ethan Pace, is it? What comes next?" Sam asked. "Because I had this dream that you told me you weren't ready for me yet. If you fall for Pace while you're getting ready, I'm not sure my good nature will hold."

"He's handsome enough to have his own show. You know that, right?" Avery asked. "But I think, instead of falling for him, I'll see how he feels about the benefits of working with independent contractors instead of hiring someone on full-time. He wants advice. I'm as qualified as I ever was to offer that."

"Uh-huh. You never needed a degree for that." Sam tapped his chin. "But what does it say that, no matter how hard you try, people keep pulling you back in? It's almost as if you were destined to be a lawyer."

Slowly but surely, that was the understanding Avery was coming to. Even when she could hardly look at the possibility of returning to the University of Chicago head-on, the universe was telling her that she needed to be a lawyer.

And it felt right.

In the spring, she'd say goodbye to Sam and weigh her options. Until then, she would distract him and fail miserably at story time, and she would pester her mother about the mysterious elder Pace and do her best to take Regina away from her worries and sadness when Sam went. She had a full to-do list for now. Law school could wait.

CHAPTER SEVENTEEN

SAM HAD KNOWN traveling with his mother would be a test of patience. He had not understood that moving into a new apartment would make him want to shove her in a closet and close the door, just so he could get a bit of peace and quiet.

At first, he'd thought she was nervous about their separation. But she just kept talking.

Then he realized the common theme to every story she trotted out, every trip down memory lane.

His mother was doing a hard sell on Avery Abernathy as the key to all his happiness.

For two weeks, he'd relied on Avery for distraction and entertainment. Even when his ribs had healed enough for him to return to the Otter Lake ranger station to meet with Ash, Avery had driven him in her mother's SUV. When he'd asked how soon she was going to get her own wheels, her vague answer was enough to make it clear she didn't want to talk about it.

There could be only one good reason for that.

Avery was planning a return trip to Chicago.

And that made him sadder than saying goodbye to the engine he'd been responsible for maintaining for more than five years.

When she and Janet had sent them off at the airport, Avery had hugged him like she never wanted to let go, but she'd never once mentioned catching up to him. If she was content where she was, they were going to continue on the same paths. That meant they were better off friends.

The sooner his mother came to terms with that, the sooner he'd have some peace.

She'd started in on how well Avery had done with her single cooking lesson, as if the ability to make lasagna was the only thing keeping Sam from claiming her as his... woman, wife, whatever his mother thought.

"Mom," Sam said as he waited for her to wind down. They were carrying in the comforter and sheets he'd picked up at a discount store. The plain apartment he'd chosen was about thirty minutes west of Boulder in a nowhere spot that might as well have been his old apartment at Otter Lake. He had a view of the woods and the two-lane road that wound up through the mountains. It was beautiful outside. Inside? It was uninspiring. He could imagine what Avery would say.

If his previous style had been "monk," this was closer to "prison cell."

But it didn't have to be completed today. His mother had already insisted they buy plates and a four-place setting of flatware. Why? He had no friends here.

At least he wouldn't have to wash dishes as often.

His mother never stopped. She paused as he said "Mom" again, but she was too busy fluffing the two pillows she'd bought to "liven up" his beige couch.

"We need Janet's touch. I should have let her come with us." She gave each pillow a chop, creating a fold down the center.

Sam raised his hand and said, "Sit."

His mother was blinking as if she didn't quite appreciate his tone, but she followed orders.

"We only have one more night together. I don't want to talk about Avery anymore." He was caught off guard at the flash of home-sickness that formed a lump in his chest. He and his mother had lived fifteen minutes apart, or less, for his entire life. How was this ever going to work?

His mother scooted back to rest against her bright throw pillow. "Okay. What should we talk about?" She was ready to be patient with him, even though she had her own plans. He could still read her face clearly.

"What if this is a mistake?" He'd surprised them both by asking the question. He'd never meant to let on to his mother that he had his doubts. She was already doing her best to pretend that everything was fine. If he didn't hold up his end of the bargain, she would be so sad.

Or that was what he thought. "A mistake? No way." The certain, hard shake of her head sent her sleek bob flying so she had to smooth her hair. "You've been training your whole life for this. You're nervous, uncertain. That's okay, but you have to know that you had this dream for a reason, baby. You are going to do good work. You are going to be safe. You are going to work hard with your team, and before you know it, you'll have an entire crew who would put their lives on the line to make sure you make it out of the fire zone, like you did at home."

Sam wanted to believe she was right, but he was still unsure.

"Listen, you haven't been tested. That's okay." His mother took his hand in hers. "You've been a lucky duck for more than thirty years and no one wants that to change, but the thing about ducks is they have to change course sometimes. They have to stretch their wings now and then. That's all this is. Like ducks, you'll remember the way home. I have no doubt." She turned away and wiped away the tears that were welling in her eyes.

"And here's a bit of good news." She clapped her hands. "Janet and I have been talking for years about planning a ski vacation. Now we got an even better reason." She poked his knee. "We can get Avery here. You tell her she'd never be good on the bunny slope and she'll be booking the plane ticket and buying the ski hat. You know it's true."

Sam snorted. It was true. That didn't solve anything.

"And if I know anything, it's that you and Avery..." His mother made kissy noises. "You two belong together. I've never seen you like you've been with her these last few weeks. I was pretty sure I was going to have to get a prescription for tranquilizer darts to keep you on that spot on the couch, but y'all played your card games and argued over what shows to watch and generally acted like best friends or...soul mates." She leaned forward. "I know which one you want it to be."

"But it isn't." Sam was afraid hoping for something that might never be would doom this move before it got off the ground.

"Did you try?" his mother asked softly. "Gotta be scary to risk a friend from way back like that."

"Does a kiss after a morning trip to watch the otters count?"

His mother frowned. "I'd say definitely, although I need to know more about this. I didn't know about such a trip or a kiss. Does Janet know?"

"You're missing the point, Mom," Sam said as he pinched the beige, beige couch.

"It was a good kiss. A great one. Still, no Avery."

"But did you ask her, son?" his mother said slowly. "Because she isn't one of those girls hunting for love under every rock. I bet you'd actually have to hit her with the rock to get her attention. It's hard when you've been through what she has."

Sam knew that. He also knew if he told his mother about the woozy conversation that he could barely remember where she'd told him that one day she'd be ready for him, there would be no stopping her. Avery would be caught in the crosshairs.

And she didn't deserve that. She didn't deserve any of it—losing her husband, losing her way, having to deal with starting over and meddling mothers and a guy who was ready to push her further than she wanted to go for a life she'd never be happy with.

"I'm still going to be a firefighter." That was the sticking point. "And she's happy in Sweetwater." Another hurdle. "Better let this one go."

His mother wanted to argue. He could see it. Instead, she chewed her bottom lip and fussed with the edge of her sweater.

But she didn't. "I don't want to mess up our last night together with a dumb argument, Sam, but you can bet you have an agent on the ground in Sweetwater." She winked. "Two, because Janet would be over the moon to call you a son."

A son? He and Avery weren't even in the same state anymore. Telling her to grab ahold of those runaway horses would be a waste of breath. He almost felt bad for Avery. Almost. The mothers might manage what he couldn't.

All Sam knew was that if Avery was here, by his side, none of these dumb fears, the homesickness or the worry could take hold. She'd brush it all away with light and fun.

"Should we drive all the way into Boulder for some good food?" His mother was already nodding yes as she posed the question. So, they would drive into Boulder. Since they'd made the commute almost every night of the week they'd been there, he wasn't surprised. "I'm going to try that sushi place this time, the one over by the college." She hit the last word hard and watched him. Then she waved both hands in the air and headed for the tiny bathroom.

Sam studied his jeans and boots. Changing would mean different jeans and boots, so what was the point? As he weighed his current fatigue against the certainty of a lecture from his mother about dressing for dinner properly, his phone dinged to say he had a text.

He wanted it to be Avery. Instead, Ash had sent him a picture of the charred area around the weather station. His note: Finally got all the flames fully extinguished. That was some surprise fire you guys stumbled into.

In return, Sam sent Ash a picture of the view from his window, the old pines with mountains rising in the distance. Wish you were here. He added the kissing emoji so that Ash would get the message's sarcastic tone. Then he swallowed hard and tried to convince himself that was how he meant it.

He was staring out the window, wondering if it was too late to pack it all in and head home, when his phone dinged again. Thinking it was Ash again, this time with a flying middle finger or other commentary on his conversational skills, Sam was grinning as he pulled it out of his pocket.

Then he saw Avery's happy face, the picture he'd saved after one of their afternoon sessions playing with the filters on her phone. There was no sign of the tense, worn-out woman from that first night up at Yanu. Here she was young and wicked, complete with small horns, and so alive.

Feed Courage. Sam read it aloud and then repeated it. "Feed Courage." It was a good message and at the time he needed it. He didn't quit. Avery Abernathy would never respect a quitter. He was going to figure out this job. That would give her enough time to make her plans. And when the time was right, he'd figure out a way to make his road and hers cross again.

All he had to do was feed Courage in the meantime.

CHAPTER EIGHTEEN

BEING FIRED FROM her part-time job was a new low Avery had never expected to experience. It wasn't that she loved working in the library. It was that she had nowhere else to go.

"We've decided to head in another direction," Astrid said slowly, almost as if she'd memorized the speech someone else wanted her to give. "The city council thinks we need to add another full-time position, one devoted to children's programs." She sighed. "I can't blame them, either. It's not my strong suit, but it's an area that needs to be covered because Sweetwater is a town with a growing family base."

Then she brightened. "I got the whole thing out and right the first time. I wasn't sure I could do it." She reached across the circulation desk. "Are you going to be okay?"

"Sure. You and I both knew it was only a

matter of time until one of us had to end this. Today Miranda didn't even want to argue about the animal-cruelty charges often leveled against the circus." Avery had chosen the circus book and then she'd spent a full two hours researching animal rescue and happy stories featuring circus acts. "She rolled her eyes at me as if I wasn't even trying."

Avery had been looking forward to a nice, heated discussion.

With a first-grader.

Life had taken some funny turns.

Astrid sighed. "Yeah, when you can't even count on things that are as dependable as the rising sun, it's time to reevaluate." Then she smiled. "You'll be fine."

Avery nodded. "I've been getting the same message a lot lately. My next step is getting clearer and clearer. I'm going to be a lawyer. Someday. Somehow."

Astrid wagged her eyebrows. "Is today your meeting with the Pace men? Because I'd like to be a fly on the wall for that."

"I'll check to see if I can let you read the contract I put together for Pace independent contractors if you'd like," Avery said, "but you've never struck me as a legal eagle."

"I do like to read but…" Astrid shrugged. "Mainly I'd like to look at Ethan Pace without him looking back. The day he walked in here, I nearly swallowed my own tongue, and that would have been a pure tragedy. No more words from Astrid. The world would mourn."

Avery walked around the desk to give Astrid a hug. "Thanks for taking a chance on me. Sorry I never got any better at the job."

"That's all right. I learned something valuable. I never imagined there was anyone in the world who couldn't read storybooks to a small group of children." Astrid patted her back. "Now I know."

Avery ran a hand down Pippi's back. "Still on hold for the library dog?"

"Yeah, I lost out on the first dog I picked out. The little girl who'd fallen in love with him scooped him right out from under me, but there'll be another. Now I've got the name. Gotta find the right dog." Astrid pointed at Avery. "And you'll always know you made your mark on the Sweetwater library. Soon as I find my Jem, I'm going to send you a photo, but don't you be a stranger around here when you go…wherever you're headed."

Avery wished Astrid could provide the answer to that. It was the only piece holding her back.

Now that Sam had left Sweetwater, some of the glow had disappeared, too.

She stepped back out onto the sidewalk. Her next destination, earlier than she'd planned since she'd been given her imaginary pink slip, was the storefront Regina and Janet had decided to flip. It had been the next project on their list before Avery's return and the Smoky Joe's detour.

Her mother was convinced Odella would never sell and Avery was inclined to agree. The café owner was as much a fixture of the town square as her dusty cookie jars. The two-piece and fruity beach drinks were on hold for now.

But the work on the old hardware store was going well, according to her mother. It had taken two days to demo it to bare walls and floors. Now it was time for the fun part.

Avery stopped to peek in the window. Regina was coming home from Colorado, but not until the last flight in to Knoxville. Her mother was driving Regina's Cadillac while dropping very clear hints it was time Avery bought her own car.

She'd have to give her mother her keys back when they rendezvoused for dinner.

Everything Regina and Janet did was planned around the right restaurant and meal.

Regina's absence left Janet in charge, not that Ethan would know, because Janet and the man who had to be Ethan's father were giggling over the building plans in one corner. Ethan was laying new wood flooring down. All by himself.

"I understand why you need to hire some help," Avery said as she stepped up behind Ethan.

He grunted and then stood slowly. "Yeah, my current guy is caught in the throes of puppy love. It's really gross around here. When is Regina back?" He yanked off the knee pads he'd strapped on and tossed them his father's direction. "Dad, can I introduce you before you propose to my new stepsister's mother?"

The older version of Ethan caught the flying pads and stacked them on the table. "You ought to be taking notes, son. Don't hate the player."

Avery raised an eyebrow. "Does he usually add 'hate the game' after that?"

Ethan's face was screwed up with disgust. "Sometimes. Please tell me holiday dinners at your house are good, sis."

Avery hissed out a breath. "Oh, do I have bad news for you, bro. Unless you're cooking it, things are going to be a real disappointment."

Ethan nodded. "Sure, I've been telling him for years to find a pretty lady, one who can cook a nice pecan pie. Instead, he goes for one who will put down new wood floor in every building she steps inside until the end of time."

Avery evaluated that critique and decided it was fair as Ethan's father marched over, his hand extended. As they shook, Avery could certainly see the appeal. If Ethan was all burning hotness, his father was rugged endurance...and some hotness. Good genes in this family.

"Nice to meet you, Avery," Michael Pace

said. "I hope you won't hold my son's bad manners against me."

"Nope, but don't believe a word my mother says about me, either." His grin was contagious and there was something in his happy expression that convinced Avery that they weren't talking about puppy love, not anymore.

She glanced at Ethan as his dad headed back to join Janet. "Want to talk independent contractors? Or should we wait for the wedding?"

His grunt could have been a laugh, but Ethan pointed at a card table with two folding chairs. "Let's talk at my desk."

Avery slipped the folder on top of the piles of paper that might be bills or invoices or who knew what. "They're pretty cute together."

"They really are," Ethan said as he flipped the folder open, "but they could be cute on their own time, you know?" He put on a pair of glasses, which only made him more handsome. Why didn't the women of Sweetwater form a conga line behind him wherever he went?

"Independent contractor, huh?" Ethan

scanned the paper. "I guess it makes sense in this case but…" He shut the folder. "I always make the decisions."

Avery blinked. This might be part of the reason the conga line had never formed.

"Right. Well, Richie, the guy you'd like to add on, wants to be able to work other jobs under his own company name. Because of that, he has his own insurance, tools, even a website. There's not much advantage to either of you to change that, so as an independent contractor, he only needs jobs and checks."

Ethan studied the mess on the card table as he considered that. "I can't count on his availability, though. The downside."

Avery had already anticipated that. "So, you could add other contractors, guys with smaller concerns who might have some flexibility. Then if Richie's booked, you can line up someone else, no harm done to either you or Richie." She fiddled with her pen. "That assumes there are more guys around who'd like to add jobs."

"I'm not sure how many I could keep busy, but…" Ethan smiled. "I'd sure like to have enough projects to make it a problem worth working on." He picked up his phone and punched a button. "Richie? Yeah, I've got the contract. We'll discuss your fee, by hour, and write that part in." He waited for Avery to nod. "And then we're good to go."

Whatever Richie said, it pleased Ethan. "Looking forward to it." He ended the call and frowned over at his father. "This was supposed to be Pace and Son, not Pace and the guy who flirts with pretty women while his son does all the work."

Avery grinned at the dry tone. "That's too long to fit on the side of your work truck, anyway."

"Yeah," Ethan said. "I don't know if you have time for lunch, but if you promise to eat and talk without a single giggle, I'll add that to the fee you and I never agreed on."

The day was so far off course already, Avery thought she should go for it. How often did she get such a handsome invitation? Then she remembered her last text from Sam. No words. Four numbers: 23.16. Avery frowned at her phone, then realized he was texting her his best time up Yanu. She hadn't timed herself, but on a day like today, when it seemed the universe was sending her messages, Avery was up to the test.

"Sorry, I've got plans." Avery considered passing the lovebirds completely by, but she was about to take her mother's car, so... "Hey, Mom, I've got an errand. I'm taking your car, but I'll be back in time to pick up Regina."

Her mother dragged her attention away from Michael long enough to study Avery's face. "Okay, baby, I'll be fine here."

Sure you will. But since her mom wasn't complaining about losing her wheels, Avery would take it.

At some point, a new car was in her future. She loved driving. If she was planning to stay in Sweetwater, she'd already have moved on that.

Wouldn't she?

Avery wasn't sure, but the drive up to the Yanu trailhead was nice. The temperature was cold, but she was prepared with layers and her old boots. As she pulled her phone out, she knew this was going to be the day. She was going to beat Sam's time. She might be the only girl to beat his time to the falls, but she would do it.

She tightened her shoelaces and then started off at a dead run, her lungs pushing hard until she settled into the rhythm of the trail. She'd done this so many times as a girl that her muscles remembered. On the steepest climbs, Avery slowed and caught her breath. On the long flats, she poured on the speed.

As she reached the rock where she'd nearly frozen in place, Avery yanked her phone out. "Yes! Under twenty-three minutes! I did it!" She ran in a small circle, arms waving in the air. If there were any bears in the area, they were backing away slowly from the crazy lady.

When she could breathe again, she texted Sam. 22.59.

Maybe he was busy. Maybe he didn't have to have an answer. Or he was taunting her from long distance to keep his promise.

Then he replied. Selfie or it didn't happen.

Avery stuck her tongue out at her phone and turned so that the falls were directly behind her, the long drop down to Otter Lake impressive at this angle. She was afraid her smile was too broad to fit, but she was pleased with the shot. She had on her dad's sunglasses. Her hair was a wreck. And there was so little of the first Avery Sam had encountered on this trail that it might have been a different lifetime.

She hit Send and sat down on the rock.

"Now then, what to do with the rest of my life." Surely the epiphany wouldn't let her down again.

She stared out over the water down in the valley and considered all the time she'd spent running these trails with Sam. Whatever happened next, he had to be a part of it.

Didn't he? There was nothing keeping her here. Nothing. Her mother loved her and Avery would never let the distance come between them like she had before.

That could be epiphany number one. She was smarter. She wouldn't make the same mistakes again.

Her phone vibrated and Avery realized that it shouldn't be working. Why was it working? Worst cell reception in the park. That was what Sam had said.

Another part of the day that felt like it was pointing her one way. Back to Sam.

She pulled her cell out. You wouldn't be

shaving your time, would you? You've been known to cheat.

Avery wrinkled her nose. Then she typed. At some point, we're going to have to lay out the rules before you send me running up a mountain. Not that she could regret it.

Draw me up a contract. I'll sign it. The next text that came from Sam showed snow on the ground. Nowhere near my best time, but my highest climb yet. 8,000 feet. In the picture, he was covered head to toe, one hand raised to give her a thumbs-up, his dark hazel eyes filled with pleasure.

He'd found his spot.

She checked the time and realized she was running out of minutes for the epiphany to appear. She had to get back to Sweetwater.

So...

Avery paced back and forth as she studied the falls and the lake and the bright blue sky.

If this wasn't the place, she could rule out others, step by step by step. She scrolled through the contacts in her phone. She counted four voice mails and at least that many messages from Maria.

The question was whether her friend would still answer after Avery had shut her out.

And if the call went through, what would it prove?

Maria answered on the first ring. "It says Avery Montague, but she fell off the edge of the earth, so who is this?"

Avery froze in her spot, afraid she'd lose the call.

"It's me, Maria." When she'd left the law program and started spending her days at Legal Aid, she and Maria had moved from supervising attorney and know-nothing kid to friends. "I've become that friend, the one who only calls when she needs something."

Maria's quiet chuckle was sweetly familiar. "So, like the rest of us, then?"

Avery waited for her to say anything else.

"I told you after Robert's diagnosis that I would do whatever I could to help. That offer hasn't changed." Maria cleared her throat. "Do you need a criminal lawyer or a civil one? I can make recommendations either way."

Avery couldn't contain the laughter. It reminded her of good times when Maria and her team of lawyers and volunteers had worked hard to win what seemed like small battles in the big picture, but, in fact, changed the world for the families they'd helped. It had been easy to celebrate each success. They'd mourned failures, too, and when Avery had needed support, Maria had been there.

Until Avery turned away. The fact that she'd answered the phone said so much about who Maria was. Avery wanted her opinion.

"Actually, I need a job. When you think of me, what do you see?" Avery asked.

"You, killing it in the first trial we had, the one about the dirty landlord who'd used one late payment as an argument to raise rent more than thirty percent. And he could do it, too. It was all in the contract." Maria added, "Not that you ever let a thing like a badly prepared contract stop you."

Avery nodded. "Okay. I'm going to text you a picture. This is the me now." Avery sent the selfie she'd taken and then put the phone back up to her ear. "Let me know when you get it."

The silence on the line convinced Avery that she'd lost the call until Maria said, "Got it. You look like a lumberjack now. Is that a plaid shirt you're wearing?"

Avery glanced down at the shirt she'd

pulled out of the closet that morning. It had belonged to her father and it felt right that she was wearing it. "It is. Is that still a lawyer you see?"

"Girl, it's like you've bought into the television story. We should all be wearing skirts short enough to flash all the business, four-inch heels, and have every case ever memorized." Maria muttered something under her breath. "There are as many different kinds of lawyers as there are people. What makes you happy? If it's those trees and that climb, you should have been focused on environmental law all along."

It seemed so obvious. Like the lightning bolt, everything had aligned.

Losing her job.

Delivering the world's most boring contract in the middle of a lovefest.

Her father's shirt, a reminder of life and family, old and new.

The race up Yanu with Sam's joke on her mind: any girl who'd win him would beat his time.

Her cell phone working when she absolutely needed it to.

And in the spot Gee had brought her and Sam to show them not to be afraid of darkness.

"Where's the best environmental law program in the country?" Avery asked, even though she had no doubt she already knew the answer.

"Well, we've got a solid program here in Chicago," Maria said slowly, "but all the exciting journal articles I've seen recently have come from Boulder. The university there has a leading environmental program and access to so many parks, reservations and the natural resources that the program studies."

Colorado. Of course it was.

"Thanks. You've been a lifesaver." Avery closed her eyes, the relief that settled over her impossible to ignore. She wasn't quite ready for Sam, but there was no doubt she was getting closer.

"All I want is to be your friend, Avery. Answer your phone the next time I call," Maria snapped.

Avery agreed and promised twice to let her know if she decided to visit the campus. There was still so much to figure out, like tuition, whether any of her credits might transfer, how long she'd be studying.

But this time, she was ready.

Then she saw the time on her phone. "Oh, man, I'm going to be late." She hit her mother's number and listened to the beeps indicating she had no cell service. Since she hadn't moved a centimeter, it should be surprising but it wasn't. "That's okay, universe. You want me to hurry and get this started. I can do that."

This time as she trotted back down the path that could have been her final resting place, Avery could smile at all the memories of her and Sam. This was always going to be home. By the time she made it back to the car, Avery had calculated that she and her mother would be fifteen minutes late to pick up Regina.

Her mother was tapping her foot, arms clamped hard across her chest, as Avery screeched around the corner to slam to a stop. To stave off the lecture, Avery said, "Yes, ma'am, I'm late. I'll slow down. We'll go right now. You call Regina to let her know we are coming."

And then she listened to her mother complain bitterly into Regina's voice mail, all the while plotting her revelation. This was going to be so good.

When Avery lurched over near the curb at the airport, Regina was sniffing into a tissue and Avery felt lower than an ant. Was she upset because they were late? Janet hopped out and wrapped her arms around Regina while Avery loaded her bags. When they were all settled back in the car, Regina said, "He's having a hard time with this move. I don't know if he's going to make it."

Avery stared in the rearview as she tried to decide if this was Regina's latest attempt at matchmaking. The running mascara was convincing enough that Avery blurted, "I'll be happy to check on him when I go for my campus visit."

The silence in the car was broken only by the thump of the tires on the highway.

"That's why I'm late." Avery tightened her hands on the steering wheel. It wasn't the only reason she was late, but everything rolled together had led to this decision, so it counted. "I lost my job today. I talked to Ethan. I climbed Yanu. My cell phone worked when it shouldn't." She could tell by the confused frowns that she was losing them. "But what happened is I know what I should be doing. Environmental law. If there's one thing my whole life has been leading to, this is it. One of the best programs in the country is in..." She trailed off and let the suspense build until her mother slapped her seat. "...Boulder. It's in Boulder. I can be a lawyer. I can argue passionately for things that matter to me. And I learn how to do it in Boulder, Colorado."

This time the silence was worrying. She'd expected happy shouts, something to indicate that everyone in the car agreed with her findings.

Finally, her mother spit, "Well, at last. You have been on my last nerve lately, Avery. It was clear to everyone who knows you that you should be a lawyer. Why in the world it took this long..." She took a deep breath. "Okay, I understand. We had to find the right place. That makes all the difference in real estate. Of course it matters in this, too."

Then she patted Avery's shoulder. "I am proud of you, even if I was considering changing the locks on you next month."

Avery rolled her eyes and then waited for whatever Regina had to add.

Sam's mother's voice was quiet when she said, "We ate dinner in Boulder every night, Avery. Please tell me this has something to do with coming to your senses about Sam, too. He's close enough for you to work things out…if you've decided you're ready."

Something about her words was a faint echo of what she'd said to Sam, convincing Avery that she'd been the topic of conversation. "Yes, ma'am. I'm ready."

Then the whoops she'd been expecting erupted and Avery was relieved and happy and so ready to get on with the next step of her life. "So here's what we're going to do. Opportunities to surprise Sam are few and far between. Can you keep a secret until after the holiday? I'll set up an appointment to meet with an admission counselor and visit Sam."

"No way." Regina was shaking her head. "Too long."

"Okay." Avery agreed. She wanted to go today. "As soon as possible." Both women nodded wildly.

"Guess I better go shopping for a real winter coat. Things are about to change." Avery pressed the gas, anxious to get home, ready to get to the next phase of the plan.

CHAPTER NINETEEN

SAM HAD NEVER been so glad to see the last arrow pointing to a trailhead parking lot in his life. To celebrate, he bent over, braced his hands on his knees and gasped for breath.

"Okay, Blackburn?" Griffith, the guy who'd be his boss whenever he started actual on-the-job training, trotted in place. "Need some oxygen?"

Did he ever need oxygen, but he wouldn't admit it. "Ribs. Giving me trouble."

Nobody was buying that. "Right. Better keep moving. The temps don't seem that cold but it doesn't take long for hypothermia to take hold." And it was clear the guy who had to be at least two years younger than he was wasn't going to let him move at his own pace. Griffith jogged as if he had all day with nothing better to do than make Sam feel like a slacker.

"You're doing good, man," Griffith said

and thumped Sam's shoulder. "You had the best time in that fitness test and I'm impressed with how you keep climbing. These mountains are hard, but you're getting there." Sam studied the guy's face, desperate to see that what he said was the truth. There was no sarcasm. No rolling eyes. The guy seemed sincere.

"Maybe I spoke too soon," Griffith said slowly. "Are you still in there, Blackburn?" Then he waved his fingers back and forth long enough for Sam to wrinkle his face in disgust. "Let's get it in gear, rook," he said.

So Sam straightened and felt the vibration of his phone in his pocket. The insulation in his jacket was good enough to keep his Adam's apple from freezing like a cube in a tray, and it had also protected his phone, so that was something.

Avery's beautiful face filled the screen. She was posed by a trailhead sign. Was it Yanu? She'd been taunting him with photos ever since the one where she'd claimed to have beaten his time. If so, there was snow on the ground that no one had told him about. Tennessee would get snow in December but it was *a lot* of snow. Then he realized she was wearing a huge orange puffy coat and a hat with dangling fringe and something embroidered on it. He enlarged the picture and then held it out to Griffith. "What kind of animal is that?"

Griffith stopped jogging and shook his head in disgust. "Buffalo. The local mascot. CU at Boulder. The Buffs?" Then he turned around and headed down the trail. "Whoever she is, she's standing down here waiting for you to get it in gear. Pretty girl like that, you don't let her wait long."

Down there? The same direction as the sign?

The surge of energy that hit was hard to control, but one wrong step and he could slide off the path into the snow or injure himself. Sam took careful steps but he didn't stop until he was gasping for air and he could see a smiling orange blob with Avery's eyes right in front of him.

"What are you doing here?" Sam managed to gasp out in between deep draws of icy cold air.

"I am freezing. That's what I'm doing." Avery unzipped his jacket and slithered her arms around his middle. "Close the jacket!"

Sam was laughing as he followed orders, glad the jacket was big enough for them both and that it put them in such close quarters. If he kissed her, what would happen?

A wolf whistle reminded him that he was still in public, the guy who'd be a crew member making a whole lot more noise than Ash ever would have.

"Really. What are you doing here?" Sam asked and studied her bright pink cheeks and the knit hat he still didn't understand.

"Campus tour. I'm going to be your neighbor." Then she tipped her head to the side. "And someday I'm going to be the best environmental lawyer I know how to be." She danced a little. "I figured it all out. I did it mostly by myself. And here I am."

Then her smile faded. "I'm not quite there, Sam, where I want to be before I get tangled up in you, but I can't stay away. I've missed you. Not like I'd miss a friend, but like I miss the guy who makes my world right. I don't want to live that way if I don't have to. So, are you willing to put up with me and my... stuff? Even if the answer's no, that's okay. Environmental law? That's for me."

"I have so many questions." Sam wished

they were somewhere inside, warm, where his brain would work properly. "How did you know I would be here?"

"Your mother said it was the closest trail." Avery ducked her head. "When you weren't home, I decided to come here."

Sam blinked slowly. "My mother. She told you where I lived. She knew you were coming. And she didn't tell me."

"She also sent leftovers. You should have seen me trying to get a container of roast through security. It took every bit of budding lawyer I had in me." Avery smiled but it didn't quite reach her eyes.

Then Sam realized he'd never answered her original question. He didn't have to. Whatever Avery wanted, he wanted, too. But he couldn't come up with the right words, so he bent and pressed a kiss to her cold lips. Kissing in Colorado was going to take some training, but they eventually warmed, and Avery tightened her arms around him.

"Is that a yes? For whatever this is, we're going for it? As friends and everything else?"

"I've heard of more romantic ways to put it," Sam drawled.

"My brain is frozen. I hope it's not permanent." Avery nodded in a "go ahead and answer" motion.

"What about the job?" Sam asked, reluctant to bring up anything that might derail the next kiss.

"Listen, I'm not going to say that I'm not worried about the job, but…" She went up on her tiptoes. "You are so good at everything you do, Samuel Blackburn. I wouldn't try this with anyone but you. I will worry, but I will be strong, too. I braved that hospital. I got what your mother needed at the hospital. I am good in a crisis. That won't change. That's the kind of girl you need. Besides that, I beat your time to the top of Yanu. You are my prize, aren't you?" Avery blinked up at him. There was not a single bit of concern in her eyes, so Sam kissed her again.

Their hard times weren't over but there was no one in the world he'd rather face them with.

"Is that a yes?" She narrowed her eyes. "I have to hear your consent loud and clear, Mr. Blackburn."

"Life with a lawyer," Sam muttered. "Yes, I'm going to take you somewhere warm. You are going to draw up the rules to the races we will run up all these new trails. You will tell me more about the law school in Boulder, and then we will come up with some sort of epic prank for the mothers."

"It'll be like old times," Avery said with a happy grin.

"Even better. It'll be like the rest of our lives," Sam said before he kissed her.

* * * * *

If you enjoyed this sweet romance, be sure to check out the next book in the OTTER LAKE RANGER STATION *series coming in 2018 and these other titles from* USA TODAY *bestselling author Cheryl Harper:*

A HOME COME TRUE
KEEPING COLE'S PROMISE
HEART'S REFUGE
WINNER TAKES ALL
THE BLUEBIRD BET
A MINUTE ON THE LIPS

Get 2 Free Books,
Plus 2 Free Gifts —
just for trying the
Reader Service!

Love Inspired®

YES! Please send me 2 FREE Love Inspired® Romance novels and my 2 FREE mystery gifts (gifts are worth about $10 retail). After receiving them, if I don't wish to receive any more books, I can return the shipping statement marked "cancel." If I don't cancel, I will receive 6 brand-new novels every month and be billed just $5.24 for the regular-print edition or $5.74 each for the larger-print edition in the U.S., or $5.74 each for the regular-print edition or $6.24 each for the larger-print edition in Canada. That's a saving of at least 13% off the cover price. It's quite a bargain! Shipping and handling is just 50¢ per book in the U.S. and 75¢ per book in Canada.* I understand that accepting the 2 free books and gifts places me under no obligation to buy anything. I can always return a shipment and cancel at any time. The free books and gifts are mine to keep no matter what I decide.

Please check one:

☐ Love Inspired Romance Regular-Print   ☐ Love Inspired Romance Larger-Print
   (105/305 IDN GLWW)   (122/322 IDN GLWW)

Name _____ (PLEASE PRINT) _____

Address _____ Apt. # _____

City _____ State/Province _____ Zip/Postal Code _____

Signature (if under 18, a parent or guardian must sign) _____

Mail to the **Reader Service**:
IN U.S.A.: P.O. Box 1341, Buffalo, NY 14240-8531
IN CANADA: P.O. Box 603, Fort Erie, Ontario L2A 5X3

Want to try two free books from another line?
Call 1-800-873-8635 today or visit www.ReaderService.com.

*Terms and prices subject to change without notice. Prices do not include applicable taxes. Sales tax applicable in N.Y. Canadian residents will be charged applicable taxes. Offer not valid in Quebec. This offer is limited to one order per household. Books received may not be as shown. Not valid for current subscribers to Love Inspired Romance books. All orders subject to approval. Credit or debit balances in a customer's account(s) may be offset by any other outstanding balance owed by or to the customer. Please allow 4 to 6 weeks for delivery. Offer available while quantities last.

Your Privacy—The Reader Service is committed to protecting your privacy. Our Privacy Policy is available online at www.ReaderService.com or upon request from the Reader Service.

We make a portion of our mailing list available to reputable third parties that offer products we believe may interest you. If you prefer that we not exchange your name with third parties, or if you wish to clarify or modify your communication preferences, please visit us at www.ReaderService.com/consumerchoice or write to us at Reader Service Preference Service, P.O. Box 9062, Buffalo, NY 14240-9062. Include your complete name and address.

LI17R2

Get 2 Free Books,
Plus 2 Free Gifts—
just for trying the Reader Service!

Get 2 Free Books,
Plus 2 Free Gifts —
just for trying the Reader Service!

Love Inspired® HISTORICAL

HOMETOWN HEARTS ♥

YES! Please send me **The Hometown Hearts Collection** in Larger Print. This collection begins with 3 FREE books and 2 FREE gifts in the first shipment. Along with my 3 free books, I'll also get the next 4 books from the Hometown Hearts Collection, in LARGER PRINT, which I may either return and owe nothing, or keep for the low price of $4.99 U.S./ $5.89 CDN each plus $2.99 for shipping and handling per shipment*. If I decide to continue, about once a month for 8 months I will get 6 or 7 more books, but will only need to pay for 4. That means 2 or 3 books in every shipment will be FREE! If I decide to keep the entire collection, I'll have paid for only 32 books because 19 books are FREE! I understand that accepting the 3 free books and gifts places me under no obligation to buy anything. I can always return a shipment and cancel at any time. My free books and gifts are mine to keep no matter what I decide.

262 HCN 3432 462 HCN 3432

Name	(PLEASE PRINT)	
Address		Apt. #
City	State/Prov.	Zip/Postal Code

Signature (if under 18, a parent or guardian must sign)

Mail to the **Reader Service:**

IN U.S.A.: P.O. Box 1867, Buffalo, NY. 14240-1867
IN CANADA: P.O. Box 609, Fort Erie, Ontario L2A 5X3

* Terms and prices subject to change without notice. Prices do not include applicable taxes. Sales tax applicable in NY. Canadian residents will be charged applicable taxes. This offer is limited to one order per household. All orders subject to approval. Credit or debit balances in a customer's account(s) may be offset by any other outstanding balance owed by or to the customer. Please allow 4 to 6 weeks for delivery. Offer available while quantities last. Offer not available to Quebec residents.

Your Privacy—The Reader Service is committed to protecting your privacy. Our Privacy Policy is available online at www.ReaderService.com or upon request from the Reader Service.

We make a portion of our mailing list available to reputable third parties that offer products we believe may interest you. If you prefer that we not exchange your name with third parties, or if you wish to clarify or modify your communication preferences, please visit us at www.ReaderService.com/consumerschoice or write to us at Reader Service Preference Service, P.O. Box 9062, Buffalo, NY. 14240-9062. Include your complete name and address.

HHBPA17

Get 2 Free Books,
Plus 2 Free Gifts—
just for trying the Reader Service!

♥ HARLEQUIN *super romance*